PERMANENTLY
BOOKED

PERMANENTLY BOOKED

LISA Q. MATHEWS

W✪RLDWIDE®

TORONTO • NEW YORK • LONDON
AMSTERDAM • PARIS • SYDNEY • HAMBURG
STOCKHOLM • ATHENS • TOKYO • MILAN
MADRID • WARSAW • BUDAPEST • AUCKLAND

Recycling programs
for this product may
not exist in your area.

Permanently Booked

A Worldwide Mystery/August 2018

First published by Carina Press

ISBN-13: 978-1-335-50671-9

To my mom, Jeanne—
aka The Mighty Quinn—librarian extraordinaire!

ONE

"WHOA, LOOK OUT!"

Dorothy Westin jumped to avoid a cascade of hard-cover books and colorful paperbacks a split second before they hit the carpet next to her Aerolite shoes. "Goodness, Summer. What are you up to now?"

"Oh, hey, I'm really sorry, Dorothy. Are you okay?" Summer Smythe, her twenty-something neighbor and sleuthing partner, hopped lightly down from the plastic-covered ottoman she'd been using to reach the top shelf of an enormous built-in bookcase. It was surprising the girl needed any extra height for the job, really. She was unusually tall, with a model's build—or, more accurately, a lifeguard's.

"I'm fine, dear." Dorothy brushed the dust and the remnants of a particularly stubborn cobweb from her powder-pink cardigan. At her age, she was fortunate to have decent reflexes, or she might have been—literally—buried in books. And well before her time, she might add.

"I need to clear these shelves off quick, so I can knock them out," Summer explained. "I'm getting an awesome home theater system installed."

"I see," Dorothy said. For this morning's project, Summer was dressed entirely in white: tiny tank top, equally miniscule shorts, and sporty tennis shoes. Not a speck of dirt anywhere—unless one counted the carpet and Dorothy's sweater. "Do you think that's such a good

idea right now? Without a steady paycheck, I mean?"
So far, Summer's aquatics director job at the Hibiscus
Pointe Senior Living Community was strictly volunteer.

"Oh, I'm working for my dad part-time now," Summer explained. "As a film reviewer, sort of. His assistant
is going to send me clips, and all I have to do is watch
them. I'm their target demo, they said. Plus, Daddy will
get a tax write-off on this place. It's going to be one of
his satellite offices."

"Ah," Dorothy murmured. She doubted Hollywood
producer Syd Sloan was in dire need of additional tax
breaks, but who knew? At least Summer got to live here
in the lovely condo he'd recently inherited from his
mother. Not exactly rent free, but still… "What are you
planning to do with all these lovely books?" she asked.

Summer swept her sunny-blond side bangs from her
face. "Oh, I dunno. I'll probably just toss them in the
Dumpsters behind the parking lot."

"You'll do no such thing," Dorothy said, horrified.
"Books are precious. Why don't you donate them to the
Hibiscus Pointe Library?" In the short time since she
had volunteered her services at the small residents' library in the main building, she'd never known Lorella
Caldwell, the earnest new librarian who had moved into
the Hibiscus Gardens section last month, to turn down
fresh reading materials.

"Okay." Summer shrugged. "I didn't think they could
fit any more books, that's all. There were whole boxes
of them piled up outside the door last night."

"Mmm." Dorothy was already perusing the piles
of discarded titles. "Some lovely art and travel books
here," she said. "And your grandma was a mystery fan,
I see. Maybe that's where you got that detective gene."

"I guess. Don't know if I have the reading gene, though." Summer peered over Dorothy's shoulder. "Hey, there's a whole series of *Citizen's Arrest* novels. I thought it was just a TV show."

Dorothy smiled and handed her a few of the paperbacks. "Why don't you try them?"

"Sure, maybe later." Summer tossed the books onto the floral couch. It, too, was covered in plastic to guard the fabric against the fierce Florida sunshine streaming through the sliding glass doors.

Sadly, the sparkling Gulf of Mexico view was wasted on Dorothy's young friend, who was deathly afraid of heights. Summer avoided her balcony more diligently than she did the Residents Board, which was forever eager to enforce Hibiscus Pointe's fifty-five-and-over minimum age requirement.

"My, look at these." Dorothy reached for another group of books that had landed upside down and carefully smoothed the pages. "Your grandma must have had every one of GH Hamel's mysteries in hardcover. She's my very favorite author."

"Wait, did you say Hamel?" Summer flipped over one of the volumes to check the author photo, which showed a dramatic-looking woman in a colorful head scarf. "I think that's Dash's mom."

"Isn't that something?" Dorothy said. "I didn't make the connection." Summer's handsome designer friend Dash lived in the Hibiscus Villas section of single-family homes with his partner, Julian, and their little girl, Juliette-Margot. He'd mentioned more than once that his mother wrote mysteries.

"You should keep those for yourself, Dorothy," Summer said. "Dash said his mom is visiting from New

York this week, I think. I'm sure he could ask her to sign them for you."

"That would be lovely," Dorothy said. "Who knows, they might even be collector's items someday."

"Oh." Summer seemed dismayed as she surveyed the collateral damage on the floor. "You think any of these others are worth some bucks? I should have been more careful."

"I wouldn't worry about it, dear." Dorothy glanced over at the digital clock on the coffeemaker near the breakfast bar. "It's almost noon. Why don't we pack all these books up and drop them by the library on our way to lunch?"

"Okay." Summer bounded toward the door. "There's a free buffet over at the tennis courts today. I'll go grab one of those hotel carts downstairs."

In less than five minutes, she was back. "Sorry, couldn't find any. People must be moving in or something."

Dorothy looked down at the trash bags she'd already half filled with books. Perhaps she could drag one at a time. "We'll have to make a few trips."

"I can manage everything at once." Summer scooped up two bags in each hand. "Oops," she said as the largest of them ripped, spilling books back onto the carpet. "Guess we'll just take a couple for now."

The wait for the elevator was interminable, as usual. Hibiscus Tower A, where Summer lived, boasted thirty-three floors. Dorothy's condo complex, Hibiscus Gardens, had only two, but the elevator there was equally slow.

When the door finally opened, they squeezed in beside one of the missing carts, loaded sky-high with bags, boxes, and luggage. Against it leaned a sixtyish woman with a curvy, country music-star figure and white-blond hair piled heavily on top of her head.

Trixie Quattrochi.

Dorothy didn't know her very well, as their hours hadn't overlapped so far at the library, but her style was quite distinctive around the tropically themed Hibiscus Pointe.

"Howdy, gals." Trixie fanned herself with a bright orange envelope. "Gotta warn you, it's hotter than a honeymoon hotel in here."

Dorothy nodded politely. The woman did look flushed, perhaps because she was overdressed for the heat. Today Trixie wore red cowboy boots, a Ski Montana T-shirt, and half a dozen heavy-looking turquoise and silver necklaces. A beaded leather belt adorned with a flashy, oversize silver buckle cinched her tight jeans.

"Nice boots." Summer was trying to peel the clingy plastic trash bags from her legs.

"Why, thank you, darlin'," Trixie said. "Gen-yoo-ine snakeskin. And this baby right here"—she tapped the enormous buckle with a long red fingernail—"is authentic, too. My sister was a rodeo queen."

Dorothy tried hard not to stare at the woman's Texas-shaped—and sized—diamond earrings. Cubic zirconia, more likely. "You're not leaving Hibiscus Pointe, are you, Trixie?"

"Heck no." Trixie patted the groaning cart. "Just goin' on a little campin' trip."

"Sounds fun." Summer's nose twitched slightly. "So where are you headed?"

Trixie pointed to her ample chest. "Montana," she said. "Best huntin' and fishin' there is. Just decided this morning to go. I'm a real spontaneous person."

"My, and you're taking all this with you?" Dorothy said. She'd never really been camping herself, unless one counted the little cabin in Maine where she and her late husband, Harlan, had spent a few lovely summers, long ago.

"Yep," Trixie said. "Almost got the ol' RV packed up."

Dorothy doubted any motor home could hold all of Trixie's bare necessities. But recreational vehicles were quite deluxe these days, offering all the amenities of home—or so the glossy ads in the back of *Now You're Golden* magazine claimed.

"Yessiree, I've got everything I need." Trixie nudged a small duffel bag with the toe of her boot. "Right here's my granddaddy's 30 Luger pistol. Never go anywhere without it."

Dorothy hastily shrank against the elevator wall. She hadn't needed to hear that.

"So, what are you gals haulin'?"

"Just bringing some books down to Lorella at the library," Dorothy said, relieved at the change in subject.

"Uh-huh." Trixie tapped her rodeo buckle again as she kept her eyes on the red numbers counting down the floors. "This thing is slower than a gator crossing the road in July."

"Ground floor," Summer announced. "Let's go, partner." She tossed the trash bags out ahead of her onto the faux-Oriental lobby carpet to help Dorothy off the elevator.

"Pardner? You must be a country gal." Trixie's bright orange lips turned up in delight as she pulled her duffel from the cart. "Where'ya from, hon?"

Summer held the elevator door open so the woman

could get herself and her belongings safely out. "California."

"Oh." This time, it was Trixie's nose that twitched.

"Would you like us to help you to your RV?" Dorothy asked.

"Nah." Trixie waved them off. "But thanks anyway. My pal Ray's gonna give me a hand."

"Have a nice trip," Summer called, over her shoulder. "Don't run into any bears."

Trixie waved her canvas bag. "No critter will stand a chance against me and General Luger."

Dorothy couldn't get to the side door of Hibiscus Towers fast enough. "I've never cared for guns," she told Summer when she'd caught her breath.

"I'm a pretty good shot," her friend said. "I won the Annie Oakley Award at this fancy summer camp my sister Joy and I went to in Jackson Hole. Our dad ditched us there while he was on one of his honeymoons. Oh, hey, look, there's Trixie's RV. And that must be Ray."

Dorothy followed Summer's gaze to the far end of the parking lot, where a reedy, greasy-haired man wearing a sleeveless olive T-shirt and a pair of battered cargo shorts smoked a cigarette outside a slightly battered motor home. The faded, swirly gold letters on the side read Happy Trailways.

"I wonder how he managed to get that through the front gate," Dorothy said.

Ray took a last drag on his cigarette and threw it to the asphalt, halfheartedly kicking at the butt with his dirty sneaker. At least he hadn't tossed it into the brown-tinged hedge behind him. Florida had been extremely dry lately.

"Caught ya!"

Trixie materialized again behind them, breathing heavily as she leaned on the cart. Her face was half-obscured by huge, buglike sunglasses bedazzled with rhinestones. "Hold on just a minute, gals."

"Yoohoo! I'm ready!" the woman called across the lot to Ray, nearly blasting Dorothy's eardrum. He returned her enthusiastic wave with a slight sneer.

Trixie shrugged, looking embarrassed, and turned back to Dorothy and Summer. "Would you do me a big favor, seein' as y'all are headed to the library?" She rummaged in her duffel and pulled out the orange envelope again, pressing it into Summer's hand with her own jeweled fingers. "We're fixin' to leave right away. Be a doll, and give this to Lorella for me, okay? It's very important."

"Um, sure," Summer said, but the woman was already halfway to the RV with her cart. Summer held the envelope up in the sunlight, squinting. "Jeez. Trixie has terrible handwriting, but I'm pretty sure I see the word *kill* here. Whoa. You think this might be some kind of threat?"

"Of course not. Don't be snoopy, dear." Dorothy took the envelope from her friend and tucked it carefully in her white leather purse. "This is confidential correspondence, between Trixie and Lorella."

"Yeah, I guess you're right." Summer hoisted one bulging book bag over each shoulder as they started across the steaming parking lot toward the main building. "Who'd ever bump off a librarian, anyway?"

THE HIBISCUS POINTE LIBRARY was dark and locked, but that was okay with Summer. Now she and Dorothy could get to lunch sooner. "Hello?" she called loudly, knocking on the door.

Nope, no answer. "Oh well," Summer said. "We can just leave the books here and come back later." Or—maybe never. Even better.

"That's exactly what everyone else has been doing." Dorothy pointed to the overflowing bags and boxes and piles of books stacked along the wall in the hallway. "I have to say, this is odd. Lorella is always here at lunch-time, in case any residents drop by."

"Maybe she's over at the buffet." Summer pulled her key card from her back pocket and slid it through the lock. The electronic key, which rarely worked any-where in the complex, at least came in handy for jam-ming things open.

"Let's take our bags inside first, and then we can move these others in, too," Dorothy suggested.

"Okay, but we'll have to work fast," Summer said. "If we don't get over to the courts before everyone else does, all the desserts will be gone."

"Really, dear." Dorothy smiled, but Summer knew she was an equal fan of Hibiscus Pointe's brownies. If either of them cooked, Summer would've asked Gre-goire, the sous-chef, for the recipe.

Dorothy flipped on the lights, which didn't work, and Summer squinted around the small, L-shaped room in the semidarkness. It was hard to believe anyone called this place a library. Not that she'd been inside very many of them, or anything. But this one wasn't very big, with a bunch of bookcases against the walls and a few rows of stacks to one side. It didn't even have that weird li-brary smell. More like cinnamon air spray.

"Goodness, what went on in here?" Dorothy frowned. "This isn't the way Lorella keeps things."

Summer took another glance around the main room. She didn't see anything wrong. A few papers on the floor, maybe, and a couple of overturned boxes.

The only sign of life was a pitcher filled with fresh pink roses on the librarian's desk. Beside it, a giant dictionary lay open on a pedestal. Probably no one ever used it. An ancient-looking globe stood on a tall cabinet with tons of little drawers. The faded poster behind it said That's All She Read.

No wonder those fancy Hibiscus Pointe brochures didn't show any pictures of the library. For what it cost to live here, the residents sure got ripped off.

There weren't even any decent magazines, unless you counted superscary health news, overpriced real estate, or crossword puzzles with all the answers written in.

Dorothy frowned. "I'm going to check out the reading room."

Summer followed as far as the doorway. The reading room held two or three beat-up leather recliners and a long wooden table with mismatched chairs. That was pretty much it. A third room, just beyond it, served as the business center. It boasted two dinosaur-age computers and an equally extinct printer.

Maybe, if anyone ever got that thing working again, she'd print a few copies of her résumé. Not that she'd updated it lately, as she hadn't held any recent paying jobs long enough to list. Her last employer, a doctor, had ended up murdered on her first day of work. But at least she and Dorothy had solved the case.

"Mrs. Caldwell?" Jennifer Margolis, the Resident Services director, hovered at the library door. The pretty, dark-haired girl, about Summer's age, was dressed in her usual Hibiscus Pointe blazer and floppy corporate tie. Ugh. Couldn't they come up with a hipper uniform?

"Sorry, she's not here," Summer called, over her shoulder.

"Oh, hey, Summer." Jennifer's face brightened as she walked in, and Summer immediately felt guilty for dissing her outfit. It wasn't Jennifer's fault. Unlike her, the girl had an actual, paying J.O.B.—and Jennifer had given her a lot of breaks lately, even fending off the Residents Board on her behalf.

"Too bad I missed her." Jennifer looked truly disappointed. "I have the first copies of the latest *What's Your Pointe?* newsletter to show her. She wrote a great article about our book club relaunch on Friday. She's so excited about it."

"That's nice," Summer said. Did anyone actually read those newsletters?

Dorothy stepped past Summer, shaking her head. "Something just isn't right," she said. "Those banker's boxes we packed for the book sale are all jumbled up, and—" She stopped when she saw Jennifer, and smiled. "Oh, hello, dear."

"Hi, Mrs. Westin, how are you today?" Jennifer glanced around the room. "It does look a little disorganized in here, doesn't it? Maybe we should turn on more lights."

"We did." Summer headed over to the librarian's desk and peered behind it. A bunch of papers were scattered on the floor, and one of the file drawers was open, with a couple of colored folders sticking out. Didn't the librarian have a chair? Yep, there it was: the black, swivel kind, lying on its side. Looked as if it was broken, too.

Ms. Ruiz back at Samo—Santa Monica High—would never let anyone mess up her library like this. "Someone's definitely been here, guys," Summer said. "And it wasn't Goldilocks."

"I'll make a vandalism report, and get Security down here right away." Jennifer reached for the cell phone at her slim waist. "When Mrs. Caldwell gets back, she can tell us if anything's missing."

"Wait just a sec. We didn't check over here." Summer jogged to the book stacks and glanced down the narrow rows of shelves. They were almost as dusty as Grandma Sloan's. But at the last section, she stopped short.

A gray-sweatered arm was sticking straight out from behind a pile of coffee table books on the floor. An old-school gold charm bracelet dangled from the wrist.

Summer's stomach pitched like a sunfish caught in a tsunami. She squeezed her eyes shut and leaned back against the nearest shelf, feeling the cool metal edge press into her back. This could not be happening again. Two dead bodies in less than two months? No way.

"I'm sure Lorella would have heard us by now," Dorothy called. She sounded weirdly far away in the tiny library.

Summer looked back at the still form on the carpet and bit her lip. "I wouldn't bet on that."

TWO

"WHAT'S WRONG, SUMMER?" Dorothy hurried toward the book stacks. The poor girl looked as if she'd encountered a ghost in the semidarkness.

With some trepidation, Dorothy followed her friend's gaze to the motionless figure of Lorella Caldwell. "Oh my goodness." Dorothy placed a hand to her heart, making a fist so it wouldn't tremble. "She's…"

"Dead," Summer said, in a near whisper. She was gripping the bookshelf behind her very tightly for support.

That wasn't possible, Dorothy told herself. Lorella always exuded such determined energy, in her quiet way.

She leaned forward, just a smidge. The librarian lay facedown on the edge of the carpet, her reading glasses askew on their beaded blue chain. A small dark-cherry stain marked her gray head, and her left arm protruded at an unnatural angle, as though she'd been reaching for something.

Or someone. Dorothy suppressed a shudder. "Maybe she's still alive," she said, trying to sound hopeful. "She might just be unconscious. Maybe some kind of spell…"

"Think maybe she's been here awhile. Doesn't seem like CPR would help, or anything." Summer gingerly knelt beside Lorella and placed two fingers to the woman's neck. "Nope. Oh, wow, her eyes are open." She quickly looked away, her face paling beneath her tan. "Sorry, that really freaks me out. It's like she's staring at me."

"Try the wrist," Dorothy said. "Sometimes it's easier to find a pulse there." Then she spotted the dried drops of crimson on the carpet. Lorella's wound was no longer bleeding. "Never mind," she said quietly.

She leaned forward to gaze more closely at the eerily still woman she'd worked beside just last week. Head wounds often bled profusely, she knew, but the bump on Lorella's head looked particularly nasty. Could she have fallen—tripped over one of these piles of books, perhaps—and injured herself?

Somehow Dorothy doubted that. Lorella's wound was at the back of her head, and she had fallen forward. But that arm… She shuddered again.

Jennifer joined them and gasped. "Oh no," the Resident Services director said, her voice barely a whisper. "Poor Mrs. Caldwell. What do you think happened?"

"Looks like someone wasn't too happy with her," Summer said. "Because there's the murder weapon." She jumped up and hurried over to a smooth gold metal bookend, lying near the far corner of the stacks.

It was shaped a bit like an Academy Award statuette, Dorothy thought. If Oscar had been female, writing a book on his lap, and stuck to an L-shaped piece of metal.

Summer gave a quick nod. "Yep. Blood."

"There's a trail of spots on the carpet and floor, too." Dorothy frowned. "They're nearly the same color, but I see them now."

"I—I'll call for help." Both Jennifer's hand and voice shook as she tried to dial.

"That's okay, I'll do it." Summer slipped her own cell from her pocket.

"Thanks." Jennifer took a few steps back. "Oh my gosh. I'm really sorry, but I think I'm going to be sick."

Dorothy hurried to put her arms around the young woman, who was now violently shuddering. "There, there, dear," she said, patting her gently on the back, as Summer gave 911 the details and answered the operator's questions. "Everything's going to be just fine."

But everything was not fine, of course. Lorella Caldwell was dead.

It was true that neither of them had really known Lorella. Summer had never even met her, in fact. But no one, especially a lovely, hardworking librarian, deserved a terrible fate like this—and it happened right here at Hibiscus Pointe, too. Who else might be in danger?

A killer had targeted one of their very own neighbors, and someone else might even be next. Dorothy had full confidence in the Milano PD, she told herself quickly, but weren't she and Summer, as residents, in a perfect position to assist with the upcoming investigation?

Of course they were. Lorella's killer needed to be unveiled and brought to justice, the sooner the better—before he or she could strike again. It didn't matter that they hadn't really known the woman. It was the right thing to do.

Jennifer was sobbing now, very quietly, in Dorothy's arms. "We can't let the other residents know yet," she said, with a hiccup. "Everyone will panic, and then the media will be here, and—"

"I'm sure people will notice the emergency vehicles," Dorothy said. "We can't very well stop those, now, can we?"

"Ten minutes," Summer called. "They're sending help from Bonita. Some big accident down by the beach."

Dorothy sighed. The Milano emergency response teams were frequently overwhelmed and forced to call upon nearby towns for help. With all the seniors in this town, and adventurous tourists, one would think they'd work ways into the city budget to avoid that. Rather than, say, gold-plated nameplates for the council persons' parking spots.

"You're right, Mrs. Westin." Jennifer stepped back and swiped at her big brown eyes, which were now heavily leaking mascara. "I guess I just panicked. I'd better go break the news to my boss and see how he wants to handle everything. Roger's going to freak over this."

"Oh, I wouldn't worry about that," Dorothy said. From what little she had observed of the frequently absent general manager of Hibiscus Pointe, Roger was more likely to be concerned about how a murder on the grounds would affect his next tee time. "Here, dear." She reached into her purse. "Let me give you a tissue before you go."

"Thanks, Mrs. Westin." Jennifer dabbed at her eyes.

As Dorothy returned the tissue packet to her purse, her hand brushed against the envelope Trixie had entrusted to Summer for Lorella.

Goodness. In all the excitement, she had entirely forgotten. Should they open it, now that Lorella was gone? Summer had to have imagined she'd seen the word *kill* through the envelope. But still, under the circumstances…

"Should I get a hold of Detective Donovan, too?"

Summer called, from the doorway. Reception was poor inside in the library. "I've got his number in my phone."

"He's off duty, but I know he's at the tennis courts right now," Jennifer said. Another line of mascara had streaked the collar of her crisp white blouse. "His grandma's playing in the tournament."

"Oh." Summer frowned.

Dorothy's friend seemed overly concerned about the detective's whereabouts, and Dorothy wasn't sure that concern was entirely due to the current situation. After their last investigation, he and Summer had seemed a bit sweet on each other, though neither of them would admit it.

It was possible the detective was still concerned that Summer had been a person of interest in their previous case. That had to have put a damper on any blossoming romance.

"Wait, isn't Mrs. Donovan in a wheelchair?" Summer asked.

"Wheelchair tennis is very popular now," Jennifer said. "The head pro over at Majesty Golf & Tennis, Garrett Reynolds, coaches her, I think."

"Well, they make you mute your cell phone at tennis tournaments," Summer said. "I'll run over to the courts and get Donovan." Without waiting for a reply, she disappeared through the doorway, but poked her head back inside a few seconds later. "The note," she said to Dorothy, breathlessly. "It had to be Trixie. Be right back." Then she was gone again.

Fortunately, Summer's words didn't seem to register with Jennifer, which was probably a good thing. No sense in anyone jumping to conclusions yet, or starting rumors about possible culprits. Besides, the Resident Services director would have enough on her plate soon.

"Someone should stay with the…um, with Mrs. Caldwell," Jennifer said. Her face was nearly as pale as the lifeless librarian's. "Would you mind, Mrs. Westin? The first responders will be here soon."

"You go ahead, Jennifer," Dorothy said. "I'll be just fine." She wasn't entirely certain of that, but Lorella shouldn't be left alone, under the circumstances.

After the young woman brought her a chair from the reading room and hurried off to find Roger, Dorothy perched on the uncomfortable plastic seat, tightly clutching her purse. What if some person appeared on the scene unexpectedly? Another resident, say, to return a book.

Or the killer.

She got up and edged a bit closer to the bloody gold bookend. If need be, she could… Dorothy shuddered. She didn't even want to think about that. Besides, it was her job right now to make sure the crime scene remained undisturbed.

Alone in the semidarkened library, with only the hum of the AC and poor Lorella for company, she drew out Trixie's envelope. Using the edge of the tiny metal nail file from her purse-sized manicure set, she very carefully slit it open. Then, with a guilty glance down at Lorella, she pulled out the note and unfolded it with a shaking hand.

The tangerine sheet, stamped at the top with an enormous silver *T*, was scented with a sinus-permeating, citrus perfume. Dorothy peered at the page closely as she tried to make out the fat, swirly—but thankfully large—handwriting in the dim light:

Miss Lorella,

Real sorry but I can't do the job for you anymore. Just got the opportunity of a lifetime and have to go for it. May be back but must tend to some rat-killing first.

Take care and watch out for The Snake,
Trixie Q.

Well. That was quite possibly the oddest note she'd ever read. Rat-killing? And…what on earth did Trixie mean about The Snake?

Dorothy looked back at the still body on the carpet, feeling a rush of sadness. Whoever—or whatever—the ominous-sounding vermin and reptile were, the warning had come too late for Lorella Caldwell.

EVEN WITH HER new Prada sunglasses, Summer had to squint against the intense Florida rays as she scanned the golf-clapping crowd at the Hibiscus Pointe Inter-Community Seniors Tennis Tournament. Where was Detective Donovan?

"Yoo-hoo, girls, you're falling behind!" a voice boomed. "Let's get these balls picked up, on the double!"

Uh-oh. Summer glanced over her shoulder. In the near court, Hibiscus Pointe's resident busybody and battle-ax, Gladys Rumway, was directing a trio of older ladies near the water station. All three wore HP polo shirts and carried plastic buckets with the palm-and-fleur-de-lis logo.

The women waved cheerfully, and immediately streamed onto the DecoTurf courts, gathering up fuzzy neon-green tennis balls.

Now Gladys was lumbering straight toward her, armed with a clipboard and a bullhorn. Not that her voice needed to be any louder.

"I see you're dressed for the tournament, missy," Gladys said, with a nod to Summer's all-white outfit. She herself wore an official-looking HP visor and an enormous white muumuu patterned with crossed navy tennis racquets. "Sorry, we don't have a junior division."

Too bad, because Summer might have been tempted to smash a serve straight off Gladys's poodle-curled head. "Is Detective Donovan around here somewhere?" she asked, shading her eyes again. "I have to find him right away. It's kind of an emergency."

"Oh yeah?" Gladys pushed her jowly face way too close. "What's going on?"

Oops. Mistake. The battle-ax had been a ginormous pain on Summer's and Dorothy's first case, following them around and getting in the way. "Um, nothing," Summer tried. "I just need to talk to him, that's all. No big deal."

"I'll handle this." Gladys lifted her bullhorn. "Attention, all players, spectators, and personnel!" she thundered. "Detective Shane Donovan, please report to the tournament director immediately. Detective Shane Donovan."

Instantly, all action on the courts came to a halt as players froze in place and tennis balls bounced uselessly in all directions. Summer cringed as she spotted the detective's grandma on the far doubles court, squealing to a stop in her motorized wheelchair, mid-backhand. Yikes. How could she have missed Peggy Donovan, with that blaring red hair, held back in a bright white headband?

Summer tried to pretend she was invisible. Every single person at the tournament was staring at her and Gladys now, and they all looked mad. Including the tall, broad-shouldered guy in his thirties standing at the edge of the wheelchair doubles court, his arms crossed.

Detective Donovan didn't even need to remove his Ray-Bans to let her know how ticked off he was at being summoned by a bullhorn. And maybe that his grandma had lost a game point.

Gladys began waving her arms wildly in the detective's direction, and he strode up the hill toward them. Summer waggled her fingers at him and tried to disappear behind Mrs. Rumway. That was pretty much wasted effort, though. She was still way taller than the battle-ax.

"Is there a problem, Mrs. Rumway?" Summer felt, rather than saw, Detective Donovan glare at both of them, behind his shades. She wasn't going to look at him. "Miss Smythe-Sloan," he added.

He still called her by her full last name, just to bug her. If only he weren't so uptight, she might be totally attracted to him. She'd thought, after she and Dorothy solved his last case for him, that maybe he was going to ask her out. But he hadn't, weirdly. "Summer," she muttered, reluctantly glancing his way.

"Right." A quick smile passed over his tanned face. Wait. Was he just messing with her? So annoying.

"This one has some kind of emergency situation." Gladys jerked her thumb in Summer's face. "So what is it, missy?"

None of your business, Summer wanted to say. She couldn't tell the detective about Mrs. Caldwell in front of Gladys. That would be the kiss of death for keeping things on the down low around Hibiscus Pointe—and all over town.

"I was supposed to get you right away." Summer resisted the urge to just grab the guy and drag him off with her. "There's an RV stuck in the parking lot."

Was that emergency boring enough to ditch Gladys?

Detective Donovan looked confused. "I'm not, uh, sure I'm the best person to—"

"Jennifer sent me," Summer added.

Well, that sure worked. He immediately turned and practically bolted for the parking lot, as Gladys stared at her in disappointment and disgust. Summer sighed. Obviously, Jennifer had a lot more pull with Detective Donovan than she did.

Quit it, she told herself. That wasn't important right now. There was a freaking dead person in the library.

"Hey, wait!" Summer scrambled to keep up with Detective Donovan. "It's a murder, okay?" she said as soon as they were far enough away from the battle-ax. "Dorothy and I think so, anyway. The librarian, Mrs. Caldwell. We already called 911."

Quickly, she told him about finding Lorella and the bloody bookend in the messed-up library, leaving out the Trixie part for now.

For a second, the guy had zero reaction. Or that was what it seemed like, anyway. Then he took off at a run again toward the main building as a bunch of sirens started up from the main road outside the complex. Summer followed, snagging a couple brownies from the welcome table by the gate on her way.

When they got to the library, Dorothy was standing—well, sitting—guard on a chair next to Lorella. Close by, a still-jittery-looking Jennifer was trying to concentrate on her phone, instead of the body on the floor. Summer noticed that, despite her nervousness, the girl had managed to freshen her makeup and let her hair loose in soft waves around her shoulders.

Huh. Well, that was weird. Unless it had something to do with...

"Detective Donovan, we're so glad you're here!" Jennifer reholstered her cell and rushed toward him, her face Desert Rose-pink again.

He didn't smile, exactly, under the circumstances, but he seemed a little friendlier now than he had at the tennis courts. "Glad to be of help, Jennifer. Hello, Mrs. Westin." His eyes swept the room, immediately zeroing in on the body. "Can you ladies tell me everything you remember about what happened?" He headed straight for the last book stack.

Summer did her own scan of the library, trying not to focus too much on the slender, tweed-skirted body on the carpet. Her sweater was wool, too, which was pretty weird for Florida. The woman could have been any Northern grandma. Totally harmless. And like Summer had asked Dorothy earlier, who'd want to kill a librarian?

No one messed with librarians, unless they were really stupid. But Trixie Quattrochi had to be pretty dumb, if she was hanging out with that skeezy Ray guy. He looked a zillion percent mean.

Maybe Ray—not Trixie—was the person who'd clobbered poor Mrs. Caldwell. Either way, all Summer and Dorothy had to do was track those two down, and prove it. If Trixie had wanted to get rid of Lorella, though, she could have just shot her with that pistol in her duffel. Unless she was worried about the noise, maybe. Could you use a silencer on that thing?

A guy carrying a resuscitation kit bumped into her, jolting Summer back to attention. All around her, the tiny library was rapidly filling with first responders and crime scene investigators. A police photographer began to snap pictures of the body from all angles, as other forensic technicians took measurements and dusted for prints. Somehow, the crowd had totally cut her off from Detective Donovan. He was taking notes on his phone now as he talked to Dorothy and Jennifer.

Cops were never really off duty, he'd told her once. Maybe that was why he liked to spend so much time on that boat of his. It was hard to reach people on the ocean.

Obviously, he didn't have any questions for her. She might as well be invisible now, like she'd wanted to be at the tennis courts a few minutes ago. Well, fine. But after she and Dorothy caught Mrs. Caldwell's killer, Detective Donovan would be sorry he forgot to ask her anything.

Had Dorothy given him Trixie's note? Yes. He was dropping that crazy orange envelope into one of the technician's brown paper evidence bags. Too bad her sleuthing partner would never have opened the letter. They really needed to know what it said, because Donovan probably wouldn't tell them.

Both of their fingerprints were all over that envelope. But at least no one would think she was a suspect this time. Before today, she hadn't even known Lorella existed—or Trixie, either, for that matter.

Sometimes she didn't pay a lot of attention to things going on at Hibiscus Pointe. But it wasn't like she was going to actually hang out with any of the old people. Except Dorothy, of course. And her partner's good friend, Ernie, and Grace, his wife, who was really sweet, and...

"Excuse me," a young cop said. She looked fresh out of the academy, with her heavy gun belt practically reaching her knees, but tough. "You're not supposed to be in here. This is a crime scene. Step outside, please."

"But I'm with them," Summer said, pointing. "I'm a witness."

"Does the detective have your name and contact info?" The cop's name tag said "Caputo."

"Well, yeah, he knows who I am," Summer said, indignant. "I—"

"He'll be in touch if he needs to talk to you." Caputo jerked her chin toward the door.

Cold.

Summer waved over the young woman's head, trying to catch Dorothy's attention. Total fail, before Caputo took a half step toward her. With a sigh, she backed out of the library and plopped herself on the floor beside the door to wait.

The carpet felt slightly damp. Either the cleaning people had just shampooed it, or it was some kind of invisible mold. Eww.

Down the hall, she could see Bill Beusel, Hibiscus Pointe's silver-haired head of security, trying to shoo a bunch of gawking residents away. He and his equally useless minion had their hands full, as the seniors pressed against the velvet rope that had been set up to block off the area near the library. And now they were all staring at her.

Luckily, Dorothy and Jennifer stepped out just then. Summer scrambled to her feet. "What did I miss?" she asked Dorothy. "Was Detective Donovan happy when you gave him the note? Did he read it in front of you?"

"I'll fill you in on everything later, dear," Dorothy said, with a tiny quirk of her eyebrow. Oh. She didn't want to talk about Trixie in front of Jennifer, probably.

Dorothy turned to the Resident Services director. "Jennifer, I know this is hardly the time, but I'd like to talk to you later about that book club launch Lorella had planned. It meant so much to her, and perhaps we can carry on her wishes. I'd be happy to help."

Jeez. What did the stupid book club deal have to do with anything? Maybe Summer's partner was trying to distract Jennifer from the dead body in the library. Or the note.

"Oh, Mrs. Westin, it's so nice of you to offer, but I couldn't impose on you to take on such a big project." Jennifer looked genuinely distressed. "Especially with Mrs. Caldwell…gone…and everything. I mean, it's true the book club idea was very close to her heart, and Roger was really anxious to build up our resident activities, but under the circumstances…"

"Hey, what did Roger say about Mrs. Caldwell being murdered?" Summer asked.

Jennifer looked at her navy pumps. "He doesn't know yet. He's out on the golf course. Um, inspecting the greens," she added quickly.

The girl sounded like she was starting to panic again. Summer felt sorry for her.

"Ah. Well, do give me a call about the book club when things settle down," Dorothy said to Jennifer. "And I'm sure Summer will lend a hand, too. Isn't that right, dear?"

What? Just what she needed. Another volunteer

job—and a superboring one, to boot. No thanks. Besides, they had a murder to solve. "Uh, yeah, sure. Dorothy, we've got to get going." Summer pulled on her friend's pink sweater sleeve. "We have to catch up with Mrs. *Luger*," she said, under her breath. Hopefully, Dorothy would take the hint about Trixie. "Like, right away."

"Please don't let me keep you, ladies," Jennifer said. "We'll talk about the book club later, Mrs. Westin."

Well, at least someone could take a hint.

"I need to track down Roger." Jennifer glanced over her shoulder at Bill trying to redirect the growing crowd, and sighed. "Guess it's too late to keep the news about Lorella quiet. But maybe we could not mention anything to the other residents about the…unusual circumstances? For now, at least."

Dorothy nodded. "I'm sure Detective Donovan would appreciate that, too. Everyone will find out the sad truth soon enough, I'm afraid."

"I knew I should have read Trixie's note," Summer said, the second she and Dorothy were around the corner. Jennifer had headed in the opposite direction, to try to help Bill get rid of the gaping seniors. "It had to have been a threat."

"More of a warning, I think."

"Wait. You mean you actually opened that envelope?" Summer stopped so fast she almost face-planted over the tips of her sneakers.

Dorothy's face turned the same pink as her sweater. "Well, yes. Under the circumstances, I felt I should."

"Good job." Summer threw her partner a grin. "I'm impressed. Hey, is that why you were trying to distract

Jennifer with all that book club stuff? So we could get rid of her and you could tell me about the note faster?"

"I wouldn't say 'distract,' exactly." Dorothy's face turned a darker pink, more like the fake tropical plant they'd just passed in the hall. "I was quite serious about volunteering." She filled Summer in on the contents of Trixie's letter.

"Whoa. There's a snake?" Summer said when her friend had finished. "Jeez, I really, really hate those things."

"Not an actual snake, I'm sure," Dorothy said. "The name was capitalized, so Trixie probably meant a person. Of the sneaky persuasion, perhaps."

"Or the killing kind," Summer said. "Trixie's got to be the murderer, I'm telling you. Or else it's her buddy Ray. Did Detective Donovan put out on an APB for the RV?"

Well, that was fun to say. She sounded very official.

"I did give him the note," Dorothy said. "He said they'd be on the lookout for the vehicle."

"On the lookout?" Summer said. "That's it?" Sounded as if the detective was in no big hurry to question the obvious prime suspect, either. Well, fine. "We'll just have to bring her and Ray in on our own, then. Hopefully, they got stuck in lunchtime traffic and haven't gotten that far yet."

She started walking again, very fast, toward the lobby, then realized she had gotten way ahead of her partner. "Whoops, sorry, Dorothy. I'll go get my car from the lot and meet you out front."

"We can't approach Trixie and Ray by ourselves," Dorothy said. "They might be dangerous. Trixie has that awful gun, remember?"

"We'll be really careful," Summer promised. "They'll never even see us. All we have to do is catch up with them, and then we can call the cops. Piece of cake."

Dorothy hesitated. "I don't know. That's not a very—"

"We've got to hurry," Summer broke in. "Ol' Ray and Trixie are probably almost to Georgia by now. Come on, we can grab a bite from the Frankn'Creams drive-through on the way."

She knew Dorothy couldn't resist their tutti-frutti shakes. And the hot dogs were pretty decent, too. "It's good to eat when you're stressed," Summer added. "You know, to keep your strength up."

In practically no time, she and Dorothy were cruising down Imperial Boulevard toward the highway entrance in her orange MINI Cooper convertible, which hadn't broken down in weeks. Beside her, Dorothy sipped her pink-yellow-and-orange-swirled shake and held on to her floppy blue sunhat with one hand.

It was terrible about Mrs. Caldwell, of course, but it felt good to be working on a case again. Solving crimes was something Summer was actually good at. And so was Dorothy. They were a great team.

"Look out, dear!" Dorothy cried as a red Fiat drew up beside them, way too close. Two sunburned guys wearing identical red muscle shirts and Oakley sunglasses leered over at them, their teeth extra white against all that red.

"Losers," Summer muttered. "Just ignore them."

The driver honked his horn before shouting something she couldn't believe any guy would say in front of Dorothy. Or any woman, for that matter.

She hit the brakes—luckily, no one was behind

them—then tapped the gas again and swerved in behind the Fiat. Yep. Out-of-state plates. Morons on a road trip.

"Pay attention to the road, not the hooligans, dear." Dorothy dabbed at a spot of tutti-frutti that had spilled on her pink sweater.

"Okay." Sensing a sudden break in traffic to her left, Summer lurched the MINI into the passing lane and sped around the Fiat, leaving the goon twins in the dust. "See? Much better."

"Mmm." Dorothy was twisted in her seat. "I'm not sure, but I think I see Trixie's RV. A few blocks behind us, turning right on Neptune."

"Hold on to your hat again," Summer said. "We're gonna make a U-ie."

Lorella Caldwell's killer was in their sights.

THREE

"I CAN'T BELIEVE THIS," Summer said. "Now we've lost them."

Dorothy tried not to wince as her friend braked at the last possible moment for still another red light on Neptune Avenue. "It does look that way," she agreed, with a sigh. The Happy Trailways had completely disappeared into the heavy midafternoon Milano traffic. "Well, they couldn't have gotten far," she pointed out. "They were headed toward the beach."

"We'll catch up with up them, no problem." Summer gritted her teeth as a trolley painted with colorful fish pulled in front of them. "I have to be a better driver than that dirtbag. And the mini is way easier to maneuver than a freaking RV."

Dorothy leaned forward over the dashboard. "There they are!" she said. "On the left, about to turn onto Benton Beach Road."

"Got 'em," Summer said. "Good spot, Dorothy."

"Give me your phone, dear, and I'll call Detective Donovan." Although her sleuthing partner had been trying very hard to talk her into buying her own cell phone, Dorothy still hadn't done so. She wasn't entirely sure they were necessary, really. Except for emergencies, of course.

There seemed to be a lot of them lately. And this certainly qualified as one.

"Wait, let's get closer first," Summer said, weaving the MINI through the other cars crawling toward the beach. "You know, to make sure it's them."

Dorothy thought that was a very poor idea. Right now there was nothing separating them from Trixie and Ray but a nasty, choking cloud of diesel. Trixie, they knew, was armed—and both of them could be dangerous.

"Look, they're pulling into the Benton Beach entrance," Summer said. "We've got 'em now. Do you have any quarters for the parking meter?"

"We don't need to park, dear," Dorothy said. "Let's just drive around the lot a bit, and wait until we see them get out. It's a lot safer that way."

"Maybe they're staying here for the night." Summer pulled up to the guardhouse, gazing warily at the yellow-and-red gate arm poised just above the MINI.

"I don't think so." Dorothy pointed to the sun-beaten sign on the side of the tiny gate house. It clearly prohibited camping, both on the beach and in the parking lot.

Summer shrugged. "A lot of people do it anyway."

Oddly, the gate house was unmanned. Was it too late in the day to collect a parking fee? The town of Milano usually required payment for just about everything, round the clock.

She frowned but withheld comment as Summer pulled the MINI into the parking space directly next to the Happy Trailways—just as the driver door opened, narrowly missing her own.

Dorothy braced herself for Ray's scowl—or worse— but it was a stocky, middle-aged man wearing a banana-yellow shirt, a canvas sunhat, and frayed denim cutoffs who emerged from the camper.

Well, that was most definitely not Trixie's friend. Dorothy let out a tiny sigh of relief. It would have been nice if they had found their two suspects, of course— but maybe not this close up.

Summer hit the daisy-decaled sun visor above her head in frustration. "Rats."

Dorothy leaned out the passenger window. "Excuse me, sir?"

He turned, wiping his face with his arm and flinging the sweat onto the asphalt. "Yeah?" he said, clearly disinterested. Then he spotted Summer, and approached the car. "What can I help you with, ladies?" he asked, placing one distinctly hairy hand on the hood.

Dorothy tried, unsuccessfully, to summon more than a shred of sympathy for the man as he yelped and jumped away from the scalding metal.

"My granddaughter and I were admiring your lovely RV," she said. "Did you buy it here in town? We're thinking of taking a little trip ourselves."

"We want one exactly like it," Summer added. "You know, with 'Happy Trailways' on the side. That's so cute."

The man's gold wedding ring flashed in the sun as he clutched his other, slightly charred paw. "You wanna tour of the inside? My name's Louis, by the way."

Dorothy detected a quiet gag from the passenger seat beside her. "No, thanks," Summer said. "We're good."

"It's a rental." A freckled woman in a khaki Australian-style hat glared at her husband as she came around the rear of the van, trailed by two children loaded down with brightly colored beach chairs, plastic toys, and swimming floats. A younger set of carrot-topped progeny was just emerging from behind the RV, lugging an enormous red cooler between them and bickering loudly.

"That's even better," Dorothy said. "Which agency did you use?"

"We just picked it up today. Cinderella Luxury Coaches, off 85," the woman said. "North Milano, I think. But don't waste your money, this thing is a piece of junk. It's already broken down twice."

"So sorry to hear that," Dorothy said. Closer up, the RV did seem worse for the wear, with one semiflat tire and a large dent below the dirty windows. On this side, the worn—or intentionally edited—letters in Happy Trailways read Hoppy Tails.

"Some dear friends of mine just rented a vehicle and they may have used Cinderella Coaches, also," Dorothy told the woman. "I do hope they won't have any trouble. They're going all the way to Montana."

"Montana?" Louis's wife glanced over her shoulder as he took off after the children, who were now pushing and shoving each other near the water fountain. "A woman in line at the rental counter said she was headed there. Told everyone she was in a big hurry, but she just kept on talking. Held all of us up."

"Was she wearing huge diamond earrings shaped like Texas?" Summer asked.

"Don't know what they were supposed to be," the woman said. "But they were big and sparkly, all right."

"Yes, that might have been my friend," Dorothy murmured. "More of an acquaintance, really."

"Pauline, get a move on!" Louis called from the wooden walkway that led to the beach. "The kids got away from me!"

"Sorry," Pauline said, with a sigh. "Gotta go. Good

luck on your trip." She adjusted the wooden bead to tighten the chin strap of her hat and hurried away over the sandy parking lot.

"Those children certainly are rambunctious," Dorothy said. "I hope their parents are able to catch up with them before they reach the water."

"I swear, I am never having kids." Summer pushed the ignition button.

Maddie used to say that, Dorothy told herself. Sadly, there was no way to know now whether her daughter might have changed her mind. "Surely you don't mean that, dear."

"Yes, I do," Summer said stubbornly, but she didn't sound quite as emphatic this time. "So, where are we headed? Guess we can forget catching up with Trixie and Ray now."

"Not necessarily," Dorothy said. "Why don't we pay a visit to Cinderella Coaches? Maybe the rental agent there can tell us something about those two. Every little detail counts."

She tried not to grip the car seat as Summer backed out of the parking space in one fell swoop.

With luck, Trixie and Ray's motor coach had turned into a pumpkin somewhere along the road.

SUMMER TAPPED HER fingers on the steering wheel. The highway was a total mess. Traffic. More traffic. Annnnd…yep, *more* traffic.

Spring break must have started early. Now there'd be a bunch of underage kids jamming the clubs every night, and all the decent restaurants would be packed with tourists.

Whoa. Did she really just think that? She used to

love spring break in Cabo, and that wasn't so long ago. Or…maybe it was.

Jeez. She was getting old.

She glanced at Dorothy beside her in the passenger seat. Her friend had to be broiling in this heat. They should have grabbed a lemonade or something from the Benton Beach snack bar.

"Hey, can you see who that is?" she asked as her cell rang. "Might be Donovan. But if it's anyone else, don't answer, okay?"

"Hello?" Dorothy said, into the phone. "Oh yes, how are you? She's right here. But she's driving, I'm afraid."

Summer sighed. "Put it on speaker, please."

"Hold on just a moment, Dash." Dorothy fumbled with the screen, then looked triumphant as the deep voice of Summer's best friend crackled into the MINI.

"Hey, Cali Girl, where are you?"

"Not home. What's up?" She loved Dash, of course, but she couldn't help feeling a tiny bit bummed that he wasn't Detective Donovan. Not that she'd expected the caller to be him, or anything. But the guy had to question her soon about finding Mrs. Caldwell, right? It was his job, for crying out loud.

Maybe he could interview her over coffee. Or drinks. Even better.

"Well, I would have asked you this sooner, but Mother just called," Dash said. "She's shown up a few days early, gods help us, and she's already on her way from the airport. Do you and Dorothy want to come over tonight for dinner? Mother is expecting a party."

"Thanks, but I may not be able to make it," Summer told him. "Dorothy and I are on a new case. I'll fill you in later, but—"

"You mean the librarian lady who just got murdered?" Dash said. "The Pointe is in quite an uproar right now. Cops and TV crews everywhere. I've been trying to peel Juliette-Margot away from the windows."

"Poor Jennifer," Dorothy murmured. "She must have her hands full."

"So what do you say, ladies?" Dash asked. "Please, please save my life and come to the dinner party tonight. You'll love Mother. And Dorothy, bring Ernie, too. The more, the merrier."

"Thank you, Dash, but are you sure we wouldn't be imposing?" Dorothy said.

"Hardly." He chuckled. "Mother's already put in her menu requests. So, cocktails at six-thirty?"

"Count us in," Summer said. "See you then."

"Wait, Dash, what would you like us to bring?" Dorothy asked.

"Just yourselves. *Ciao* for now." He clicked off.

"Well, it will certainly be lovely to meet the great GH Hamel," Dorothy said. "But goodness, we can't show up empty-handed. We should at least get some flowers on the way home."

"Okay," Summer said. "I'm sure we'll pass a few grocery stores. Hey, look, there's a sign for Cinderella Coaches," she added as they finally reached the off-ramp for North Milano. "See the one with the revolving glass slipper?"

Oops. Hopefully, Dorothy wouldn't notice those other signs next to it. Miss Kitty's Gentlemen's Club and Greenwood Discount Cremation Services. Summer didn't know which one was worse.

But Dorothy was frowning at something else. Her attention seemed focused on the strip mall just off the exit, where another silver slipper—glittering like a disco ball—revolved on top of a tall pole in the middle of the parking lot. "What on earth is going on here?" she said.

"Looks as if Cinderella Coaches is going out of business," Summer said. "Or else there's a sudden big demand for Happy Trailways motor homes."

At least five RVs and a few sad-looking SUVs were in the process of being hitched up to wreckers. A white stretch limo was already being towed from the lot exit. Some poor bride was going to be in for a nasty surprise.

Summer pulled into the entrance near a nondescript brick building. The sign in the window said "Cinderella Coaches and Luxury Vehicles"—with OUT OF BUSINESS stamped over it. "Well, that was fast," she said. "Wonder if Trixie and Ray will get to keep their RV."

"I doubt it," Dorothy said. "How very odd, that people were renting from this place just a few hours ago."

"Must have been an unexpected closing." Summer leaned over the steering wheel to peer at the posted notice on the door. "Yep. IRS."

Dorothy sighed. "I guess we won't be questioning the rental agents, then. We might as well go ahead and buy those flowers for tonight."

"Okay," Summer said. "Next stop, Publix."

Unfortunately, the entrance to 85 was closed for construction, so she had to navigate another round of traffic on the parallel truck route. At this rate, they'd be lucky to make Dash's for dinner at all.

"Wait a minute," Dorothy said, twisting in her seat. "Was that Jupiter Boulevard back there?"

"No idea," Summer said. Everything in this part of town looked the same to her. Strip malls, outlet stores, fancy car dealerships, elaborately landscaped entrances to gated communities and golf and tennis clubs.

Downtown was another story, of course. Close to the beaches, the trendier parts of Milano boasted trendy boutiques, uber-hip restaurants and clubs, and famous art galleries. Not that she cared much about the galleries. They were a dime a dozen around here. But sometimes they hired model types—usually male—to hand out white wine and hors d'oeuvres.

"I seem to remember Lorella mentioning she lived off of Jupiter Boulevard before she moved to Hibiscus Pointe," Dorothy said. "Somewhere behind the Jupiter Crossings Mall, which we just passed. Maybe we can talk to some of her other former neighbors."

"Okay." Summer took the next left turn. "Put my phone on speaker again, so we can find out her old address."

After several rounds of the neighborhood under the equally-clueless direction of the cell phone's virtual assistant, they pulled up to the curb outside of 831 Jupiter Court. The pointy, two-story tan and brown house with the criss-crossed windowpanes looked totally out of place on the crowded block of little pink houses with Spanish-tile roofs.

"That is one ugly place," Summer said. "Like the witch's cottage from Hansel and Gretel."

"It's called a Tudor home, after the royal Tudor family in medieval times," Dorothy told her. "The style was most popular around the beginning of the twentieth century, though. You've never seen one?"

Sometimes Dorothy sounded a lot like a librarian herself. "Maybe," Summer said. "But this one looks kind of haunted, if you ask me."

"Nonsense." Dorothy was already getting out of the car. "Let's see if there's anyone home."

For the zillionth time that day, no one answered the door. And once again, Summer felt relieved, just like she had at the library. Look how *that* had turned out.

"Let's go try the neighbors," she said, glancing around at the other houses. All the ones besides Lorella's had teeny, tiny pools. Did people actually swim in those? They were more like hot tubs, without the jets.

Stepping off the crumbling stone porch, she almost ran smack into a short, dark-haired guy carrying a large pair of hedge trimmers. He'd appeared out of nowhere.

Like a ghost.

"What are you doing here?" the guy demanded, in a low, gravelly voice. He narrowed his already-squinty eyes, closing and unclosing the clippers.

Why was he doing that? Maybe the guy was some kind of psycho killer, like the ones in those late-night horror movies? She tried to block Dorothy's view, as her friend came up behind her.

"We're friends of Lorella Caldwell," Dorothy told the creepy guy, giving Summer a tiny push aside. "It looks as if she isn't home, and we're so disappointed."

"Mrs. C doesn't live here anymore," the guy said. "I take care of this place for the new owners while they're up North. The Johnstons."

Summer glanced back at the deserted house. By the looks of things, he wasn't doing such a hot job. Back in LA, he'd be fired pronto. "Are they coming back, uh, soon?" Hopefully not, for his sake.

The guy shrugged. "Dunno. They're always changing their minds. You gotta leave now."

"Oh, of course." Dorothy made no move to go.

"Sorry to have bothered you. So you worked for Mrs. Caldwell, too?"

"Yeah. Nice lady. Real quiet. No visitors, except for that brother of hers. That's who he said he was, anyway."

"Brother?" Summer said. "Does he live in Milano?"

"Dunno," the guy said. "Drove an old black sports car with Florida plates. Just caught him here the other day, snooping around in the bushes. Coulda got his head chopped off." He held up the clippers, and demonstrated on a small, dead branch hanging over the porch railing.

Yep. This guy was definitely a psycho. Either he didn't know his old boss was dead, or...maybe he'd tracked her to Hibiscus Pointe and killed her himself. Maybe Lorella hadn't paid him or something.

"How odd that he wasn't aware his sister had moved," Dorothy said, thoughtfully.

"I set him straight on that," the caretaker said. "He won't be coming around here again."

Lorella's brother was probably buried somewhere under the dead rosebushes. "Well, guess we'd better get going," Summer said, quickly. "Come on, Dorothy."

"Thank you so much for your help, sir," Dorothy called over her shoulder, as Summer hustled her friend as fast as she could down the uneven walk. The stones were barely visible through the scratchy, brown grass. Lorella must have taken Milano's rarely-enforced watering restrictions pretty seriously.

Things were a little different back at Hibiscus Pointe. The fountains there spewed twenty-four-seven and the grass was greener than the felt on the mini-putting green outside the main building.

Maybe that was one of the reasons Lorella decided

to move there. Or maybe she just didn't want to take care of her ugly, haunted house anymore. Who could blame her?

Summer was just opening the car door for Dorothy when she spotted a pair of eyes peering over the wood fence. Kind of like the nosy neighbor guy on that old TV show *Home Improvement*, where you never saw the rest of his face. But this person, judging from the curly white head with the pink visor, had to be a woman.

"Hold on a sec," Summer said to Dorothy. "I'll be right back."

She jogged toward the fence—by now the psycho guy with the clippers had disappeared around the side of the witch house—and the white-and-pink lady had vanished, too.

Summer peered over the faded brown fence. She was careful not to touch it, because it was probably full of splinters.

The woman on the other side was crouched down in a row of red and yellow tulips, pretending to be invisible. "You know I can see you, right?" Summer asked.

Lorella's former neighbor stood up and took a few steps back into her yard, half tripping over a flat of unplanted purple pansies. She just stood there, blinking nervously a few times. "Are you the Johnstons?" the woman asked, finally.

"Nope," Summer said. "We're friends of Mrs. Caldwell's. Well, my grandma is, anyway." No need to mention Lorella was dead, in case Nervous Nellie hadn't heard yet. "Did you know her?"

"No, not at all," Nellie said. "I mind my own business, you know."

Yeah, I bet, Summer thought. "You don't know where Mrs. Caldwell's brother lives, do you?"

"Lorella doesn't have a brother," Nellie said. "No family at all."

Summer didn't find that idea depressing, like everyone else seemed to. She had plenty of family, thanks to all her dad's marriages, and she couldn't stand any of them. Except her sister, Joy, of course, and their dad, when they weren't trying to mess up her life.

Her mom, Harmony, was okay, too, but who knew where she was these days? The crystal store on the pier must not have worked out so well. "No brother, huh? That's funny, I thought I met him once."

Nellie pulled her pink visor farther down over her face and stepped back toward the fence. "Oh, you mean the young man who was always visiting," she said, in a gossipy voice. "That's not Lorella's brother. He's her boyfriend."

"How young?" Summer asked. It was hard to imagine Mrs. Caldwell as a cougar.

Nellie leaned in closer. "Not a day over sixty."

Huh. Well, that was no big deal. Lorella had to have been in her seventies. "Yep, that's the guy we need to talk to, all right," Summer said. "Do you know his name?"

"Oh yes." Nellie nodded eagerly. "It's Charles Bell. He teaches at Santa Teresa Community College. Lorella used to work there, you know, in the English Department office." The woman was straight up against the fence now. "If you ask me, I think the two of them were having an affair."

"So he's married?"

"Well, I don't have all the details," Nellie said. "Lorella wasn't much of a talker. But I can just tell those kinds of things, you know? That man was definitely poking around here, just the other day, and she moved away about a month ago. She must not have told him she was leaving."

Was Lorella's younger boyfriend a stalker? He had to have been up to something. Summer brushed a damp strand of hair off her face. It was a good thing she never burned, because the sun was even more broiling now. Dorothy had to be getting really hot back there in the car. They needed to put on the AC and buy her a bottle of water somewhere.

"Hey, it was great to meet you and everything, but I've got to go," she said to Nellie. "Keep an eye on things around here, okay?"

"Oh, I always do," the woman said. She sounded proud about it, too.

"If Lorella's boyfriend shows up again, call the police, okay?" Summer added. "He might be dangerous."

Had this Charles Bell guy needed to get rid of Lorella because of their steamy affair? Maybe she'd threatened to tell his wife. Or—

Three sharp honks sounded from the MINI. Oops. Dorothy was looking a little impatient, fanning herself with her hat.

Summer ran toward the car and leaped behind the wheel without bothering to open the door. Piece of cake.

She'd always wanted to do that, like the two crazy brothers in those old *Dukes of Hazzard* reruns she watched at three in the morning, when she was getting in from the clubs.

"Hey, guess what?" she said to Dorothy. "We've got ourselves another lead."

FOUR

"MRS. WESTIN!"

Dorothy heard Jennifer before she saw her step off the elevator on the second floor of Hibiscus Gardens Building One. The Resident Services director ran toward her down the carpeted hallway, her arms full of books, canvas tote bags, and brochures.

"Hello, Jennifer. Let me help you with those, dear." Dorothy shifted the wine bottle and bouquet of flowers in her arms, and reached out to take the tote bags and at least a few of the heavy-looking hardcovers from the young woman's grasp. "*War and Peace*? My goodness."

"These are Lorella's materials for the book club launch," Jennifer said, still a bit breathless. "I was hoping maybe, if you and Summer were still willing to take things over…" Her voice trailed away, sounding hopeful.

"We'll be happy to help out," Dorothy said, unlocking the door and ushering Jennifer inside. "Just set the rest of those things down somewhere in the living room."

"Thanks, Mrs. Westin. Wow, you have your condo fixed up so nicely. The layouts are all the same in the Gardens, but yours looks so cozy and— Eek!" Jennifer jumped back as a swift, fiery orange ball of fur, claws, and teeth flew toward her from the couch. "Oh my gosh, what is that?"

Dorothy hurried over to shoo her large-boned, unrepentant tomcat toward the bedroom. "That's Mr. Bitey. He's a bit jittery around guests sometimes. I do apologize if he gave you a fright."

"Mr. Whitey?" Jennifer's worried brown eyes shot around the room. "But he's, um, orange, right?"

"No, the name really is Bitey." Dorothy sighed. "I adopted him after his owner moved into assisted living. He was something of a forever-home placement challenge, the cat rescue people mentioned. But the two of us get on swimmingly now." As long as he received prompt meals and frequent snacks.

"Oh. That's nice." Jennifer settled herself gingerly on the floral couch, discreetly arming herself with a crocheted pillow.

"Has there been any more word on what happened to Lorella?" Dorothy set the bottle of wine she'd bought for Dash's dinner party down on the counter and began to unwrap the sadly wilted grocery store flowers from their plastic wrappings. Hopefully, she could revive them with a burst of cold water.

"Not really," Jennifer said. "Detective Donovan told me they need to notify the next of kin. I don't think Mrs. Caldwell had any family, though."

"No children or siblings?" Dorothy asked. "A brother, perhaps?"

Jennifer shook her head. "Not that I know of. This is why it's so important for people to fill everything out on their New Resident Let's-Get-to-Know-You forms."

"Do you still have the form Lorella gave you when she moved in to Hibiscus Pointe?" Dorothy stuck the bouquet into a vase and added one of the little vitamin packs she kept on hand for floral emergencies.

"I do, back in my office," Jennifer said. "I keep all the residents' information in those big loose-leaf binders on the bookshelves behind my desk, sorted by year, and also alphabetically. But I'm afraid the contents of those are strictly confidential."

"Oh, of course." Hibiscus Pointe kept their resident files more secure than most doctors Dorothy knew. But wouldn't Jennifer need to turn over any information she had at all on Lorella Caldwell to Detective Donovan?

The Resident Services director picked an invisible piece of lint from her skirt. Dorothy carefully snipped the stem of a particularly morbid-looking daisy, waiting.

"I looked at Lorella's form quickly this afternoon, but it was mostly blank," Jennifer said. "Of course, if anyone really needed it, a lot of the get-to-know-you information for new residents goes into our *What's Your Pointe?* newsletter when they move in."

"Ah yes." Dorothy busied herself gathering up dead leaves from the sink. "I'll have to dig up my back copies." That might be quite a job. Lately, she'd been placing them in the giant green recycling bin at the end of the hall on a fairly regular basis. After she'd read them, of course.

"So tell me more about Lorella's plans for the book club relaunch," she said, bringing two glasses of ice water out to the living room. Mr. Bitey, she noticed, had reasserted himself a paw's length from the corner of the couch. She seated herself next to Jennifer, just in case she needed to head the jealous kitty off again.

"Well, we didn't talk about them much, really," Jennifer said. "Specifically, anyway. But I do have what Mrs. Caldwell wrote in her article." She reached carefully across the couch, with a wary glance at Mr. Bitey, and took a brochure from one of the tote bags. "Here's a copy of tomorrow's newsletter. Mrs. Caldwell was hoping for a good turnout of residents for the organizational meeting on Friday. But I've heard the last time we had a book club here at Hibiscus Pointe, things didn't go very well."

No, they certainly hadn't. Dorothy quickly perused the article. "It says here that the club will meet twice each month. My, the reading list sounds quite…ambitious."

Perfect for anyone who felt inspired to read and discuss some of the longest classic novels ever written within two weeks.

"Did you go to any of the meetings when Helen Murphy ran the book club here?" Jennifer asked. "That was before I started working here."

"Yes, I was a member," Dorothy said. In its previous incarnation, the Hibiscus Pointe Book Club was a deadly dull affair, and entirely too exclusive, in her view. Strongly opinionated members were unwelcome, as were those whose reading tastes failed to meet with Helen Murphy's approval.

In a few short months, Helen had found herself in a book club of one. Fortunately—or perhaps unfortunately, in Summer's case—she'd taken up the reins of the Residents Board. Everyone agreed that position was much better suited to her directorial talents.

"Mrs. Caldwell was really serious about the classics," Jennifer said. "I guess that's not a big surprise, since she worked over at Santa Teresa College."

So Lorella and Charles Bell had once been colleagues. "My, I see all kinds of literary gems here," Dorothy said, glancing down at the book club reading list again.

Wuthering Heights, Jane Eyre, Anna Karenina…each to be read within two weeks. "I assume she was in the English Department, then?"

"Yes, as an administrative assistant," Jennifer said. "That's what she listed on her information form. But she had a PhD, I think."

Interesting. Lorella hardly seemed like the sort of person who might find herself in any kind of serious trouble, Dorothy told herself. But obviously, someone had wanted her out of the way—permanently.

Had Lorella startled that same person in the stacks, up to no good? But why would anyone be involved in some nefarious activity in such a small—and very public— place? There wasn't much traffic in the library, and even less in the business center, but still…

Most likely, the killer had grabbed a weapon from somewhere in the library to do her in. No one carried heavy gold bookends around with them.

It definitely seemed like a crime of passion, as if the person hadn't planned the murder. He or she must have acted in some sudden, uncontrollable fit of rage. But… hadn't the murderer struck poor Lorella on the back of her head? She might not have seen her attacker coming. Dorothy hoped not.

What might the person have been angry about? Money? Family matters? A romantic entanglement?

Again, neither of those seemed likely to apply, in Lorella's case. By all appearances, the librarian had lived quietly and frugally, and had no family. But one never knew… Could Charles Bell have killed her in some jealous rage or lovers' quarrel? And who was The Snake that Trixie had warned her of, before she quickly decamped in her rented RV with an unsavory companion?

"So, what do you think, Mrs. Westin?"

Dorothy snapped to attention. Jennifer was looking at her expectantly, and she hadn't heard a word the young woman had said. "Sorry, dear. I'm afraid I lost track of our conversation, for a moment or two."

She hated lending the idea she was inattentive to conversation—or worse, prone to "senior moments." But sometimes age did come in handy.

"That's okay, Mrs. Westin," Jennifer said. "I don't think any of us are ourselves today, after"—her Rose Quartz lips quivered slightly—"what happened to Mrs. Caldwell. Do you think we should cancel the first book club meeting on Friday?"

"Absolutely not," Dorothy said. The sooner she and Summer got things rolling, the better. The book club would be a perfect cover for learning more about Lorella Caldwell's shadowy world. Her murderer might even show up to the meetings. Maybe the person hadn't gotten what he or she wanted yet. Or maybe they were eager to ensure that whatever secret Lorella might have stumbled upon had gone to the grave with her.

"That's only two days away." Jennifer still looked worried, but then, the poor girl was always concerned about something. "The newsletter comes out tomorrow, and as you can see it's already printed, but maybe I could—"

Dorothy reached over to pat Jennifer's arm. "No need to change the date," she said. "Summer and I will pull something together for Friday. Carrying on with the book club as Lorella planned will be a lovely tribute to her, don't you think?"

"I guess you're right," Jennifer said. "I'm not sure that there will be any kind of other memorial."

"There, then that's settled." Dorothy sat back on the couch and took a sip of her ice water.

Jennifer's cell phone sounded at her waist, and she quickly silenced it. "It's Roger," she said, with a sigh. "I'd better go."

"Of course." Dorothy rose to see her guest out, expertly blocking Mr. Bitey's paw with her shoe to prevent him from shredding the young woman's panty hose—or worse. "You try to have a nice evening, now, Jennifer. Everything will be just fine."

SUMMER STRODE CONFIDENTLY to the edge of the diving board, made a half pirouette, and bounced once or twice on the balls of her feet above the sparkling pool. The cloudless, late-afternoon sky was equally blue, and not even the slightest breeze rustled the palms.

Perfect.

She brought her arms up, chest level, then over her head, and bounced again, almost breaking the diving board as she launched herself high into the air. After an effortless double somersault, she executed a sharp jackknife and entered the water with crisply pointed toes.

No splash, of course. Just a cool, refreshing rush of H_2O. And hopefully no more disturbing flashbacks of Lorella Caldwell's dead, staring eyes.

She navigated the length of the pool underwater and emerged smoothly at the shallow end. Pulling herself up onto the ledge, she stretched out for a minute or two, letting her body soak up the fading heat of the concrete.

Summer loved this time of day, when all the residents were pregaming for their formal, five o'clock dinner in the Canyons Dining Room and she had the whole pool to herself. Usually, she headed back to her condo afterward for a nap—and maybe a snack and some binge TV—before mapping out which bars or clubs to hit after eleven.

But tonight was Dash's dinner party, she reminded herself. He and Julian were always tons of fun—well, Dash was, anyway—and Juliette-Margot was the greatest kid ever. They'd have a good time, even with his mom there. Maybe, since ol' GH-aka-Georgiana Hamel was such a famous mystery writer, she could even give her and Dorothy a few detective tips to help them with their new case.

Summer had never met Dash's mom, but she'd already figured out that she was older, and that he'd been adopted. From the way her son talked about her, Georgiana sounded a little intimidating. But interesting, at least.

Not like all her most recent stepmoms. How many of those mindless, gold-digging bimbos had her dad married lately, anyway? She'd have to ask Joy, because she'd lost count. And their own mom, Harmony Moon Smythe-Sloan—well, she was more like a sister, really. A kind of spacy one, who traveled around and dropped in and out of other people's lives whenever she felt like it.

Luckily, Syd was on marital hiatus right now. He must have gotten some sense knocked into him when he hit the Big 7-0.

Something—or someone—was blocking her sun. Summer's eyes flew open, and she gazed up at the tall, tanned figure of Detective Donovan.

Did he ever take off those Ray-Bans? He should, because he had really nice blue eyes. Sort of the same shade as hers, come to think of it.

"Jeez, you could have said something." Summer sat up, being careful not to let her tiny, lime polka-dot bikini top slip. It had gotten a little loose after that last dive.

"Sorry." He held out a rolled navy-and-gold-striped Hibiscus Pointe towel from the unmanned cabana. "I brought you this."

"Thanks," Summer said, wrapping it quickly around her waist. "So, what are you doing here?" He wasn't exactly dressed for a dip, in the same khakis and polo shirt he'd been wearing earlier. Even behind the shades, she could tell he was tired.

"Looking for you," he said. "I couldn't seem to reach you on your cell, so I figured the pool was my best bet."

Summer glanced back at her phone, lying on the wet concrete next to her straw pool bag. Whoops.

"Let's sit down over there, okay?" The detective pointed toward two lounge chairs at the opposite corner of the pool. "I got us some lemon waters from that fancy dispenser."

Well, that was nice of him. Was he just going to ask her stuff about finding Lorella this morning, or could this turn into something a tiny bit more social? He sounded all business right now, but she could be wrong.

She usually was, around this guy. All the others she could pretty much read like…well, a book. Usually, guys came right up and hung all over her. They never stopped talking about themselves, and a lot of times they treated her as if she were stupid.

That was where *they* were wrong.

Detective Donovan, on the other hand, never said anything about himself, so she had to stay alert for clues. It was kind of fun trying to guess things about his personal life. So far, the actual solid facts were: he wasn't married, his grandma lived at Hibiscus Pointe, he liked to fish on his boat, and he ate as much junk food as she did.

In other words, she had pretty much nada.

He averted his eyes as she readjusted her towel and plopped herself down on one of the lounge chairs. How could he be so uptight? Or maybe he was just shy. But he was a cop, for cripes' sake.

Maybe he'd been burned by some girlfriend or fiancée in the past. That had to be it. He was vulnerable and emotionally wounded.

Were those attractive qualities in a guy? Maybe. Or maybe not. She'd never had any boyfriends like that.

Just total jerks. Including the one who'd almost gotten her sent to jail back in New Jersey. And Donovan knew all about that, thanks to her background check when she was sort of a suspect in a case down here—that she and Dorothy solved.

"Long day, huh?" she tried, swirling the lemon slices in her cup. The water still tasted like chlorine. She was working on Jennifer to get Hibiscus Pointe to switch to salt water for the pool, too, but so far no dice. What did they put all those extra resident fees toward, anyway?

Probably a bonus for Roger.

"You could say that. Goes with the job, though." He finally smiled and pushed up his shades. Yep, those baby blues were intense, all right. "So, tell me, how well did you know Lorella Caldwell?"

Summer drew back. Not again. He didn't seriously think she had anything to do with this murder, did he? "I didn't. Never even saw her before in my life."

He pulled out his phone and gave it a tap. "Are you

sure? You still live in the complex here, don't you? Why is that, by the way?"

His tone was even, but Summer's face burned. Okay, so maybe it was kind of weird that she lived in a retirement complex with a bunch of old people. But that didn't mean she was some lazy freeloader, or hiding from anything.

"I like it here," she said. "The facilities are pretty good. They have a lot of dumb rules, but the people are really nice."

She cringed as Gladys Rumway, all dressed up for dinner in a show-stopping yellow pantsuit and matching headscarf, led a group of chattering women past the pool gate toward the main building. Gladys's beady eyes widened a half slit as she took in Summer and the detective together at the pool, before turning back to her wannabes, probably to make some gossipy comment. "Well, most of them are okay," Summer muttered.

The detective took a sip of his lemon water. "You're planning to move out soon, though, right?"

"Move out?" Summer bristled. Well, he had a lot of nerve. Where did he live that was so great? His own grandma lived here.

Detective Donovan cleared his throat. "I mean, didn't you say this whole old-folks thing was just a temporary arrangement, until you found a real apartment?"

"No," Summer said. "I mean, yes." This was a lot like being grilled by the Residents Board. And it was, by the way, even less of Shane Donovan's business than theirs where she chose to live.

He was right, though. Originally, she hadn't planned to stay here very long. Just until she got back on her feet after moving to Florida and things cooled down on all that other stuff. She'd planned to make her exit from Hibiscus Pointe before the second rent check to Syd was due.

But the truth was, she was getting sort of used to the place.

Besides, she couldn't leave Dorothy now. How often did you find an amazing friend, detective partner, and grandma, all rolled into one?

"It's not like I'm stuck here," Summer said. "I can move out anytime I want. And it isn't as if this is my whole social life, or anything," she added. "I like hanging out with Dorothy, that's all. And Ernie and his wife, Grace. And Dash, and a whole bunch of other people."

She could count them on two and a half fingers: Esmé, who worked 24/7, Mia, who was off on an extended cruise after her ex-fiancé ended up dead, and—sort of—Jennifer.

One corner of the detective's mouth twitched slightly, revealing a very small, extra dimple she hadn't noticed before. "Hey, whoa, I'm sorry," he said. "I didn't mean it to come out like that. Let's start over. I just need to confirm that you still live here. You know, for the case."

Right. Obviously, he thought she was a loser. "I told you before, I'm the aquatics director here now," she informed him. "I teach swimming and fitness classes and we're starting up a water ballet team soon." If Helen Murphy got her way.

"You're quite a diver, too." Detective Donovan jerked his head in the direction of the board. "I was watching you earlier. Pretty impressive."

"Thanks." Now he knew she was good at two things: water sports and solving crimes. That was progress.

"I'm doing some film reviewing, too," she added.

"Oh yeah, that's right," he said. "Your dad's that Hollywood bigwig, right?"

Okay, now that was really annoying. He didn't have to sound so snotty about it. She'd never told him about Syd. He'd found out himself, when he was checking out her background when she was a suspect in that other case. "Sort of," she muttered.

Why did she care what this guy thought of her anyway?

"Okay, so let's get back to business here," Detective Donovan said. "Why don't you start by telling me exactly when and how you found Mrs. Caldwell?"

Summer told him all the details she could remember, starting from her and Dorothy bringing the books down to the library, to the elevator ride with Trixie Quattrochi and her gun, to the weird warning about The Snake, and learning about Lorella's possible professor boyfriend from her old neighbor. Dorothy had to have told him the exact same story, but the detective was taking notes anyway, on his phone. "Did you find Trixie and Ray yet?" she asked.

Detective Donovan ran a hand through his dark brush cut. "No, but we will. And we'll be speaking with this Professor Bell also."

"I bet Trixie and Ray weren't really going to Montana," Summer said. "I mean, she made such a big deal about it, she was probably lying. You know, to throw people off. That way, everyone would look for her in the wrong place."

"Possibly," Detective Donovan said. "But in any case, I'd like to ask you and Mrs. Westin to refrain from pursuing any possible suspects on your own. We appreciate your efforts, but that's our job. Got it?"

Well, he sure wasn't very grateful. She and Dorothy were trying to help, and they'd already made more progress on the case than the Milano PD. "Mm-hmm," she said.

"No, seriously. We don't want anyone getting hurt." He smiled again. "Hey, *I* don't want *you* getting hurt, okay?"

Summer hugged her knees under the towel. "Okay." No point in ticking him off. He'd be really happy when she and Dorothy solved the case. Maybe he'd get to take a few days off and go out on that boat of his. He might even take her with him.

"Hi, guys!"

The pool gate swung shut behind Jennifer with a clang as she crossed the pool area toward them, carrying a paper plate covered with aluminum foil.

Summer sighed. Just when she and the detective were finally making some progress. She had to hand it to Jennifer, the girl always had great timing. Like Radar O'Reilly in those old *M*A*S*H** reruns, who always knew what people wanted before they did.

So those had to be cookies. Yum.

"I thought you might not have had any time to grab lunch today, Detective, so I brought you a hot prime rib sandwich from the dining room." Jennifer placed the plate on the little wrought-iron table between the lounge chairs and removed the foil. "It's okay if you don't want to eat it now. I had it packed to go, just in case."

Detective Donovan's face lit up like the Christmas tree on the Third Avenue Promenade back home in Santa Monica. "Thank you, Jennifer. This is really nice of you. I've had nothing but coffee all day."

Jennifer beamed as he unrolled the cloth napkin with the silverware she'd also thought to bring, and dug in.

"Um, I didn't realize you were here, too, Summer, or I would have brought more."

"That's okay." Jennifer looked really nice again, Summer noticed. She was still wearing her pencil skirt, but she'd ditched the blazer and undone a button or two on her starched blouse. Oh, and the little scarf was gone, too. One paisley silk corner was sticking out of the Resident Services director's factory-store purse.

She had to be off duty now. And obviously, the girl had a ginormous crush on Shane Donovan. Well, she, Summer, was no boyfriend stealer. Time to go.

Detective Donovan paused midfeast. "Sorry, I think I got carried away. Does anyone want some fries or anything?" He pointed toward the steaming plate with his knife. "Happy to share."

Those fries did smell amazing. "No, thanks," Summer said, trying to get herself up gracefully from the lounge chair with her towel still in place. "I'm going to a dinner party tonight, actually, so I have to save my appetite."

That would be a first. She never lost her appetite.

"Oh, okay," Jennifer said, sounding unsure. "Have fun."

"I'll be talking with you again soon, I'm sure." Detective Donovan waved his fork.

Count on it, Summer told him silently as she headed to retrieve her phone and pool bag. He'd need to congratulate her and Dorothy when they hauled in Lorella Caldwell's killer.

FIVE

"*BON SOIR*, MADAME DOROTHY. You are late."

Dorothy smiled down at the little girl in the purple taffeta party dress and matching Mary Janes who greeted them at the door of the Hamel-Bernard residence. "You're right, Juliette-Margot," she said. "Please accept our apologies."

Their handsome host, thirtyish Dash Hamel, shook his head as he came up behind his daughter, martini in hand. "That wasn't exactly the etiquette we've been working on," he said.

"Juliette-Margot is *très désolée*," the little girl told Dorothy, just as Summer and Ernie Conlon came up from parking the car across the elaborate Spanish-style courtyard. "That means 'very sorry' in French." She turned back to her father, with a slight frown. "But it is seven-thirty, Papa. Juliette-Margot has been waiting forever."

Dash sighed. "Please come on in, everyone."

"My fault, JM." Summer stepped through the doorway, in her simple, perfectly fitted lime-green shift.

"That's okay." The little girl took Summer's hand—the two had matching pink pedicures, Dorothy noticed—and gazed up at her adoringly.

"Cute kid, but why does she call herself by her own name like that?" Ernie whispered to Dorothy as they followed the rest of the group through the tiled foyer.

"I'm not sure," Dorothy said. Juliette-Margot was almost six, with her own, very definite sense of style. "But it's quite endearing, isn't it?"

"Yeah, sure. I guess." Ernie, dressed in checkered golf pants and a red polo shirt, handed Dash the Publix flowers, the bottle of wine, and a box of mint-liqueur chocolates. He had carefully slicked back his salt-and-pepper hair for the occasion. "Thanks for letting me join you all."

"Glad to have you," Dash said, with an easy smile. He wore a casual but perfectly tailored navy blazer, a crisp white shirt, and immaculate khaki trousers. "Mother loves a party. The bigger, the better."

"Whatever is keeping you, darling?" a deep voice called from the lanai off the spacious, open living room. "Are those your friends you promised? Do come out here so I can meet them."

"*Grandmère*, this is Summer," Juliette-Margot said, taking Summer by the hand and pulling her out onto the lanai festooned with white Japanese lanterns.

Georgiana Hamel, perhaps a decade younger than Dorothy—or perhaps not, judging from her taut, un-lined skin and carefully chiseled cheekbones—was ensconced in a black-lacquered palm chair, wearing a flowing bloodred caftan. Her hair was done up in a matching head scarf. One equally red curl hung down the middle of her forehead, directly between her highly arched, painted eyebrows.

GH Hamel was one of the few authors Dorothy had seen in person whose book jacket photo exactly matched her actual appearance. Certainly, no one could ever miss her in a crowd—even in New York.

"Hello, darling," Georgiana said to Summer. "Aren't

you a looker! Dashiell has told me so much about you."
She smiled, her heavy gold bracelets clattering as she
grasped Summer's wrist with long, red-taloned fingers.
A large bloodstone displayed in an intricate gold setting adorned her the middle finger of her right hand.

"Um, nice to meet you." Summer seemed nervous,
physically caught between Dash's adoring little girl and
his intimidating mother.

Not intimidating, Dorothy corrected herself. Dramatic, maybe. Perhaps Georgiana had been on the
Broadway stage before she'd embarked upon her writing career.

"And you are the lovely Dorothy Westin—and you,
of course, are Dorothy's *very* close friend, Ernie Conlon." Georgiana settled back in her chair, looking a tad
smug.

Goodness. Dorothy felt her face grow warm as she
glanced at Ernie. The two of them were indeed dear
friends, but strictly nothing more. Ernie was married to
a wonderful woman, Grace, who had Alzheimer's. The
Conlons had a full-time caretaker living with them now,
so Ernie was able to leave the condo for short spells, but
he was entirely devoted to Grace, of course.

"Nice to meet you." Even Ernie's hand looked small
in Georgiana's grasp.

"I'm such a big fan of all your books," Dorothy said.
"Especially the last one, *Good Night, Sweetheart.* I was
on the edge of my seat."

Georgiana took a lengthy sip of her Manhattan.
"Thank you. I always try to maintain suspense at the
highest pitch possible, until the very final page. That's
what keeps my readers coming back for more."

GH Hamel wasn't the most modest person Dorothy

had ever met. But the author was enormously success-ful and clearly worked hard at her craft, so she'd earned the right to boast a bit. She just had one of those large personalities.

Much like, say, Gladys Rumway.

"Now, Mother," Dash said, handing Dorothy a glass of Chardonnay and Ernie a Scotch on the rocks. "I thought you said you didn't want to talk about writ-ing tonight."

"True," Georgiana said. "Trust me, I had plenty of literary discussion at that delicious independent book-store I stopped at on the way from the airport—what was the name of it, now? Ah yes. Murder by the Sea."

"So, did anyone recognize you?" Summer shook her head as Juliette-Margot offered her a silver hors-d'oeuvre plate of escargots steamed in heavy garlic and butter.

"Well, of course." Georgiana seemed a bit taken aback by the question. "They were surprised, I sup-pose, but very glad to see me. I signed a few stacks of my new book for them—hot off the press from my publisher. They were still in the boxes at the back of the store, in fact. Technically, the on-sale date is—"

"Mother," Dash warned.

Dorothy hid a smile. Georgiana had only been in town for a few hours, and her son already sounded tired.

"So you didn't tell them when you were coming?" Ernie asked.

Georgiana gave a dismissive wave. "Oh no. I rarely give advance warning of my promotional appearances. So much more amusing that way. And I never have to worry about people not showing up for one of my signings."

My, Dorothy thought. What an unusual approach. And perhaps a bit inconvenient for the poor booksellers.

The author leaned forward in her chair. "I jest, of course. I like to keep booksellers on their toes and make sure my books are highly visible. Also, it helps keep the crowds and the writer's cramp from all those signings at manageable levels."

Somehow Dorothy doubted that GH Hamel preferred the presence of fewer fans. In fact, she suspected Georgiana failed to schedule her bookstore visits because she enjoyed the high drama and flurry of a spur-of-the-moment arrival.

"I'll be sure to sign a copy of my new book to you, though, Dorothy," Georgiana added. "I'm going in more of a historical direction on this one. The title is *Murder in the Moorlands*, and it's about a penniless young American woman who must solve a nineteenth-century murder at the family seat in Devonshire to earn an unexpected inheritance. In the process, she wins the heart of a handsome duke."

"Thank you, it sounds fascinating," Dorothy said. "I so enjoyed that setting in *The Hound of the Baskervilles*."

"Yes." Georgiana frowned. "But that's where any remote similarity to the Sherlock Holmes tale ends," she added, with a sharp adjustment of her head scarf. "Each of my books is a unique, precious gem, to which my fans and reviewers—not to mention my sales—attest."

Oh dear. Dorothy's face grew warm. She hadn't intended to insult one of her favorite authors. "Of course," she murmured. Georgiana herself was certainly unique.

Dash stood up. "I'm going to check in with Julian in the kitchen. He's usually the sous-chef, but he insisted on preparing everything himself tonight. You know, so I could spend more time chatting with you all and Mother."

"I'll go with you," Summer said, quickly.

"No, no, my dear," Georgiana said. "I need to hear everything from you and Dorothy about your highly intriguing adventure this morning. A murder right here at Hibiscus Pointe, imagine. One never knows what dastardly deeds are done, behind the gilded gates of these Florida communities."

"Juliette-Margot, come with Papa to the kitchen." Dash frowned over his daughter's delicate blond head at his mother. "*Grandmère* needs more ice for her drink."

"Thank you, darling," Georgiana called over her shoulder. "Two ice cubes, please, remember? Medium-sized."

"So give me all the details, ladies," she added as soon as Dash and Juliette-Margot were out of earshot. "Did you know the victim? How exactly did you find the body? Was it a terribly gruesome scene?"

Beside her, Dorothy heard Ernie sputter slightly over his Scotch. GH Hamel certainly seemed eager for details. "I'm afraid we can't offer you much information," she said. "Neither Summer nor I knew Lorella—well, that's not entirely true. I had just started working with her in our little Hibiscus Pointe Library—and everything unfolded so quickly..."

The front door chime—Beethoven's Fifth—sounded from an artfully camouflaged speaker over Dorothy's head, thankfully cutting her off.

"I'll get it!" Summer called loudly, from the direction of the foyer.

"Hi there, I'm Carrie Dunbar." Dorothy could hear

the newcomer's perky voice all the way out on the lanai. "I'm a new author—well, sort of new—with Planet Press, and this is my assistant, Parker Pruce. We just heard GH Hamel was here, and I'm her hugest fan. Do you think we could meet her?"

SUMMER HESITATED, GLANCING behind her for help. Dash and Julian were still in the kitchen. "Um, I think Georgiana's a little busy right now. This is kind of a private party."

"Oh, that's okay," the young woman said, pushing straight past her. Mud-brown hair, no makeup, a T-shirt that said Write On! Ask Me About My Book, and mom jeans that didn't fit. She looked about Summer's age, but it was hard to tell. "We'll just say hello for a second."

Jeez. What was her name? Carrie Something.

"Hey, Carrie, wait, you can't go in there!" Summer called after her as the woman bolted straight down the foyer toward Dash's living room. She must have seen there were guests out on the lanai.

And she sure moved fast for someone who didn't look in shape.

"Sorry," the other woman—Parker?—muttered, behind Summer. "I tried to talk her out of it, but she was just so excited."

Summer sighed. "Yeah, I can tell. Come on in."

Carrie's tall, superskinny assistant was dressed all in black, a weird choice for Florida, especially when it was still daylight. Black linen jacket, black pencil skirt, black heels, funky black glasses. Her hair was jet-black, too, professionally relaxed and cut in an asymmetrical bob that angled lower in the front.

No way she'd gotten that style in Milano. New York,

probably. Everything about Parker looked sharp, narrow, and pointed. Her dark skin was flawless.

"And who have we here?" Georgiana sat straighter in her palm chair, raising one crazy eyebrow way above the other. She reminded Summer of the normal witch's snooty mother-in-law in *Bewitched*. Endora.

"You have no idea what an honor this is." Carrie rushed forward and stuck out her hand to Dash's mom. "I'm an author with Planet Press, Carrie Dunbar, and I'm kicking off my first live promo tour here in town. My book is *A Killing Fog*—maybe you've heard of it?"

Georgiana looked bored but shook the eager woman's hand. Carrie's nails, Summer couldn't help noticing, were bitten all the way down to the quick.

"*Enchantée,*" Georgiana said. "I've never heard of you. Or your book, I'm afraid."

Ouch.

Carrie didn't seem bothered. "I know you went to Wellsmount College," she rushed on. "I did, too, but the tuition was too high, so I transferred back here to Santa Teresa."

"Really." Georgiana raised her glass of melted ice. "There's no place like home, I suppose, right, Dorothy?" She turned back to Carrie. "Are you and your friend here for our little dinner party, too?"

"Oh, sorry, I forgot, this is Parker," Carrie said. "She's my author assistant—well, independent PR person, really—from New York."

Bingo on the haircut, Summer told herself. Parker didn't seem like much of a PR person, though. She was hanging back in the doorway, texting on her phone. Not much of a multitasker.

"Thanks so much for asking, but we really couldn't

impose, Ms. Hamel. Can I call you Georgiana?" Carrie threw her a fake-shy smile. Obviously, the worm was looking for an invitation.

"If you must." Georgiana gazed over Carrie's shoulder as Dash stepped past Parker, balancing a tray of drinks and a silver ice bucket.

"Oh, hello," he greeted the party crashers. "I don't believe I know you ladies. Are you friends of Mother's?"

Carrie introduced herself and her assistant all over again.

"We were just in the neighborhood, actually," Parker finally spoke up. "We were supposed to have a suite at the Beachside. It turned out they were overbooked, but they have some kind of arrangement with Hibiscus Verandas for overflow guests."

Dash looked even more confused now. Summer hadn't known, either, that any local hotels sent people here. What a drag, to get stuck in a retirement community rental condo for your vacay. But wait a sec…

"Didn't you say you're from Milano, Carrie?" Summer said. "Why doesn't Parker just stay at your place?"

"No, I went to college here," Carrie corrected. "I'm from outside Orlando, actually." She looked back at Georgiana. "So we don't really have any dinner plans. We were going to eat at the hotel, but…"

How obvious could that frumpy little con artist be? Summer stole a quick glance at Dorothy, but she couldn't quite read her friend's expression. Ernie was concentrating on a bowl of honey-roasted peanuts.

Dash caved, as Summer knew he would, and set two more places for dinner. Hopefully, there would be enough food to go around, because she and Ernie were both starving by now.

It was a really good dinner, too—coq au vin, which Micheline, her dad's favorite personal chef, used to make for her and Joy whenever he was away. Which was a lot. And there was plenty of yummy garlic bread to sop up the wine sauce.

Parker was the only one digging into the salad, but by the time she picked away the egg, bleu cheese, bacon, croutons, anchovies, black olives, and tomatoes, there wasn't much left, except a ton of lettuce.

Carrie, Summer noticed, was too busy hanging on Georgiana's every word to eat much, either.

"So, tell me, girls, what have you heard about the unfortunate incident in the main building today?" Georgiana leaned forward. "My son has forbidden us to talk any more about writing."

"I really don't think we should discuss that *other* subject over dinner, either, Mother." Dash glanced at Juliette-Margot, who was making an elaborate fort out of her green beans almondine.

"Awful, isn't it?" Carrie said. "We just heard about the whole thing this afternoon when we got here. And it was especially sad because Lorella Caldwell was such a big fan of mine."

"You don't say." Georgiana gave Dash a nod and tapped her wineglass for another refill.

No one, not even Carrie's PR person, took the opportunity to ask Carrie anything about her killer fog book, Summer noticed. Well, she sure wasn't going to bring it up.

"It's too bad I never got to meet Lorella in person," Carrie added. "I got in touch with her a few weeks ago and she offered to introduce me to some important people at Santa Teresa."

Dorothy offered Juliette-Margot a pat of butter for her green bean fort. "Didn't you mention you were an alumna there yourself, Carrie?"

Nice, Summer thought. Dorothy was onto Carrie and her fibs, too.

"There are so many literary influentials in Milano," Carrie went on, as if she hadn't heard the question. "That's one of the reasons I decided to launch my author tour here."

Beside Summer, Parker gave an angry little snort over her mountain of rabbit food. Dorothy was rubbing her temples and Dash looked as if he had a really bad headache, too. But Georgiana was leaning toward Carrie again, like a cat sizing up a cockroach—probably gathering material for some clueless character in her next novel.

"I just love to get out and meet people in person," Carrie blabbed on. "I don't really like to toot my own horn or deal with small stuff, though. That's why I hired Parker."

Her assistant gave a particularly hard stab at her lettuce. She had to have a tough job, Summer told herself.

"Well, I devote my energies to writing. At the end of the day, that's what's most important to my readers." Georgiana sat back in her chair, and reached for the e-cigarette holder next to her dessert fork. Dash shook his head. Luckily, Julian had already escaped from the party to finish some pressing work in his study, or he probably would have blown a gasket.

Dorothy put down her crystal water glass. "Speaking of readers," she said, "Summer and I are carrying on Lorella's plans to revive the Hibiscus Pointe Book Club. Our first meeting is this coming Friday, in fact."

"How very thoughtful," Georgiana said. "Would you like me to make an appearance, to help kick things off? I happen to have some short speeches prepared, for these sorts of things."

Summer could have called that one. And an even more thrilling offer from Carrie in—wait for it—three, two—

"I could make a presentation, also," Carrie jumped in. "I'm sure Mrs. Caldwell would have wanted me to."

Right. Summer didn't know about poor Lorella, who was probably silently screaming from wherever she was, but this pushy Carrie person was driving her crazy.

"How very kind of you both to offer," Dorothy said. "Our membership will be quite small to start, though, so it may not be worth your valuable time. We could do a larger, joint reception down the road, perhaps. With the first meeting set in two days, I don't think we'd have enough time to publicize…"

"Oh, that won't be a problem, Ms. Westin." Parker turned to Summer. "You could put some flyers up around the complex tomorrow, right? I would, but it'd be better if you did it, since you're a resident. Some people don't like outsiders posting notices."

No point in informing Parker that a lot of people around Hibiscus Pointe didn't consider her a resident. Summer glanced at Dorothy. She wasn't sure her friend wanted to host this author reception deal, either, but they were trapped. "Uh, sure."

"Jennifer did give me some flyers this afternoon," Dorothy said. "And there's the article Lorella wrote for the Hibiscus Pointe newsletter tomorrow. That's all we have for promotion, I'm afraid."

"We can update the flyers," Parker said. "And maybe

you can get them into resident mailboxes, as well," she added to Summer. "I'll handle the online end."

What a pain. But maybe if they made a bigger deal out of this meeting, and more people showed up, she and Dorothy could solve this case faster. And then she could quit the whole book club thing. She'd have to find a way to do it without hurting Dorothy's feelings, though.

"I'm so excited to make a joint appearance with the great GH Hamel," Carrie said as Julian reappeared at the party with a tray of little pots filled with chocolate mousse. "I just can't believe it."

"Likewise." Georgiana looked as if she'd just chugged a whiskey sour. "As I always say, the more the merrier."

SIX

"SORRY, JENNIFER, BUT that's your job. I've got other fires to put out, okay? You need to clean this whole thing up, or the board will be screaming."

Summer flattened herself against the wall outside the Resident Services director's office, straining to hear the conversation above the sounds of hammers and drills. And she really hoped the Please Pardon Our Appearance— We're Renovating! sign behind her head didn't mean wet paint. She'd just bought this T-shirt online from Kitson.

The guy with the whiny voice had to be Roger. Summer hadn't actually heard the complex manager say a single word since she moved here. The only place most residents ever even saw Roger the Dodger was either on Hibiscus Pointe's private links or in his super-airbrushed photo in the *What's Your Pointe?* newsletter. There was a Manager's Corner section every week, where he supposedly answered people's questions and responded to suggestions.

Of course Jennifer wrote the whole thing.

"Things have gotten way out of hand with resident accounts," Roger went on. "This particular delinquency was a primo example, and now what are we supposed to do? Do you think you can get things cleaned up by the time I get back on Monday?"

Resident accounts? Uh-oh. Summer sent a quick text to Joy to see if she'd spring for rent again this month.

Her sister would be pretty ticked off, but she couldn't take a regular—well, paying—job right now, with the new case and all.

"I'll take care of it, Roger," Jennifer promised, but her voice sounded a little wobbly. "I'm sure we'll get a check eventually. She just didn't seem like such a bad person. I had no idea…"

Of course not. Because she, Summer, was a really good person. But it was nice of Jennifer to have her back.

She checked her phone. No answer from Joy yet. Summer edged away from the wall and hurried down the hall.

Now wasn't the best time to talk to Jennifer. Even if it meant she couldn't use the free Hibiscus Pointe office copier for that new flyer Parker had given her this morning. And she wouldn't get to find out if anything happened between Jennifer and Detective Donovan.

Oh well. It wasn't like she cared that much, anyway. Like Roger, she had more important stuff to do right now.

Like find Lorella Caldwell's killer—before the Milano PD.

THE SILVER PANCAKE was much more crowded than Dorothy had anticipated, especially for late morning on a weekday. But so many people at Hibiscus Pointe had recommended the cranberry crepes that she had her heart set on them.

This was a working brunch, since she and Summer planned to discuss book club logistics. With the Hibiscus Pointe Library still cordoned off for the investigation, they'd chosen a new locale: the Events Room at

Hibiscus Towers. Hopefully, it wouldn't be too large a space for their visiting authors.

The hostess called yet another party, an elderly couple with two walkers and one uniformed aide between them. Summer, wearing a stylish, droopy T-shirt and rather low-rise yoga pants—had she worn those to bed?—came over to sit next to Dorothy on the waiting bench. "Brought you a paper," she said.

"Thank you, dear." Dorothy began to skim the pages, holding it away from her no-iron white blouse. The *Milano Morning Sun* never carried much news. The free local daily was mostly filled with advertisements, estate sale announcements, and real estate opportunities. But her eye stopped at the crowded Deaths section.

There it was: Lorella Caldwell's obituary. The short write-up included a small, grainy black-and-white photo, which had to be three decades old.

Summer was looking over her shoulder now. "She looked almost the same when she was younger as she did when…we found her."

Dorothy squinted at the page. Maybe the printing quality of the *Milano Morning Sun* was to blame for the blurriness of Lorella's photo. "Well, let's see. She was from Massachusetts, a former professor at and graduate of Wellsmount College. Goodness."

"Never heard of it." Summer inspected her pedicure. "Oh, wait. Wasn't that the school Dash's mom went to? And Carrie, sort of? They were talking about it last night."

"Yes, indeed," Dorothy said. "Quite a coincidence, don't you think? Wellsmount is a very small, prestigious college in New England. It was once an institution for female students only, but they went coeducational in the late eighties, I believe."

Summer shrugged. "Before I was born."

"Oh. Of course." Where on earth had the years gone? It seemed like just yesterday that Maddie had graduated from Ball State. Before she and Harlan knew it, their daughter had gone on to graduate school for meteorology, taken up photography, and then earned her pilot's license. A restless ball of energy, their Maddie.

If she hadn't gotten involved with flying, and chasing those dangerous storms across the country, maybe she would still be alive. But there had been no talking her adventurous daughter out of it—not that Dorothy had tried, really. That wouldn't have been fair to Maddie. But if she'd ever realized…

Summer leaned closer over Dorothy's shoulder. "It definitely doesn't sound like Lorella had any family. No brother."

Dorothy sighed, thankful that Summer had pulled her from her thoughts. "Yes, it's very sad. And Jennifer was right. No memorial, either. And no listed cause of death. Just 'unexpectedly.'"

"I wonder why she went to work again, after she retired," Summer said. "I would never do that."

"She may have needed the money," Dorothy said. "Or perhaps she decided to stay involved with education, in a less pressured position. It's also possible she wanted to meet new people."

"Lorella wasn't very social," Summer said. "Oh, wait, you mean, she wanted to get a boyfriend? Like that stalker Charles Bell?"

"Not necessarily," Dorothy said. "Older people need community. My Harlan was quite bored, for a while, after he retired. That's one of the reasons we moved to Hibiscus Pointe."

"Don't you ever get bored?" Summer asked.

"No." Dorothy refolded the *Morning Sun* and smoothed the pages. "Well, not often. Bored people are boring themselves, and wasting precious time. I have my friends, and my books, and"—she smiled at her detective partner—"our cases to solve."

"Oh. Right." Summer smiled back.

"Lorella was a very private person, I suppose, but she seemed very committed to sharing her passion for literature with the world," Dorothy said. "Her students at Wellsmount, for instance, the college here in Milano, and even us residents at Hibiscus Pointe."

"So, okay, what about Georgiana and Lorella both going to Wellsmount?" Summer craned her neck, looking for the hostess. "Dash's mom is probably about Lorella's age, right? Maybe they were there at the same time."

Dorothy sat up straighter on the bench. "You're entirely right, dear. Why didn't we think of that at dinner?"

"Because Carrie wouldn't shut up." Summer consulted her phone. "Okay, it says here that GH (Georgiana) Hamel is sixty-five years old. I bet she's way older. Hey, my dad did a couple of movies based on her books. Huh. Maybe they know each other."

"How interesting. You'll have to ask." Dorothy reopened the paper and glanced back at the obituary. "Lorella's age is listed as sixty-nine. With Wellsmount's small student body and their mutual interest in literature, there's a very good chance she and Lorella were acquainted also."

"It's weird Georgiana didn't say anything, then," Summer said.

Dorothy frowned. "Yes, it certainly is."

The hostess finally called their names and they followed the petite, dark-haired young woman in the Silver Pancake T-shirt to a booth at the far end of the noisy restaurant. Apparently, everyone else in town had heard about the cranberry crepes.

Dorothy's anticipation took a dive as she and Summer slid into their booth—directly behind Gladys Rumway and three other Hibiscus Pointers. Oh dear. Hopefully, none of the group would notice them.

"Dorothy!" Gladys boomed, startling the young busboy who was bringing a tray of water glasses. Summer reached out and steadied it just in time.

"Thanks," the boy said, in overly obvious admiration.

"No prob." Summer threw him a grin. "I've been there."

Despite her impressive powers of observation, Gladys didn't seem to notice the near miss. "We were just talking about you," she told Dorothy. "Heard it's going to be quite a book club meeting tomorrow. I used to be president of our club up North—reelected every year, by the way. I'd offer to show you how it's done, but I'm busy working the Caldwell investigation for the Milano PD, as you know."

What a lot of hooey. And Gladys wasn't the grand mistress of discretion. Dorothy glanced around at their fellow diners, but they all seemed busy with their own conversations and plates of delicious-looking crepes.

Summer twisted in her seat, resting one long, tanned arm along the top of the booth behind Gladys. "Hey, Mrs. Rumway," she said. "Great job in swim class the other day. Next time maybe we can try using the kickboard. Juliette-Margot made it all the way across the pool."

Gladys's friends tittered before she silenced them with a haughty glare.

Oh dear. Surely Summer hadn't meant to insult Gladys. She'd probably just been trying to change the subject. But she had effectively silenced the woman, at least—for a moment or two.

"No need for you to worry, Dorothy," Gladys said, pointedly ignoring Summer. "I'm gonna have this whole Caldwell thing case-closed in no time, so you can keep focusing on the book club."

"Thank you, Gladys. I do appreciate that." Dorothy took a sip of ice water so she wouldn't have to bite her tongue.

Summer picked up one of the greasy menus the hostess had left, using it as a screen as she leaned across the table. "Don't listen to her," she said to Dorothy. "We're way ahead of that amateur."

"I'm not worried about who solves the case first." Dorothy took another sip of ice water. "The important thing is bringing Lorella's killer to justice, one way or the other."

Just after the waitress took her and Summer's orders, Gladys and her companions began to gather their handbags and sweaters. "You girls go on ahead," Gladys told the other women. "Jeannie, why don't you pay my tab, and I'll pick up yours next time? I just have to talk to Dorothy for a minute."

Dorothy braced herself as Gladys leaned casually—and rather heavily—against the post behind her booth, draping Dorothy in excess fabric from the sleeve of her floral blouse. "Didn't want the girls to hear this, because it's just between us detectives," she said. "Keep this confidential, okay?"

"What is it, Gladys?" Dorothy said wearily.

The woman triumphantly twirled the plastic wrapping off a toothpick she must have taken from the hostess booth on her way in. "Just got the scoop from my cousin Merle, first thing this morning," she said. "He volunteers down at the PD, remember?"

"Yes, I believe I do," Dorothy said. Gladys always mentioned it at every opportunity. Admittedly, Merle sometimes offered valuable pieces of information— when he didn't get his facts wrong.

Gladys paused for dramatic effect. "Spit it out, Mrs. Rumway," Summer said.

Dorothy drew back.

"You know the bookend that the murderer used to clobber Lorella?" Gladys nearly popped an ornamental button as she drew herself up. "There wasn't a single fingerprint on it."

"How interesting," Dorothy said. "Thank you for sharing that with us, Gladys."

"You're welcome." Gladys modestly patted her poodle-style hairdo. "Just makes solving this case more of a challenge, but I'm up to it."

Their waitress reappeared at the booth, looking slightly out of breath. "I'm really sorry, ladies, but we're all out of cranberry crepes. The table behind you got the last ones. I've brought your menus back, in case you'd like to order something else."

"Oh, that's too bad," Gladys said. "Ta-ta for now— see you back at the Pointe." She leaned back in over the booth. "And I have to tell you, those cranberry crepes were beyond fabulous."

"She really didn't have to rub that in," Summer said, after Gladys and the waitress had left. "Jeez."

Dorothy picked up her menu again. "Well, it may not have been Gladys's intention, but she did give us what might be a very helpful clue."

"You mean, about the fingerprints?" Summer still looked glum.

Dorothy nodded. "Yes. The bookend that killed Lorella had a highly polished surface. None of the bloodstains in the carpet looked smudged and the library didn't have curtains. With that amount of blood, even if the killer was carrying a handkerchief or something else to clean the murder weapon, there's a good—"

"The person wore gloves," Summer broke in. "So the murderer must have planned to kill Lorella ahead of time. They didn't have a sudden, big fight or anything."

"Exactly." Dorothy returned her attention to the other breakfast entrées. Radish, sausage and cauliflower omelets? Nauseating.

Summer tossed her menu aside. "I don't feel like breakfast anymore. And we really need to find that professor guy. Want to go grab something from Westminster Dog House?"

"Excellent idea," Dorothy said. With Lorella's killer still at large, there was no time to waste—and no way to tell who might be his or her next victim.

SEVEN

"THIS PLACE LOOKS really new," Summer said as she and Dorothy drove through the perfectly landscaped, Mission-style campus of Santa Teresa College. "Like, perfect."

"It is," Dorothy said. "It was just accredited last year."

"I took some classes after high school," Summer said. "My dad wanted me to major in business, but it didn't work out. There's the library. Should we park there?"

"No, try the admissions building, on the other side," Dorothy said. "It's spring break, I believe, so there are spots everywhere. But we don't have a sticker."

"Worse than the beach," Summer muttered. "Do you think Professor Bell is even going to be here, if everyone's gone?"

"It's worth a try," Dorothy said. "Let's go in and see whether we can get a campus map. A lot of prospective students and their parents visit campuses this time of year, so the administrative offices will be open, at least."

A familiar cloud of dread surrounded Summer as they entered the admissions building. She'd never actually been rejected from any schools, or kicked out—Syd and his money saw to that—but she'd never felt as if she belonged there, either.

"Hello," Dorothy said, to the sporty-looking young woman in perfect cornrow braids and a Santa Teresa

T-shirt at the reception desk. "We'd like some information about your English literature program."

Summer felt her friend's nudge. "Um, right…"

The student gave her a big, friendly smile. "Oh, you're one of our graduate applicants, then?"

Summer felt her face grow hot. Not only did she feel really stupid right now, but she seemed old to this girl.

"No," Dorothy spoke up. "I am."

"Fantastic." The girl reached toward a big stack of folders on her desk and handed one to each of them. "This should give you a start, and of course we have a lot more info online. You'll find a CD inside, a campus map, and cards for our admissions counselors. I'm Andee, so feel free to ask me any questions during or after your visit, too, okay?"

Andee's cheeriness wasn't the fake kind Summer hated, she could tell. She really needed to improve her attitude. "Thanks," she said, taking the folder. "This is great. I might apply, too. Maybe not for a few more semesters."

"Great." Andee looked really happy. So did Dorothy, Summer noticed.

"By the way, do you know whether Professor Charles Bell is in today?" Dorothy asked the student. "I was hoping to ask him some questions in person."

"I'm not sure," Andee said, "but I can check for you. He's been at the library a lot lately." She reached for the phone.

"Oh, no need to call," Dorothy said. "We'll just stop by his office, and the library is on our route, I see. Thanks so much for your help."

"Bye!" Andee called after them. "Have a wonderful day at Santa Teresa, and see you next fall!"

In some alternative universe, Summer thought, when she and Dorothy were safely out in the hallway. It was plastered with posters of carefully posed students pursuing every academic, cultural, and sports activity under the Florida sun.

Whoops. There was that negative thinking again. She'd really have to work on that.

As they made their way down the orange-tiled front steps of the admissions building, the mission bells rang from the clock tower of the enormous church in the center of campus.

"One o'clock, and we have so much to do today," Dorothy said. "Why don't we split up to save time? I'll take the library, to find any useful book club materials we might use, and see whether anyone there knew Lorella. You can chat with Professor Bell."

Summer sighed. Sometimes detectives just had to suck it up for a case. "Okay."

No way was she posing as a student, though. Unless she really had to. Too many professors she'd known had offered her extra tutoring during extra-private office hours. And she already knew this guy was a stalker.

Rose Hall, located right next door to the modern-style library, seemed way out of place on the supersunny campus. It was one of those dark old buildings with the little pointy roofs, like a bigger version of Lorella's old place—Tudor-style, Dorothy had said. Maybe it had been her home away from home.

Summer checked the directory in the lobby and jogged up four winding flights of stairs to the faculty offices. Charles Bell's office was the first one on the left and the door was open, so she knocked and walked in.

She still hadn't figured out exactly how to play this,

but maybe it would be better to just wing it. Most of the time, things never went exactly as she planned anyway.

There were actually two offices behind the door, one for the administrative assistant and, just past it, a larger one for Charles Bell.

It looked as if whoever had taken over Lorella's old job had stepped out, judging by the half-empty tea mug and reusable lunch bag in the middle of the desk in the first office. Hopefully, the assistant—it had to be a she, judging from the unicorn heads on the lunch bag and mug and a bunch of photocopied unicorn prints on the back wall—wouldn't be back any time soon.

The professor's door was open, too. Looked as if Stalker Charlie was absent. Hopefully, Dorothy would find him in the library. But maybe she could snoop around a little, before the Unicorn Lady showed up and kicked her out.

The whole office smelled like woodsy pipe tobacco. And everything about it was dark, thanks to the one tiny window with those crisscrossed panes. It had a pointy ceiling, though, which was kind of cool, and Professor Bell's messy desk was tucked in an alcove. Summer headed straight toward it, leaving the lights off so it wouldn't look like she was snooping.

The room was jammed with papers, files, and books, especially the desk. Where did he keep his computer?

She leaned in closer to scan the book titles.

100 Shades of Passion—Make Your Readers Beg for More!
How to Write a Best-seller Without Really Trying
In the Mood:
Romance 101 for Writers

Fishing for Writers:
Catch a Publisher and Release Your Book
You Can Promote Your Novel (Without Killing
Yourself)

Yikes. No one could be that desperate. Was this the sort of stuff Charles Bell taught in his classes?

Definitely not, she realized, after a glance at the reading lists posted to three crowded bulletin boards above the professor's desk. English 101: Introduction to the Novel, English 222: Romanticism and the Rise of Industrialism in England, 1800-1850, and English 400: Sturm and Drang: Intuition and Emotion vs. Rationalism.

What a snooze. As Summer shuddered and turned away, she spotted a battered leather pocket calendar on the corner of the credenza behind the desk. Excellent. Now she could see exactly what the professor had been up to, day to day, for the whole year.

Which was only three months so far, unfortunately, but still… No, wait, it was an academic year calendar. Excellent.

As Summer reached to snatch up the little book, her fingers brushed something cold and solid, mostly hidden by a huge pile of paper. It was a fancy, smooth gold bookend, in the shape of a woman holding a book. And it looked exactly like the one she and Dorothy had found near Lorella Caldwell's body in the Hibiscus Pointe Library.

Bookends always came in pairs. Was this the mate to the one that had killed Lorella? She didn't see any other gold lady statues in here. But the office was so jammed with stuff it was impossible to tell for sure. It could be anywhere.

Summer blinked as the fluorescent overhead lights suddenly came on in the room."I hope you can explain what you're doing in here," a man's voice said. "But I doubt it."

Busted. Summer turned slowly, keeping one hand on the credenza behind her. If he made a move, she'd grab the bookend and bean him the same way he'd clocked Lorella.

He was taller than she'd expected, somehow. And not even that bad-looking, for his age. Tanned, with a decent head of hair, which was long and flecked with a few distinguished streaks of gray. Not a bad dresser, either, though the navy blazer he wore over his casual, strategically faded jeans wasn't as pricy as Dash's.

She could probably take him mano a mano. For sure with the bookend.

"Oh, sorry." Summer threw the professor the careful smile she used to keep old guys at bay. "It's Professor Bell, right? I just saw this really funky little statue here"—she nodded over her shoulder—"from the doorway and I ran in for a closer look. Is it an award or something?"

"Hardly." Now he was staring at her in disgust, kind of the way Captain von Trapp looked at Maria in *The Sound of Music* when she showed up at his villa in those ugly clothes.

Not that she could blame him. She *had* sounded pretty dumb. But it was all she could come up with on the spur of the moment. "Oh, I see now, it's a bookend," she said. "Jeez, guess I'd better make that Lasik appointment. Where could I get some like this? I just inherited a whole bunch of books from my grandma, so I could really use them."

The professor sighed, just a tiny bit. "They sell them at every J.P. Booker bookstore. And online."

At least he wasn't moving from the doorway. Summer didn't budge, either. The more distance between them, the better, until she got some answers from this guy—and found the other bookend.

Or not.

"You aren't one of my students, are you?" he said. "I'm sure I would have remembered you."

"Oh gosh, no." Summer waved. "But I love romance books. And I finished school ages ago." Well, that last one was true. She reached into her bag and held up one of Parker's colorful flyers. "I just stopped by to invite you to a party."

Professor Bell crossed his arms. "Thank you, but I don't think so."

Oops. He'd taken that way wrong. "I'm from Hibiscus Pointe," Summer said. "Lorella Caldwell, our librarian over there, really wanted us to invite you."

Aha! The guy's eyes were practically bugging out of his head. Lorella's name had definitely gotten a reaction out of him. "Hibiscus Pointe? Isn't that a…senior community? What are you—"

"I work there." Summer cut him off. Again, totally true. "I'm really sorry about Lorella," she added. "It must have been a horrible shock."

"Yes," he murmured, glancing back through the doorway at her old desk. "We do miss her around here."

"Did you know Lorella well?" Summer asked.

One side of the professor's mouth quirked, just a little. "Only professionally," he said.

Liar, Summer thought. Why was he sneaking around her old house, then?

"Professor Bell?"

A thirtysomething woman with frizzy purple hair and huge, round glasses came up behind him, blinking. Judging from the big-eyed, cutesy unicorn twins on her sweatshirt, she had to be his new assistant.

He sighed, turning. "Yes, Jocelyn?"

"I have to leave early today," she said. "My landlord's trying to evict me again."

For what, Summer could only imagine. Probably fifty thousand unicorns in her apartment. But who cared? This was her chance to make an exit. And maybe snag the bookend, in case it turned out to be evidence. His office was such a mess he'd probably never miss it anyway.

She plucked the little statue—way heavier than she'd expected—from underneath the papers and tucked it in her bag, just as the professor turned back around.

Had he noticed? She pushed the bookend farther down, and her fingers touched on Parker's flyers. Phew.

Summer strode across the office and stepped past the professor and Jocelyn, who was still whining to him about her housing probs.

She'd been there, and she felt sorry for the frizzy unicorn freak—sort of—but no way was she hanging around this creepy office any longer than she had to.

"Here's the info for that book club event, in case you change your mind. GH Hamel is the guest speaker, by the way." Summer handed the flyer to Professor Bell and kept on walking.

"Wait!" he called after her. "GH Hamel is in town? The novelist? She'll be there?"

"Yep," Summer said, without turning around. "See you Friday."

She wouldn't care if she ever saw the pompous professor again, actually, but she and Dorothy needed any possible suspects to show up at the book club deal. And Charles Bell definitely qualified.

So far, Dorothy hadn't had much luck at the bright, modern Santa Teresa library. There was no sign of Professor Bell, and the assistant librarian had his hands full setting up computer stations for a group of visiting seniors.

"Hello. May I help you?" a woman about Dorothy's age asked, from a set of nearby carrels. She wore a maroon and gold lanyard with a name badge that said "Volunteer," with "Millicent" hand-printed beneath in smaller letters.

"Thank you," Dorothy said, walking toward her. The carpet was the same dark red Hardware Station pattern as the one in the Hibiscus Pointe library, she realized with a chill. "I'm wondering, do you have a book club here at Santa Teresa?"

"Sorry, not yet," Millicent said. "But it's funny you asked. A former Santa Teresa staff member photocopied quite a stack of materials on that very subject, but she wasn't able to pick them up."

"Oh, could I take a quick look at those?" Dorothy asked. "I might be able to get a few ideas. I'm starting up a book club myself."

"Please take everything you can," Millicent said. "It's gathering dust on a shelf behind the main desk. I'll get them for you."

The silver-haired woman, limping heavily on her

left side, led Dorothy back to the information area. She lifted a section of the counter, ducked beneath it, and disappeared for a moment or two. "Here you go," she said, dumping an enormous Santa Teresa Bookstore bag in front of Dorothy. "All yours."

"Thank you, this will be so helpful." Dorothy wished she could sort through the materials a bit, rather than lugging the entire bag, but she didn't want to sound ungrateful. "Tell me, that former staff member—was it Lorella Caldwell, perhaps?"

Millicent's eyes watered slightly. "Yes," she said. "She passed just the other day, I read in the paper. Very sad. Did you know her?"

"Yes," Dorothy said. "Lorella was a lovely person."

"I only spoke with her a few times, I'm afraid," Millicent said. "She wasn't very outgoing. But she often came in with Professor Bell." A slight shadow of disapproval crossed her face.

Was the library volunteer implying that the two of them were romantically involved? Dorothy wasn't sure. "Oh, of course," she said. "Lorella was his administrative secretary, wasn't she?"

"Well, yes." Millicent leaned closer across the counter. "But if you ask me, I think there was some hanky-panky going on there. They always had their heads together over in a corner."

"Really?" Dorothy shifted uncomfortably. She loathed this kind of gossip, and her Aerolite shoes were feeling a bit tight. Weren't both the professor and his secretary unattached? And they worked together, for heaven's sake. Maybe that was the library volunteer's objection.

"The professor is very highly regarded on campus."

Millicent was really warming up now. "He was practically Ivy League. And he's writing a novel. It's very hush-hush, but he told me himself."

"You don't say." Dorothy slid the heavy bag of book club materials onto a metal cart that another aide had thoughtfully abandoned by the desk. She knew plenty of people who were writing books. Or planned to, some-day.

"Maybe now the professor will have fewer distractions," Millicent said. "True artists need their space to create."

Had Professor Bell told her that, too? Dorothy wondered. In any case, she needed some space herself right now. "Thank you again for your help, Millicent," she said, pointing the cart toward the library's main doors. "I'll put all this wonderful book club material to good use."

How could the library volunteer have been so unkind—and unfair—to Lorella? The poor woman had just died. No, she'd been *murdered*, Dorothy corrected herself. Much, much worse. And solving the mystery of her death was the only way she could find justice for Lorella now.

Dorothy had just stopped the cart at the sliding glass doors when Summer burst through the entrance. "Hey, Dorothy," Summer said, taking the book bag. "What's all this?"

"Oh, just a few things for the book club," Dorothy said, ignoring her friend's wrinkled nose. "Did you speak with Professor Bell?" she added, with a quick glance behind her.

"Oh yeah. He's a real winner. I'll tell you all about our little meeting when we get to the car. I've got some-thing pretty interesting in my bag to show you." Summer reached out with her other hand to help Dorothy negotiate the steps. "Hey, there's a Hibiscus Pointe Book Club flyer on the bulletin board back there. Did you put that up? I only had that one left in my bag from this morning, when I was going to ask Jennifer to make copies. I gave it to the professor. He was pretty interested once he found out GH Hamel would be there."

"I didn't post anything." Dorothy twisted her neck to view the announcement tacked to the Santa Teresa bulletin board with maroon and yellow push pins. "It's a Hibiscus Pointe-only event."

"Not anymore," Summer said cheerfully. "Parker or Carrie must have beaten us to it." She squinted a bit, then frowned. "Huh. That flyer's different than ours. It says we're serving free food and drinks."

"We most certainly will not," Dorothy said. It was a good thing Summer had a hold of her arm, or she might have toppled over in surprise—and horror. "We don't have any budget for refreshments."

"It's worth a try," Summer said, guiding Dorothy smoothly toward the steps. "Maybe Jennifer can talk Roger into springing for a few more bucks. But if you ask me, I think free food and drinks is a great idea. A lot more people will show up, so we don't have to worry about a big audience for Dash's mom. And, uh, Carrie."

"I suppose you're right." Dorothy sighed.

"Plus, we know we have one of our suspects coming. And maybe even proof he killed Lorella." Summer stopped to open her bag and moved aside a messy stack of book club flyers. "Check this out. Ta-da!"

A shiny gold bookend in the shape of a woman. "Oh my goodness. Is that the mate?" Dorothy asked in horror.

"Could be," Summer said. "Turns out these are really common, though. They sell them all over the place. So we still have to figure out where Trixie is and invite her, too. I still think she's the real murderer. Ol' Professor Charlie seems like a wimp to me."

Dorothy glanced at the darkening sky behind the Santa Teresa bell tower and the vine-covered walls of Rose Hall. The earlier brilliant sunshine had disappeared behind the clouds, and she felt the humidity pressing hard upon her on all sides.

"We'd better hurry up," Summer said, "or we're going to get poured on."

In more ways than one, Dorothy told herself, as they quickened their pace down the Spanish-tiled library steps.

Lorella's killer was out there somewhere. And if he or she wasn't found soon, anyone at Hibiscus Pointe might very well be next.

EIGHT

"Come on, now, Mrs. Rumway," Summer called down to the lazily drifting whale in the pool. "How about a little more effort? You've totally mastered the dead man's float."

Gladys remained motionless, her flabby arms and legs stretched out like a stubborn starfish.

Summer leaned closer. "Please?" she tried, loudly.

Her beginner swim class had been extra challenging today. For some reason, neither of her students was paying a single shred of attention. Maybe it was because of the gloomy gray skies. It still hadn't actually started raining, and there wasn't any sign of thunder or lightning.

That'd wake the battle-ax up and force her out of the pool. Or maybe she should blow the lifeguard whistle around her neck.

"Mademoiselle Summer," her younger student said, tapping on her leg from where she sat on the pool steps, her wet kickboard across her knees, "did you hear Juliette-Margot say she's getting a puppy?"

"That's nice," Summer murmured, her eyes never moving from Gladys as the woman continued to float in her brown-and-mustard-yellow-striped, skater-style resort swimwear. There was a reason they called that style a tank suit.

The battle-ax could go under any minute and she'd

already been rescued once, a few weeks ago. If she'd just put on her big-girl briefs and learn to swim… But at least she wasn't talking anymore about how she was going to solve Lorella Caldwell's murder.

That had taken the first fifteen minutes of class.

"Maybe a poodle," Summer heard Juliette-Margot say as she tuned back in. The kid was so excited she should pay more attention. "One of those big, pretty ones. They're French, you know."

"Mm-hmm." No way were Dash and Julian ever going to agree to that, with their designer-showcase house. Dash met with clients there.

"And they don't shed, *Grandmère* says."

Summer was just about to call an end to class, storm or no storm, when she spotted Helen Murphy walking toward them in an A-line white sundress, her skin glowing its usual Tropicana shade and her blond hair styled into a tight helmet.

"So glad I caught you, Summer," the Residents Board president greeted her.

Summer sighed. Helen was always trying to catch her in something so she could get her kicked out of Hibiscus Pointe. "Do you need something, Mrs. Murphy?"

The woman smiled her thin, red Joker smile. Or maybe it was more like the Grinch's, if he'd had bad plastic surgery. "In fact, there is. I'm wondering what kind of progress you've made on the water ballet organizational front."

Nooo. Not again. Helen had been bugging her about it ever since Summer took the aquatics director job. Coaching a bunch of seniors to compete against other retirement community teams in synchronized swimming would be a nightmare.

Way, way worse than the book club. She should get paid for that kind of extra stuff, right? Besides, she and Dorothy were already much too busy, with the investigation and all.

"Water ballet?" Gladys suddenly jackknifed up in the pool, spraying water everywhere. "I'm in. When do we start?"

Luckily, a faint, low rumble of thunder sounded before Summer had to come up with an answer. *Saved*, she told herself. "Out of the pool, please, Mrs. Rumway. Quick, there may be lightning soon. You, too, Juliette-Margot," she added, reaching down for the little girl's hand. "We need to go. Don't hold on to the railing, Mrs. Rumway. It's metal."

As the battle-ax lugged herself up the pool steps, Summer hustled Juliette-Margot past Helen toward the nearby covered cabana, where Dash had left his daughter's towel and pool bag. "We'll definitely talk about this later, Mrs. Murphy," she called over her shoulder. "You'd better get inside somewhere now. Safety first."

Helen didn't look happy, but the woman was already beelining for the main building. For one thing, she probably didn't want to get her hair wet. It also looked as if she was anxious to avoid the more dangerous storm— Gladys, who chased after her, blabbing about water ballet sign-ups and dripping all over her.

Summer breathed a deep sigh of relief as she wrapped a shivering Juliette-Margot in her beach towel. It was probably just a matter of time before she had to start up that team, or Helen would be back on her case because she wasn't fifty-five, so she wasn't supposed to be living here.

"So, will you help me name Juliette-Margot's new puppy?" the little girl asked. "I thought maybe Alphonse."

Jeez. Where did the kid come up with a weird name like that? "Sounds perfect," Summer said, pulling a pink terry cover-up over Juliette-Margot's damp blond curls. "So when are you getting this doggy?"

"She's not." Dash stepped into the cabana. "Juliette-Margot, what did your daddy and I explain to you about that?" He rolled his eyes at Summer over his daughter's head. "Mother's big idea. And a very poor one, even for her, I might add."

"But, Papa…"

"Sorry, *cherie*, no buts," Dash said. "Case closed. We'll get you one of those nice, clean, quiet robot dogs. You can train it and everything, okay?"

Juliette-Margot's eyes filled with tears, and Summer felt sorry for the poor kid. She'd never had a pet, either. Not that she'd wanted one, really. Besides the fact that she was allergic to them, animals made her nervous in general. Especially Dorothy's cat, Mr. Bitey.

"Listen, Summer, can you do me a big favor?" Dash asked. "Our nanny's sister just had a car accident and she had to take the afternoon off. Do you think you could watch Juliette-Margot right now while I meet with a client at the house? It'd only be for a couple of hours. Julian's in court today, Mother is writing and can't be disturbed, and I'm up the creek."

"*S'il vous plait?*" Juliette-Margot gazed up at Summer, her tears drying up as fast as last season's lipstick.

Oh wow. How could she say no to that hopeful, lispy voice? The kid sounded exactly like the cute little sister in *ET*.

"Sure," Summer said to her. "Um, what should we

do?" she added to Dash, over Juliette-Margot's head. She'd never babysat for anyone before. Except maybe a few ex-boyfriends.

"I don't know. Anything, really. Go get an ice cream or something," Dash said as a few gentle raindrops began to hit the cabana's canvas roof. "I should be done by the time you get back. I'll owe you, okay?" He checked his Movado watch and smiled apologetically. "Gotta go."

"No prob," Summer said. "I've got this." She hoped.

Half an hour later, she and Juliette-Margot sat in the MINI Cooper outside Alice's Ice Cream, eating their massive cones as the rain pounded the roof. "Isn't this fun?" Summer asked.

"*Oui.*" Juliette-Margot plucked the little elephant animal cracker out of her Caterpillar Hookah-Looka Crunch. "*Grandmère* says I can still have a puppy, even if my papas said no. She says I can get whatever I wish for, if I never, ever give up."

"That's not always true, JM," Summer said, pushing the ignition as she balanced her cone in the other hand. Was it wrong to burst a little kid's bubble like that? Probably. "I mean, your *grandmère* is right about never giving up on stuff, but...sometimes you end up with something else that's just as good, but maybe a little different than you expected."

"Better than a puppy?"

"Well, sometimes."

There was no point in mentioning there were also those times in life when you ended up with something different—and really, really bad. Like being murdered, for example. Lorella Caldwell could never have expected that would happen to her. Or...had she?

So far, there was no way to tell.

Summer flipped on the windshield wipers as she pulled out of Alice's driveway onto Bonita Beach Boulevard, swerving to avoid a white, windowless van that sped up to cut her off. *Jerk.*

"Are you okay?" she asked her seemingly undisturbed passenger.

The little girl nodded. She hadn't lost a drop of her ice cream. "That's why Juliette-Margot's papas make her sit in the backseat."

Oh no. How had she forgotten the numero-uno rule of car safety for kids? "You're right," Summer said. "I'm really sorry. We'll pull over so you can climb into the back."

It was official. She was the worst babysitter ever. Was Juliette-Margot too big for a car seat? Dash would have mentioned it to her if she needed one, she was sure. He and Julian were superprotective of their daughter.

"Look, alligators! And a big snake." Juliette-Margot pointed excitedly out the window as Summer turned into the next strip mall entrance and brought the MINI to a stop in the nearest parking space.

"What?" Summer twisted to see a huge white sign painted with sun-faded black letters that screamed 20-Foot Snake! and Camo's Exotic Pets and Supplies. An ugly cartoon serpent twisted across the top of the sign, with a wily-looking alligator at each side. They held smaller signs that said Live Gators! and Meet Camo—Free!

"Can we go in and see them?" Juliette-Margot asked.

"Not on your life," Summer said. "They probably aren't real, anyway." She hoped not, anyway. "Hurry up and climb into the back, okay, JM? We need to get out of here."

Camo's Exotic Pets and Supplies looked like it had

once been a strip bar, with its nondescript square shape and blacked-out, barred windows. A neon green Open sign buzzed in the window.

All the other businesses around the place were either closed or out of business. No surprise there. Who knew what kind of lowlifes hung out at Camo's?

As Summer gave Juliette-Margot—still carefully clutching her ice cream—a boost over the console between them, she heard a car door slam.

Incredible. A skinny guy in a black heavy metal T-shirt and cargo shorts was getting out of a white van parked near a group of tall weeds in the far corner of the parking lot. It looked like the same van that had almost creamed them outside Alice's.

And the guy looked exactly like…Ray.

Summer started the MINI, being careful to rev the gas as little as possible, and leaned forward across the dash to see better. Yep, it was him, all right. And he was headed straight into Camo's.

Was Trixie waiting in the van? Summer was dying to find out, or to follow Ray into the creepy animal store. Well, sort of. But she couldn't, even for a peek, not with Juliette-Margot in the car. If those two were dangerous—and there was a really good chance they were—she had to get the kid out of here.

The door closed behind Ray. "Hey, JM, hand me my phone," Summer said. "It's in my bag there next to you."

"Juliette-Margot cannot find it."

"Okay, just give me the whole bag," Summer said. She needed to call Detective Donovan, pronto.

She couldn't find her cell at first, either, until her hand brushed against it between the leather and the torn lining. Jeez, outlet bags were worthless.

And just her luck. The phone was totally out of juice—she didn't have a car recharger anymore and she'd left her other one plugged into the wall back at Dorothy's condo.

Not only could she not call Detective Donovan, but if anything bad happened with Ray or Trixie, she couldn't call 911, either.

"Do you have your belt on nice and tight, JM?" Summer asked. The second the little girl nodded, she peeled—carefully—out of the parking lot with a MINI Cooper—level roar.

Trixie and Ray weren't going to get away this time.

"IT'S NOT YOUR FAULT, DEAR," Dorothy said to Summer as her friend opened the door of the MINI for her in front of Camo's Exotic Pets and Supplies. "You did the right thing by coming straight home and keeping Juliette-Margot safe."

"I know," Summer said, sounding glum. "But the van is gone now."

"Well, I'm sure Detective Donovan has already been here," Dorothy added, even though she wasn't quite as confident on that count. The detective had been out when they called him from her condo, and they'd had to settle for leaving an urgent message with Merle.

It wouldn't surprise her if Gladys had beaten all three of them here to question Ray and Trixie. Hopefully, she wouldn't end up like poor Lorella.

"So, should we just walk in?" Summer hesitated at the black metal door. "I am not looking at any snake. Or gators, either, even if they're baby ones."

"Of course," Dorothy said. "Ray doesn't know us, and we're just browsing."

"Do you think he's going to believe that, with all these creepy animals?" Summer asked. "Even Ray can't be that dumb. And what if Trixie's in there with him? She'll recognize us for sure."

"We could always say we had a ladies' room emergency, then, I suppose," Dorothy said. "And if Trixie is here, of course, we'll politely ask her what happened to her Montana plans."

Summer took a deep breath. "Okay," she said. "But if there are any snakes loose in here, we're leaving."

"Nonsense," Dorothy murmured. "These exotic animal businesses are strictly regulated. I'm sure they do regular inspections." She tried not to notice the Enter at Your Own Risk sign behind the bars of the window to the right.

"I have a very bad feeling about this," Summer said as she pulled the door open and they stepped inside.

It took a few moments for Dorothy's eyes to adjust to the darkness. The store was jammed wall to wall with plastic cages, terrariums, aquariums, and enormous wire crates inhabited by snakes, lizards, spiders, and all types of unusual creatures. A few were spotlit with individual, differently hued bulbs.

She tried not to look too closely inside some of the cages. Most of the animals were either in hiding or camouflaged by the sand, branches, and plants in their personal habitats.

The words Danger: Highly Venomous did jump out at her from some of the little plaques above the displays.

An even bigger sales draw for some buyers, no doubt.

"It's superhot in here," Summer said. "Like a rain forest or something." She glanced around nervously. "Where do you think they keep the big snake?"

"You mean Camo?" a teenage boy in a baseball cap asked from a slipcovered recliner in the corner of the store. He had his feet up on the edge of an enormous glass aquarium filled with tiny green turtles as he read a dark-looking comic book. "Sorry, the snake ain't here right now. The gators are outside, though, if you want to see them."

"No, thank you," Dorothy said.

"Uh, where is this giant snake thing?" Summer asked.

The young man shrugged, absorbed again in his comic book. "Dunno."

"What do you mean, you don't know?" Summer looked as green as the turtles. "Like, he got out or something? How could you lose him? The sign says he's twenty feet long."

"*She* got out." The bored employee turned a page. "No big deal, it's okay. My boss always finds her. Ray's real good at that. You folks should come by again tomorrow."

Dorothy placed a calming—and hopefully deterring—hand on Summer's shoulder. "Oh, we're sorry to have missed Ray," she said. "We've heard so much about him. How long has he owned this place now?"

"Forever, I guess," the young man said. "He just stopped by about an hour ago, to see if Camo showed up on her own. But other than that, I ain't seen Ray for a while. He's been out in the field."

"When do you expect him back?" Dorothy asked.

The employee tipped the brim of his cap up slightly and regarded her with a level expression. "That's what the cop guy who was in here before you asked, too. Hey, I don't ask any questions. I just cover the store and clean the cages. I don't deal with the big clients. You know, the private collectors."

"Right." Summer shook off Dorothy's hand and approached the giant aquarium with the baby turtles. "These little guys are really cute," she said, peering closer. "I know someone who's looking for a pet."

The young man shrugged. "Can't go wrong with a red-eared slider. They're pretty easy to take care of."

"How big do they get?" Summer asked.

"Not very."

"Okay, I'll take one." Summer pointed to a turtle plastered against the wall at the top of the aquarium, tiny bubbles emerging from its nostrils and floating across the surface of the slightly cloudy water. "Juliette-Margot's going to love you," she told it.

Dorothy hurried up beside her friend. "Summer, I don't think buying the child a turtle is a very good idea," she said.

The employee took a small net from the wall beside his chair and scooped the flailing animal out. "Good choice," he congratulated Summer. "This one's got a nice, hard shell. That means it's healthy."

"You should ask Dash and Julian first, at least," Dorothy tried. "Owning an animal is a serious responsibility."

Summer gave her a reassuring smile as the young man put the turtle in a small white box that looked like a Chinese take-out carton with air holes. "Oh, I totally know that, Dorothy. But those two are so overprotective of Juliette-Margot I know they'll all take great care of this little guy, too."

Dorothy sighed, and Summer talked the employee into throwing in a free plastic pet container with a hot-pink lid and a sample shaker of turtle food. "You can get more instructions online," he said.

"Awesome," Summer said. "By the way," she added,

handing over her credit card, "does your boss have a girlfriend named Trixie?"

"Sorry, cash only," the young man replied. "There's some lady who's with him a lot, but I forget her name. Real fancy hair, kinda loud, lots of jewelry?"

"That's the one," Dorothy said as her friend checked her wallet and bit her lip. She unsnapped her purse and stepped up to hand Ray's employee a twenty-dollar bill. "Will this cover it?"

"Sure," he replied. "Anything else you need?"

Dorothy gazed over his shoulder at the assortment of cheaply framed photos hanging on the back wall. They all showed Ray with various terrifying creatures, mostly snakes, hairy spiders, alligators, and spiked lizards. The photo in the center, however, featured the multitattooed, exotic pet business owner with the largest snake by far, wrapped around his shoulders, his arm, and what looked like a large barrel. Even more of the animal—dark-colored, with patterned brown splotches bordered in black and piercing eyes—trailed along the ground.

Oh my. That had to be Camo. Which of the creatures was more cold-blooded? Dorothy wondered. The snake or Ray?

"No," she said to the young man in the ball cap. "We are definitely all set, thank you."

When Dorothy and Summer stepped outside, the rain and cloudy skies had finally cleared, leaving the air smelling so much fresher. Or maybe it was because they had just emerged from the swampy, choking humidity of the exotic pet store.

"So, do you think Ray was 'The Snake' Trixie was talking about in that letter she wrote to Lorella?" Summer asked as they headed toward the car. "It's probably his nickname. He had a really gross snake tattoo halfway down his left arm in those photos."

"Well, it does seem entirely possible that Ray might be The Snake," Dorothy said. "But why would Trixie have gone anywhere with an unpleasant man like that, if she was warning Lorella about him?"

"I know," Summer said, sneaking a peek into the carry-out carton, where the turtle was desperately scratching the cardboard with its tiny claws. "It makes no sense. And I can't see Lorella having anything to do with a guy like Ray anyway."

Her phone rang, and Summer fished her cell from her back shorts pocket. She'd have to talk fast, because she hadn't gotten much juice on the portable charger on the way over. *Donovan*, she mouthed to Dorothy, handing her the turtle box. "Hello?" she said, into the phone. "Yeah, sure, we were just—"

Something rustled loudly in the bushes, and Summer stopped talking. "What is that?" she whispered to Dorothy.

Dorothy had heard the noise, too, but she'd hoped it was her imagination. The odd leaf rustling started up again, moving closer.

Summer stepped over to the edge of the parking lot, leaning forward as she peered into the weeds and dry foliage. "Aaahh!" she screamed, dropping her phone on the broken asphalt and making no move to retrieve it. "Oh my gosh, something's staring at me!"

Before Dorothy could react, her friend reached down, grabbed a pink flip-flop from her foot, and fired it into the bushes. "Dorothy, run!" she cried.

NINE

DOROTHY SET A microwaved plate of dark, congealed spaghetti in front of Summer on the breakfast bar. "Eat this nice dinner Ernie brought us up from the dining room, dear. You'll feel better."

"Thanks." Summer stared dejectedly at the pasta as she wound it up with her fork. "You know what this reminds me of? Snakes."

"Now, now, none of that," Dorothy scolded. She'd rarely seen her friend lose her appetite, even for dismal Hibiscus Pointe Canyons leftovers. "I doubt it was that awful Camo creature you saw in the bushes. Your mind was probably playing tricks on you."

"Nope," Summer said. "It was a really ginormous snake, all curled up, with evil, beady eyes. I'm a hundred percent positive." She sighed and checked her cell phone beside her plate again. "That thing made me break my phone and"—she held up a bare, tanned foot—"lose one of my favorite flip-flops. Plus, by the time Detective Donovan gets our message, Camo will have gobbled up half of Milano. And probably Trixie and Ray, too, before we can question them."

Dorothy smiled, although for some reason, the prospect of Ray being swallowed by a giant python seemed less horrific than it should have. "Why don't we try to focus on the brighter side right now?" she suggested. "Tomorrow is our book club launch, and we're sure to have plenty of opportunities to interact with possible suspects. Do you think we should mention the event to the detective? Perhaps he'll want to sit in."

"No," Summer said. "Let's just handle this ourselves. It's not like he's been superresponsive or anything so far. Obviously, he doesn't want our help."

Goodness, why was Summer sounding so discouraged this morning? That wasn't like her at all. Perhaps the fright from the snake. "I don't think that's the case," Dorothy said. "We've just had a few timing issues."

The door buzzer sounded, and Dorothy stumbled over Mr. Bitey to answer it. That cat never failed to miss a chance to protect his territory from any and all visitors. He would have made a perfect guard dog, should she ever have required—or wanted—one.

Jennifer waved at her through the peephole. "Hi, Mrs. Westin," she said. "Just dropping off the printed copies of the new reading list you requested for book club."

"Why, thank you, Jennifer," Dorothy said, opening the door. "My, that was fast. Please come in."

"Hey, Jennifer, how's it going?" Summer pushed away the offending spaghetti.

"Not great," the Resident Services director said, with a sigh. "It's been a challenge fielding all the media calls, and we've had to put on extra security staff to man the gatehouse at the front entrance. But Shane—I mean Detective—Donovan has been a big help keeping things under control."

Summer snorted and leaned over to scrape her plate into the sink, flipping the switch for the noisy, grinding disposal. What a waste of good food, Dorothy thought. Well, maybe not *good*, exactly, but still…

"You and the detective are really close, huh?" Summer reached for the bottle of dish detergent and applied an extra-large amount of liquid onto her plate and silverware.

"Oh no." Jennifer smoothed a strand of shiny dark hair back under her navy headband, coloring very slightly. "Well, I mean, I guess we're very friendly. In a professional sort of way, of course."

"Uh-huh," Summer said. "That's nice." Her usually sunny smile seemed a bit wobbly.

Dorothy frowned. Her sleuthing partner was certainly not acting very professional right now. What on earth had gotten into her?

"One good thing is, Roger left this morning for a tournament in Miami," Jennifer went on. "So I have a little more time to spend reassuring residents. Some of them are very concerned about their safety."

No surprise there, Dorothy thought. Maybe it was a good thing she hadn't accepted Ernie's invitation to join him and Grace in the dining room tonight. She couldn't imagine the gossip and alarmist discussions that had to be coursing through Hibiscus Pointe right now.

On the other hand, why shouldn't people be concerned about their safety? That's exactly why it was so important for her and Summer to assist the Milano PD in solving Lorella's murder as quickly as possible.

Jennifer set the box of photocopies down next to Summer on the breakfast bar. "I made a few extra of these, Mrs. Westin. You and Summer got so many flyers up we may have more people than we originally expected."

"Those weren't ours," Summer told her. "Well, some of them were, maybe, but we had some extra help, I think. By the way, any chance we might be able to up the refreshment budget a tiny bit?"

Jennifer bit the side of her lip. "I did notice that you were advertising food and drinks. I don't think we actually had much of a budget for that. But since Roger's not here to approve things, I guess I could make the call to add in some more brownies from the kitchen and maybe a few extra bottles of wine from the Events Catering Department. Just keep the receipts on anything else, okay?"

"Wonderful," Dorothy said. "Thank you, Jennifer."

The phone at the Resident Services director's waist buzzed and she checked it quickly. "I'd better go," she said. "There's a news crew pulled up in front of the main building. I don't know why Bill let them in."

"He was probably sleeping," Summer said, and Dorothy shook her head at her behind Jennifer's back. There was no sense in upsetting the young woman more.

As she opened the door to see Jennifer out, she was surprised to see Detective Donovan and his grandmother Peggy in the hall.

"You beat us to it. We were just about to ring the bell," Peggy said, from her wheelchair. Behind her, the detective gave Jennifer a wave as she hurried down the hall.

Goodness, her condo was Grand Central Station today. "Peggy, Detective, how nice to see you. Won't you come in?" Dorothy opened the door as far as possible to accommodate the wheelchair. Summer rushed to help, but Peggy gave a sudden, extra push to the wheels, nearly running over the girl's bare toes.

"I just wanted to talk to you about the book club tomorrow, Dorothy," Peggy said, rolling into the living room, where Mr. Bitey regarded her from behind a potted rubber plant with narrowed eyes. "Maybe you can clear up a few things for me. I don't want to waste my time reading those racy novels."

Detective Donovan cleared his throat. "We were out to dinner," he said, sounding apologetic. "And we happened to run into Mrs. Rumway."

Peggy leaned forward in her wheelchair, her green eyes fiercely bright. "Gladys told a whole table of ladies that you were kicking things off with *Passions and Lace*. I don't care how much the author talked it up on *Good Morning, Milano*, it's not the sort of thing I care to read." She sat back again and crossed her arms. "I'm a police procedural fan, all the way. Daughter of a cop, was married to a cop, my four kids and now my grandson here, all cops. So you can see why I—"

"We also stopped by to check on you and Ms. Smythe-Sloan," Detective Donovan interjected smoothly. "I was concerned when your first message got cut off, and then that next one from the station that you'd had a near run-in with a possible snake."

"*And* Trixie's accomplice Ray," Summer said. This time she didn't bother correcting him on the formal address, Dorothy noted. Maybe she'd given up.

"Well, I'm glad to see you're all right." Detective Donovan remained standing beside his grandma's wheelchair. "We'd already issued APBs for all three of them, but no reports have come in yet. We did check out the area around the exotic pet store, and questioned the employee on the premises, but there was no sign of any giant python."

"It wasn't my imagination," Summer insisted. "The thing was a monster, all wound up in the bushes. And I definitely saw Ray, too. He was there—didn't the kid in the ball cap tell you that?"

"Yes, the young man corroborated that his boss was there," the detective said. "And I've been in touch personally with my contacts at Fish and Game to check out the business for any illegal activities. They'll keep searching for that missing python, too. We did put out the APB, but they're the ones to officially handle that."

"To think that such a huge, dangerous creature could be slithering around Milano," Dorothy said, with a shudder.

The detective nodded. "We've had reports about all kinds of exotic animals, some of them no longer wanted pets, breeding in the area. Many are released directly into the swamps, which is a perfect habitat for snakes in particular, but they're prevalent in every part of the state now. Even heavily populated areas such as this."

"Let's talk about something else." Peggy turned back to Dorothy. "About these book club selections, for instance. Do members have any say in this at all?"

Oh dear, Dorothy thought. The detective's grandma certainly had a way of getting directly to the point of things. "In fact, Peggy, I have a list of possible titles right here," she said, heading to pick up a sheet from the breakfast bar. "I thought we could all discuss it at our first meeting tomorrow."

"Thanks, I'd like to take a look at that, if you don't mind," Peggy said.

"I don't believe there are any police procedurals on there at the moment," Dorothy said. "But perhaps you could suggest a few titles."

She definitely felt another headache coming on. This whole book club business might prove to be more difficult than she'd expected. No wonder Lorella had been so stressed before her death.

THIS IS SO *AWKWARD*, Summer thought as she stood next to Detective Donovan while Dorothy and his grandma discussed book club plans. She'd already tried to bring up the investigation, and he'd shut her down pretty quick.

"So, do you read much?" she asked him, hoping he wouldn't ask her the same thing back.

"Not much, I'm afraid," he said. "I wish I had more time, but the job and keeping tabs on Nana over there"—he jerked his head in the redhead's direction—"doesn't leave me much time. When I do get a break, I usually head out on the boat."

"I'm more of a movie person, myself," Summer said.

"Oh, right, your dad is that bigwig Hollywood guy. You mentioned you were doing some work for him."

Summer felt her face flame. Super. So now he thought she'd been trying to remind him about Syd, like some kind of humble bragger. "Sort of," she said. "I need to get my home theater system installed."

"It's been a while, but if you have the system already, I might be able to help you out with that," the detective said as his grandma went on talking poor Dorothy's ear off about all the books she'd read over the past year and a half. "I used to work for Top This when I was in college. Just let me know."

"Really?" Summer said. "Wow, thanks, that'd be great. I bought the system and everything, but I haven't had time yet to make an appointment for the guys to come by. You know, with the case and all."

His dark eyebrows shot up like Pop Tarts out of a toaster. "I thought we agreed you were going to stay out of the Caldwell investigation."

Nope. She definitely hadn't agreed to anything like that. You'd think he'd be a little more grateful, considering that she and Dorothy had practically delivered Lorella's murderer—or murderers, if you counted Trixie—to him on a Hibiscus Pointe silver platter. Like, hello? Who was it who'd found Ray today, anyway?

"You know, I'd hoped it was a coincidence that you stopped by that exotic pet store," Detective Donovan said.

Seriously? He thought she was into weird, creepy animals sold by murder suspects? "I was buying a cool little turtle for my friend's kid," Summer said, in what she hoped was a dignified voice.

Wait a second. Why was the detective's grandma watching her from the corner of her eye like that, as she talked to Dorothy?

"I remember you," Peggy said, suddenly twisting fully toward Summer. "You're that girl who cost me the tennis tournament championship yesterday."

Jeez.

"I'm really sorry about that, Mrs. Donovan," Summer said. "But it was an emergency. They didn't let you play match point over?"

"No. Gladys was quite emphatic on that, once you and my grandson left." Peggy pursed her lips. "Never mind," she said, with a wave. "I'll win it next time. I usually do."

"Sorry," Detective Donovan muttered under his breath. "She gets carried away sometimes."

"I heard that, Shane Junior," Peggy said, but Summer saw her smile just a little. "And you're right, young lady. Under the circumstances, with that poor librarian bumped off like that, it doesn't amount to a pile of—"

"You know, Peggy," Dorothy broke in smoothly, "you've made some excellent suggestions for additions to the reading list. We don't have time to get it reprinted, but why don't you give me those titles again and I'll write them down to bring up at the meeting tomorrow?"

"Good idea," Peggy said. "I bet I could get that nice Resident Services director to print up more copies for us, though. Such a sweet and helpful young woman. Pretty, too." She winked at Dorothy. "I told my grandson here he'd better get off his butt and ask her out, before she gets snapped up by someone else."

"Nana, please." The detective's face was as red as a stoplight. Maybe the Milano PD should switch him to traffic duty.

"Well, who else are you going to date around here?" Peggy demanded. "It's slim pickings, I tell you, even for a nice, good-looking young man with a hero's job."

Ooookay. This was her cue to go, Summer thought. Before things got any worse. Obviously, Detective Donovan's grandma hated her. And the guy could ask Jennifer on a date anytime he wanted, if he hadn't already. She was totally over him. Even if he looked extra cute when he was embarrassed.

"Hey, Dorothy, I'm going to run to SuperMart," she said. "We might need a few extra things for those book club refreshments."

"Well, don't overdo it, dear," Dorothy said. "We can make do with whatever the Hibiscus Pointe catering staff comes up with, I'm sure."

"Got it," Summer said, picking up her bag from the counter on her way to the door. "See you later, guys."

She was just crossing the parking lot from Hibiscus Gardens when her cell rang. Miracle of miracles, the rest and reboot must have worked. The screen was still cracked, though.

Maybe Dorothy had thought of something else they needed. "Hello?"

"Hey, Cali Girl," Dash said. "This is a rescue call."

Jeez, what now?

"I can't stand another minute with Mother," he said, dropping his voice. Summer envisioned him glancing over his shoulder. "She's driving me to drink, right along with her. Do you want to hit the town with me and Esmé later? She asked us to meet her at Chameleon when she gets off work."

A night out did sound good. She needed a break, with all the crazy stuff going on. It might help clear the stress and make her sharper for the book club sting tomorrow. "Okay," she said. "I'll get ready now and pick you up. I know it's early, but I need to do a quick errand before the place closes, okay?"

"No problem," Dash said. "I'm desperate. And by the way, thanks so much for that blooming turtle. So far it prefers the master bathtub to its aquarium."

Gross. But Juliette-Margot sure had been thrilled when she presented her with the little guy in his clawed-through carton. "Sorry, you're breaking up," Summer told him. "See you in a few."

It took her almost an hour to shower and get ready, because she couldn't find the strappy gold Grecian sandals she needed to go with her sparkly gold top and black-and-gold miniskirt.

She felt almost like Trixie when she added swingy chocolate diamond earrings and checked herself out in the mirror. Ugh, too much. She slipped off the earrings and tossed them back on the dresser. No jewelry tonight.

Twenty minutes later, with Dash cramped up in

the passenger seat, Summer pulled the MINI into the packed SuperMart parking lot.

"You're kidding," Dash said. "SuperMart? That's your big errand?"

"Yep." Summer jumped out of the car and leaned her head back in through the window. "Better than hanging out with your mom, right? Are you coming?"

"Thank you, but no," Dash said. "I'll just wait here and people watch."

Summer tried to stay focused, ignoring a few stares as she grabbed giant tubs of lemonade, daiquiri, and piña colada mixes. People acted as if they'd never seen anyone dressed up before. Well, that was their problem.

She'd have to hit a liquor store later for the vodka and rum. They probably wouldn't need much of the hard stuff, since most of the seniors didn't drink much, but it would be good to have plenty of nonalcoholic options. Hopefully, Jennifer could round them up a bunch of blenders.

Summer was headed toward the checkout area, tossing a bottle of cool blue nail polish and a package of TP into her cart on her way, when she spotted a huge display of red plastic drink cups. Might be a good idea to pick up some of those, too. Less cleanup, and these were recyclable.

She grabbed for the nearest pack at the same time the burly guy next to her did, and his elbow knocked straight through the cardboard display. "Watch it," he growled, snatching the cups and heading for the chips aisle.

Summer didn't respond. She was too busy staring at the SuperMart customer on the other side of the display. White jeans, cowboy boots, curvy figure, obvious wig—strawberry blond this time. No rodeo buckle, but she was wearing massive Texas-shaped diamond earrings.

The woman saw her, too, and made a break for the exit doors, squeezing her way through the crowd. Some shoppers seemed confused, and others annoyed—but most were just plain oblivious.

"Trixie, wait!" Summer ditched her cart and took off after her. "I just need to talk to you. It's me or the police!"

Well, it would be both, actually. No sense in mentioning that now, though.

Lorella's ex-assistant ignored her and kept on running. Summer had almost caught up with her when Trixie pushed a cart full of screaming, unattended toddlers in her path and ducked past the SuperMart greeter out the sliding doors.

"Hey, get away from my kids!" A woman whirled around with her half-read checkout magazine and grabbed the cart. "What's the matter with you?"

"Really sorry," Summer mumbled, ducking into the next aisle and squeezing past the Next Lane Please sign. She had to catch Trixie.

Unfortunately, Ray's sort-of girlfriend moved faster in those boots than Summer did in her slippery new sandals. By the time Summer reached the parking lot, Trixie was nowhere in sight.

She had to be here somewhere, Summer told herself. No way could she just disappear, with her crazy looks, even in a crowded parking lot.

Wrong. Trixie was gone.

Summer wanted to kick herself for not alerting Security on her way out the door. But the SuperMart employee had been busy checking each and every shopper's receipts and she'd figured she was better off on her own.

Drat. Maybe, if she drove her car up every aisle in the parking lot, she'd spot Trixie. Or maybe she should zoom to the nearest exit—unfortunately, there were two, she noticed—and wait for the woman to leave.

Trixie had run away as soon as she saw her. That meant she had to be guilty, right? She obviously knew Summer and Dorothy were onto her—about lying to them about her big trip to Montana, anyway. And Trixie had to be aware by now that Lorella was dead. Did she know she was a suspect in her boss's murder? Probably, if Detective Donovan had shown up looking for her and Ray at that nasty exotic pet store.

Dash was taking a preclub nap in the MINI, oblivious of the pounding techno music on the radio, as Summer jumped in behind the wheel and pushed the ignition.

"Whoa, what's the deal?" he said, sounding a little dazed as she roared carefully up each section of the parking lot. "Watch out for those two old folks," he added. "Over there, on the left, And the curved screen TV carton, behind that red pickup."

"No worries, I've got this," Summer told him. Except she didn't. She was right back where she'd started. Trixie was gone.

"Call Detective Donovan," she instructed her cell phone assistant.

This time, he answered, for once. "Trixie didn't leave town, for sure," Summer said, skipping the hellos. "I'm at the SuperMart on Blue Heron Boulevard and I just saw her. And…she got away again. I lost her. But this means both she and Ray are definitely hiding out in town. And Trixie's somewhere around here right now."

"Thanks for the tip," the detective said. "But we have a team already on it." He paused. "Summer, please. Go home, okay? I've asked you more than once not to get involved, for your own safety."

Go home? What was she, a little kid? She clicked off, without bothering to say goodbye. She'd just seen him, and he hadn't mentioned anything about Trixie, except to say the cops had put out an APB on her. Now they were on alert for two snakes. Or three, if you counted Ray.

Did Donovan's "team" really know Trixie was *here*, right this very second? Or was the detective just pretending he even knew for sure Trixie was still in Milano? Well, it didn't matter. Either way he was a jerk.

Why didn't he ever take her seriously?

"Hey, are you okay?" Dash asked, wide-awake now. "You look a little…thundery."

"I'm fine. We're out of here." Summer revved the MINI to take them far, far away from SuperMart.

How could she have ever thought Shane Donovan Jr. was remotely attractive? Now she was totally glad he and his grandma were more interested in Jennifer than her. In fact, she was going to scout out another, much better guy for Jennifer. Starting tonight, maybe. The girl deserved a decent boyfriend.

And it was game on for the case, Detective.

TEN

DOROTHY WOKE FROM a fitful sleep to the insistent ring of the phone she'd recently had installed next to her bed.

She already regretted that decision, but the woman from the Resident Wellness and Safety staff had recommended a multihandset system, in the highly unlikely case of some unspecified emergency.

"Hi, Dorothy?" a perky voice chirped. "Good morning! It's Carrie Dunbar. I didn't wake you, did I?"

"Not quite," Dorothy said politely. "What can I do for you, Carrie?"

"Well, thank goodness it's Friday, right? Book club day! Just wanted to see if there's anything else you think we'll need, or anything more Parker and I can do to get the word out."

Definitely not an emergency. Dorothy wearily rubbed her already throbbing temples. Perhaps a Tylenol or two would be in order for breakfast. "I don't believe so, Carrie."

This young woman was going to be very disappointed in today's resident turnout. If the equally enthusiastic Lorella Caldwell hadn't succeeded in raising the literary engagement level at Hibiscus Pointe, then really, who could?

It might even—somehow—have cost the librarian her life.

"So Parker's had a zillion bookmarks printed and

we're bringing a few cartons of books and a bunch of promotional tchotchkes. Do you think that will be enough? I've got some cute little chocolates with my website printed on them, but we'll take those out at the very last minute so they don't melt in the heat or anything."

"Oh, that sounds just wonderful, dear," Dorothy said. And definitely overkill. Goodness, she hoped Georgiana wasn't going to be miffed that this eager young author was offering so many of her own, extra promotional materials. Would the great GH Hamel feel she was being overshadowed?

No, she assured herself. Discriminating readers would not be swayed by colorful bookmarks and fancy chocolate. They'd make their own book choices, based on literary merit. And Georgiana would understand that, of course.

"Hey, Dorothy!" Summer stepped into the condo, balancing a cardboard tray with two cups of coffee and a bag of pastries, and pulled the key Dorothy had had made for her out of the door lock.

"So sorry, Carrie, I'm afraid I have to go," Dorothy said as Summer expertly avoided Mr. Bitey's claws extended from somewhere behind the antique hutch in the living room. "I have a guest. But I'll see you this afternoon."

"Oh, okay." Carrie sounded disappointed. "Parker and I will be there early to help set up. Just let me know if you think of anything else for us to do. You have my number, right?"

"I do." Dorothy tried not to glance at her nightstand, where she'd left the business card she'd used as a bookmark last night. It showed a rather unflattering photo of Carrie—wearing a tiara, no less—beside her contact info. A blurb along the bottom edge of the card read *Soon to be the international, bestselling queen of romantic suspense!*

That was certainly an attention-getting marketing approach. And perhaps a tad optimistic, at this early stage in her career as an author.

"Don't you think, Dorothy?"

Oh. Carrie was still talking, and Dorothy hadn't heard a word she'd said. "Bye now, dear," she said as she dropped the phone back on its cradle. The young woman probably hadn't even noticed.

"Carrie again?" Summer wrinkled her nose and set one of the coffee cups down on the nightstand. "It's way too early to deal with her."

Dorothy sighed. "I have to agree with you there. I was considering Tylenol for breakfast."

"Well, I brought you a half-caff latte and a snack, but we have to hurry," Summer said. "We have some investigating to do."

"Right now?" Dorothy said, gratefully taking the coffee.

"Yep. As soon as you can get ready, okay?" She handed Dorothy her silky blue dressing gown from the end of the bed. "On my way here, I went up to get the free pastries in my building and I saw a bunch of Hibiscus Pointe staff people cleaning out Trixie's condo."

"Are you sure it was hers?" Dorothy headed toward her closet.

Summer took a swig of her triple-shot mocha. "Oh yeah. I've been by her place a couple of times, scoping it out in case she came back. But I would have known it was hers anyway. There was a whole bunch of Texas stuff—a big lamp with antlers—and road maps and tons of cans outside the door. Plus Lone Star beer and superhold hair spray."

"Maybe we could check some of those maps and see if Trixie and Ray marked their route as they were planning their trip," Dorothy said. "It's worth a try, anyway."

"Good idea," Summer said. "Oh, and do you think I could have a couple of those Tylenol? Dash and I had kind of a crazy night."

By the time she and Summer made it over to Tower A, the cleaning staff members were nowhere in sight, but Trixie's door was still open. A rolling cart just outside it in the hall held a supply of trash bags, towels, mops, and cleaning supplies.

"We'll have to work fast," Summer said. "They'll be back. They're probably just dumping the trash."

"There's still quite a bit of it left," Dorothy observed, nudging a crumpled pack of Marlboros with the toe of one Aerolite Racer. An odiferous cloud of cheap perfume wafted from a broken, horsehead-shaped bottle on the carpet and a sad trail of rhinestones led into the condo.

"Hey, Dorothy, check this out," Summer called, from beyond the door.

Dorothy hurried inside to where her sleuthing partner stood over a messy lineup of shopping bags, overflowing with papers.

"Bills, mostly," Summer said, holding up a handful of pages. "Unpaid ones. They're all marked 'Past Due' and there are a bunch of disconnection notices, too."

"Goodness," Dorothy said, rummaging through the bags. From the looks of things, Trixie was indeed in dire financial straits. "How do you suppose she managed to afford this condo?" No doubt she was a renter, but Dorothy didn't want to mention that, in case Summer's feelings might be hurt.

Not to mention that financial matters in general were usually something of a sore point for her young friend.

"She didn't," Summer said. "There are tons of past due alerts from Hibiscus Pointe here, too. Oh, and yep, here we go. An eviction notice, from two months ago."

"I wonder whether that's why Trixie was in such a hurry to leave," Dorothy said. "It could have had nothing to do with Lorella's murder."

"She could have stayed awhile longer, I bet," Summer said. "It takes months for landlords to actually get rid of you. Unless it's Joy. Then you're out in two seconds."

Dorothy sighed. Her friend was still smarting from her sister's strong encouragement to move out of their shared home in New Jersey. "Look at the bright side, dear. If you hadn't come down here to Florida, we wouldn't have met."

"True." Summer bounced over to give her a quick hug. She smelled like coconut, as always, and strawberry lip gloss. Then she broke away and frowned. "But Trixie was getting paid to work at the library, right? She must have started getting a few paychecks, at least. Maybe she promised Hibiscus Pointe she'd pay them back soon."

"Or they offered to give her a break on her rent," Dorothy said.

"Well, they're not doing anything like that for anyone else." Summer tossed the eviction notice back into the bag over her shoulder. "I work at the pool for free and you know what the deal I got was? They said they wouldn't kick me out because I was 'underage.' Not yet, anyway."

"Remember, positivity," Dorothy said lightly. "Perhaps Jennifer can tell us whether Trixie had some kind of special financial arrangement." She doubted that, though. As recent events in particular had shown, the Resident Services director took the confidential aspects of her job very seriously.

Which was a good thing, really. Except when one needed to establish motive for murder.

"I heard Roger telling Jennifer there was some kind of major delinquency problem with someone's account," Summer said. "Maybe it was Trixie, then, and not me. Phew. I still need to double-check with Joy that we're okay, though."

"Mmm." Dorothy riffled through another stack of Trixie's old mail. "These go back quite a ways," she said. "I wonder why she even bothered to keep them. Unless she planned to pay them off eventually, of course."

"Nah," Summer said, with a wave. "She's a hoarder, probably. Did you see all that crazy stuff she got into the RV?"

"You looking for something, ladies? No one lives here anymore."

Dorothy turned toward the voice from the doorway. A tired-looking, dark-haired woman dressed in the navy-and-tan uniform of Housekeeping Services set down a bucket filled with bottles of bleach and Faux-Breeze.

"Oh, hello. We were looking for Trixie Quattrochi," Dorothy said. "To wish her well on her trip. But it looks as if we're too late."

The housekeeper wiped her arm across her perspiring face. "Yeah, you are. And she's not coming back. Good riddance, I say. That one never let me in here to clean, and now look at the place."

"Pretty bad," Summer agreed. "Hey, did you find anything interesting in here when you were clearing things out?"

"Depends on what you call interesting." The housekeeper shuddered slightly. "I didn't look too close, after that stuffed dead raccoon. A coupla antler lamps. And, oh yeah, a box of big plastic owls. The guys took everything straight to the incinerator. They're on their way back for these last few bags."

"We could get rid of them for you," Summer offered, just as two men in Hibiscus Pointe uniforms arrived with a rolling Dumpster and threw the bags in.

"I guess we'd best be going." Dorothy took one more glance around the now-empty condo. Trixie must have managed to take all her flashy jewelry, at least. Except, apparently, for the overly large turquoise and amber necklace peeking out from the side pocket of the housekeeper's dress. "We'll be out of your way."

"Where to now?" Summer asked as she and Dorothy stepped out into the hall. "Trixie didn't have any neighbors. This part of the Towers is being renovated or something, because no one else lives here. I checked it out on Wednesday night after we got back from Dash's party."

Dorothy sighed. This entire section of condos did appear uninhabited. No floral wreaths on the doors. No welcome mats. No fancy gold nameplates. "Why don't we go back to the Gardens and see if we can talk to any of Lorella's neighbors?"

Earlier, the entire end of the hall in proximity to the deceased librarian's condo had been crime-taped by the Milano PD—and then blocked by a folding metal grate. Overkill, perhaps, Dorothy thought. But effective in keeping out rubberneckers.

Not to mention—very inconveniently, she might add—amateur detectives.

They had just made their way over to Hibiscus Gardens and turned the corner toward Lorella's former residence when Summer muttered something under her breath. "Look who beat us here," she said. "Ol' Mr. Bill."

Dorothy sighed. Sure enough, the security chief was headed their way from the other entrance, lugging a medium-sized plastic animal carrier. She waved, and he gave a small, pained smile as he continued toward them down the hall.

Bill stopped and knocked on a door just two condos down from Lorella's. The person who answered unlatched a thick gold security chain and poked out her white, pink-curlered head. "Oh, good, you're here just in time," she said. "My show is about to start."

Dorothy rushed over behind Bill, who set down the animal carrier and wiped his brow. "Oh, hello," she said to the woman. "I'm Dorothy Westin, and this is my friend, Summer. Could we talk to you for a moment?"

"Sorry, I really can't," the woman said as the theme song for *Afternoons with Eleanor* drifted out from a TV inside, along with the faint odor of cigarette smoke. "And don't let the…"

Something fast and furry brushed Dorothy's ankle, and Bill jumped aside. Behind them, Summer reached down just in time to nab a small, skinny gray cat.

"Got him!" Summer said triumphantly.

"Her," the woman in curlers corrected.

Dorothy reached out to give the animal a pet, but it shrank back against Summer and ducked its head. Poor thing.

The woman opened the door a bit wider and Summer tried to hand the frightened kitty, paws frantically flailing, over to its owner. "Here you go."

"You can keep her if you want, young lady," she said. "Because I can't."

"What? You mean, for good?" Summer threw Dorothy a panicked look that mirrored the cat's.

"That's why I'm here." Bill picked up the carrier again. "She was Lorella Caldwell's cat and I'm taking it to the Milano Animal Shelter."

Oh dear, Dorothy thought. No lost or unwanted pets lasted long there. "You'll do no such thing," she said, extracting the shivering cat from the crook of Summer's elbow. "I'll keep her until we can find her a good home."

"Fine. Her name's Guinevere, by the way." Margaret pulled her floral housecoat closer around her tiny frame. "The cops must have let her out the sliding doors onto Lorella's porch and she got over on mine and broke all the vines in my upside-down tomato planter. I just ordered it off the TV, too. She's a nuisance, if you ask me."

Bill was already halfway back down the hall. "Thanks, Mrs. Westin," he called. "You're a generous woman."

"Wait, ma'am?" Summer said, sticking her sneaker inside the woman's door just as it began to close. "We really need to talk to you for a sec. About your neighbor, Lorella?"

"Didn't know her." The woman nudged Summer's

foot back with her own matted lavender slipper. "Just her cat."

Dorothy's mouth dropped open as the door closed firmly and the clatter of metal chain was drowned out by wild applause from the studio audience of *Afternoons with Eleanor*.

Well, that, it seemed, was that.

"EASY-SLEAZY," SUMMER ANNOUNCED as she slid open Lorella's glass door and stepped into the dead woman's condo. "What did I tell you? The cops messed up. Everyone always forgets to lock the porch entrance."

At least Lorella's place was on the ground floor of a two-floor complex. Any higher, and she wouldn't have even tried.

"Good job," Dorothy murmured. "Be careful of Guinevere, now. She must be even more frightened now."

Summer peered warily into the cat carrier, and the little animal blinked back at her. She was kind of cute, actually. Not all ornery, like Mr. Bitey. "She's okay."

Maybe she could convince Dash to adopt the kitty for Juliette-Margot. She'd already gotten them that turtle, though. And cat fur might not go so well with the Hamel-LeBlancs' designer furniture and white rugs.

Lorella's condo was small and superneat, even after the cops had gone through it—if you didn't mind all the books stuffed in every room. The place was full of clunky, ugly old furniture—the creepy, dark, carved kind that would have been perfect for...well, one of those creepy Tudor houses. Or maybe Professor Bell's office.

That was what the place reminded her of, except

Lorella's bookshelves were perfectly organized. But that wasn't a huge shock. After all, the woman was a librarian.

Summer felt a little guilty as she and Dorothy snooped around, but she tried to be as respectful as possible about the dead woman's stuff.

There wasn't much in any of her drawers, and hardly anything in her closet. Mostly heavy materials like wool and tweed. She must not have gone outdoors, like, ever.

No makeup in the bathroom, either, except for a jar of superthick face cream that looked as if it had been bought in 1948, a tub of generic petroleum jelly, and one classic red lipstick.

The tube was Chanel. And beside it stood a bottle of Chanel No 5—the perfume version, not the less expensive toilet water spray.

Nice, Summer told herself. Lorella had some secret indulgences. She tried the lipstick out on the mirror. It really was a cool, vintage-type color, but she hardly ever wore red.

"That shade is called Pirate," Dorothy said. "I used to wear it myself," she added, sounding a little sad.

"Yikes, it looks like blood." Summer quickly tried to wipe the lipstick from the glass with her finger. "The cops will know someone was here if they come back."

"It looks as if Lorella turned the master closet into a little office," Dorothy said, stepping back into the bedroom. "There's even a desk in here."

"Her computer's gone," Summer said, joining her friend and running a hand over the desktop. "See, no dust over this big, square spot."

"Except now there's a streak of red lipstick," Dorothy pointed out.

Oops. Summer reached for a few tissues from the dispenser on the desktop and rubbed it off. "Hey, there are some files boxes behind here," she said, ducking under the desk. "Like the ones Lorella was using at the library. Nothing's labeled—just a bunch of folders and a few Moleskine notebooks. Probably all her old professor notes. The police must have gone through them already, I guess."

"I'll be right there, dear. Maybe we can take a few with us, and come back later to double-check the rest for clues, just in case." Dorothy was busy perusing the headboard of Lorella's bed, which had bookshelves built into it. No surprise here. The librarian must have run out of room for all her books.

"Just look at all these Angelina St. Rose titles," Dorothy added. "My friends and I used to head to the bookstore to buy the latest ones the minute they arrived."

"Huh." Summer crossed the room to peer over her friend's shoulder. "I actually read some of those when I was a kid. My first and third stepmoms were big fans. They didn't want me to have them, though."

"Well, I can understand that," Dorothy said. "Angelina St. Rose is a bit racy for younger readers, wouldn't you say?"

"I guess," Summer said. She'd read some of her stepmoms' other books that were a lot worse.

As Dorothy continued to look at all of Lorella's books, Summer made her way through the rest of the bedroom. Beneath a fake red rose in a vase, a small ivory and gold jewelry box caught her eye. She carefully lifted the lid.

Rats. It was empty. Summer was about to put the lid back on, but her finger caught a tiny tab. Some kind of secret compartment? She pulled on it gently and her mouth dropped open. Underneath the blue velvet liner was a gorgeous bloodstone ring in a fancy gold setting.

Where had she seen a ring like that before?

"My, that looks like the one Georgiana was wearing at the party," Dorothy said, coming up beside her with a tote bag of file folders.

"Yeah, you're right," Summer said. How could she have forgotten that? The ring Dash's mom had worn was a little bigger, maybe. But otherwise the same. How could Lorella Caldwell and GH Hamel possibly have anything in common?

It was a really weird coincidence that the quiet librarian and the famous mystery writer had the exact same taste in jewelry.

But they didn't. Georgiana wore huge, swingy earrings, and from what Summer could tell, Lorella had owned a single pair of pearl posts.

She took out her phone to snap a picture of the ring as Dorothy headed toward the sliding doors. "Let's go, dear," her friend said. "We still have a lot to do before the book club meeting. But we'll come back."

"Okay." Summer put her phone away and slipped the bloodstone onto her ring finger. Pretty tight. But hey, her pinky was a perfect fit.

Maybe she should take this with her, in case it was needed for evidence somehow. The cops had probably missed it in that secret compartment. And she could always put it back later, when she and Dorothy returned.

Summer pocketed the ring, picked up the pitifully meowing Guinevere in her carrier, and followed her sleuthing partner through the sliding doors.

ELEVEN

DOROTHY CHECKED HER reflection in the mirror on the back of her bedroom door. She had chosen her freshly dry-cleaned, peach linen suit—the one that always made her feel attractive and confident—to wear for the book club kickoff.

A bit formal, perhaps, but as her mother had always insisted, it was better to be overdressed than underdressed for special occasions.

Unfortunately, she could very well be late to her own party. Her mother had a few expressions for those occasions, as well—which did not, as Dorothy recalled, include "better late than never." But she'd been at her wits' end this afternoon, wrangling two very unhappy felines.

"Bitey, stop that!" she scolded as she walked into the living room and discovered the orange tomcat chasing poor Guinevere around and around the ottoman. Fortunately, Mr. Bitey was not quite as nimble as the tiny gray kitty. "Get over here, young man."

He didn't pay a scrap of attention, but Guinevere made a break for it and tried to hide behind Dorothy's shoes.

"All right, that's it," Dorothy informed both rascals. The three of them would be here the entire afternoon, at this rate. Fortunately, Summer was already over at the Magnolia Events Room, helping Jennifer and Parker set up.

She reached down to grab Guinevere and carried her toward the powder room, with Mr. Bity hot on their heels. Thank goodness she hadn't worn hose, as she'd initially considered, or they would be in shreds by now.

"I'm sorry to do this to you," Dorothy told the little gray cat as she placed her on the powder room floor and firmly shut the door. "But you'll be better off in here." She'd already put down food, water, and a makeshift litter box for her guest.

As Dorothy left, she could hear Mr. Bitey scratching at the powder room door, but she'd just have to deal with the damage later. She had exactly ten minutes to get over to the Towers.

"Hi, Dorothy!" Carrie Dunbar, her braids rather unsuccessfully bobby-pinned on top of her head, smiled broadly from four feet away in the hall. "I've been waiting for you."

Dorothy touched a relieved hand to her chest. "Heavens, you gave me such a fright."

"Oh, I'm really sorry. I heard you talking to those people inside your condo, and I was just about to knock. Sounded as if there was something crazy going on in there." Carrie picked up the canvas book tote—custom-printed with the same tiara-ed photo as her business cards, Dorothy noted—from the carpet beside her, supporting it with both hands. "Wow, this thing is heavy. I've got so many of my books in here, you know? Parker said we had enough already, but I figured we might need some extras."

"Mmm." Dorothy headed toward the elevator at a brisk clip. Hopefully, she had remembered to tuck that travel-sized bottle of Tylenol in her purse.

Carrie practically skipped along beside her, even with the loaded book bag. "I wanted to walk in with you, Dorothy, since you know everyone. I'm on the agenda, right? I know *A Killing Fog* is my new book, but I really want to give a sales boost to my first one, *Debut for Death*, too."

"Of course," Dorothy murmured, stabbing at the elevator button.

"I have a few ideas to present them both, maybe right after Georgiana's," Carrie went on as the doors finally opened. "What would you think if I started with—"

"You know, Carrie, this is just a small, introductory book club meeting, really," Dorothy broke in. "No doubt all of our new members will be eager to learn more about your novels, but overselling things might not be wise, at this point." Or at any point, she added silently.

"Oh." Carrie looked a half-smidge deflated. "Right."

"Why don't you consider redirecting your energies a bit, dear? Maybe toward promoting literature and reading in general?" Dorothy suggested. "For a start, of course."

"Uh, sure." Carrie readjusted the weight of her book bag to one hip, hitching up the side of her pleated tan skirt. "By the way, Parker and I are putting together a few fun, low-key promo events this week at some trendy spots around Milano. Do you and Summer want to join us? And maybe, since you guys know Georgiana and her family so well, you could get Georgiana to come along, too."

"Why, thank you," Dorothy said. "We'll see."

Mercifully, an empty Hibiscus Pointe shuttle bus picked them up as they emerged from the building and delivered them directly to the Towers. If Dorothy had been forced to listen to this young woman's chatter for another five minutes, she might very well have thrown herself under it.

When she and Carrie arrived at the top floor of Tower B, Dorothy was astounded to see that the Magnolia Events Room was packed with residents—and outsiders, too. Gracious, how did that happen?

Lorella would have been so pleased.

"Great turnout," Carrie said. "I can't believe all these people are here to see me."

"And GH Hamel, perhaps," Dorothy reminded her, lightly. "Not to mention they're expecting a book club launch."

The young woman had the good grace to blush. "Oh, I meant that. But isn't Parker just the best publicist ever? It must have been all those flyers. I am so glad I hired her. She's worth every penny."

"Yes, she's certainly doing a marvelous job," Dorothy said, scanning the crowd. The publicity assistant was circling the crowd with her tablet, handing out promotional bookmarks and obtaining signatures for something. Carrie's email list, no doubt.

Summer, dressed in a splashy, Hawaiian-themed shift, was popping maraschino cherries into her mouth as she set up blenders for daiquiris and piña coladas— goodness, that would be noisy during the meeting, Dorothy suddenly realized—while Jennifer directed the catering staff in pouring bottles of wine and sparkling water. Faux-silver trays lined with cookies, blondie brownies, cheese, crackers, and grapes lined the serving tables, which were draped with golden tablecloths.

Quite the "do." Hopefully, the meeting itself would be met with equal enthusiasm.

She should start making her way toward the podium, Dorothy realized, tamping down tiny embers of nervousness. People were beginning to find seats. If only Harlan and Maddie could see her now. She did so hate speaking in public, but this was for a very good cause.

And if reestablishing the Hibiscus Pointe Book Club would help solve Lorella's murder, it would be worth a few moments of personal discomfort.

Was this how the shy former professor and librarian had felt when she was forced to face the public? And if she had stayed buried in her books, as she'd clearly preferred, would Lorella have been running this meeting today?

Dorothy smoothed her suit and made her way toward the central aisle toward the podium, still thinking of her predecessor.

The racy romance novels, the bold Pirate lipstick, the gorgeous bloodstone ring, the secret relationship with a younger man... The dead woman clearly had had her passions. And it was up to her and Summer to uncover whatever lurked behind them.

SUMMER GRABBED A red plastic cup from the stack on the table beside her and poured herself a piña colada tester. Not bad. "Want to try one?" she asked, filling a cup for Jennifer.

"No, thanks," Jennifer said. "I can't drink when I'm working."

"Oh, right." Summer wiped the sticky coconut crème from her fingers with a Hibiscus Pointe paper napkin. "I'll just leave it here, in case you change your mind later. I need to make sure Dorothy's okay up there. She looks a little nervous."

"Well, hurry back." Jennifer glanced toward the door. "GH Hamel hasn't arrived yet, and people are getting restless. I think we're going to have to put out more drinks soon."

"Guess we could have made some bucks on this," Summer said. "Too late."

"Well, that's a good idea anyway. People could charge alcoholic drinks to their resident accounts, like they do at dinner." Jennifer uncorked another bottle of Chardonnay. "We'd make a fortune, and it might even help me get Roger off my case. Next time, for sure."

There wasn't going to be a next time, Summer told herself. Not if she and Dorothy could solve Lorella's murder today, anyway. But first they needed their suspects to show up.

She headed toward the podium, where Dorothy was trying to deal with that prune face Helen Martin, but stopped when she heard a commotion near the Events Room entrance.

Summer blinked in the sudden bright light. WMLO reporter Felicia Hernandez and her TV crew had just walked in, cameras already rolling. Who had called the media? Well, that was a no-brainer. Carrie and Parker were right there at the door to greet them.

Someone else was posted near the entrance, too. Yep, Professor Charles Bell had shown up. Was he trying to get on TV?

Summer glanced Dorothy's way again. Uh-oh. Peggy Donovan had rolled up to the podium now, too, and it looked as if she was taking on Helen about something. Poor Dorothy was trying to intervene.

Jeez. Well, her sleuthing partner would want her to go after their suspect, for sure.

The professor, wearing a different navy blazer and the same pair of jeans, didn't seem to be paying any attention to the news crew. Instead he kept looking out into the hall, clutching a beat-up-looking leather man bag.

Summer made it over there just as there was another burst of activity and GH Hamel swept into the Magnolia Events Room, followed by Dash and a black lace–clad Juliette-Margot.

Nice dress, Summer thought. She wouldn't mind getting one like that for herself. She was pretty sure they made that one in grown-up sizes.

Georgiana wore a red silk tunic over black silk pants, ropes of giant white beads, and a candy-cane-striped head scarf.

Oh, and that bloodstone ring. Summer peered at it more closely. Yep, exactly like Lorella's.

"Move back, please, everyone!" Parker started shooing people—including her own client Carrie—off to the sides of the room to make way for the famous author.

Georgiana played the part, too, as she nodded and gave the crowd a royal wave or two. Elbow held steady and twist of the wrist, to cut down on arm jiggle.

"Daiquiri, please," Summer heard Georgiana mutter to Dash, but he was already on it. She quickly grabbed Juliette-Margot's hand so she wouldn't get trampled by her grandmother's fans.

The kid didn't seem that worried. "Juliette-Margot brought this for the book club meeting," she said, holding up a picture book with a messy-looking girl about her age on the cover. "See? *Eloise*. She speaks French, just like me."

"That's nice." Summer kept her eyes on the professor. He was shifting around, looking nervous, as people began to find seats.

"Ms. Hamel?" He suddenly broke toward Georgiana, trying to pull something out of his bag. Looked like some kind of package.

Summer pushed Juliette-Margot behind her. Did the guy have a bomb?

Just as Summer was about to make a move, Parker stepped up and blocked the professor. "No questions now, please, sir. We have time built in for Q&A at the end of the authors' talks."

"I have to give GH Hamel something," he said. "It's very important."

Summer was about to warn Parker when she realized the package was just a couple of superthick manila envelopes, held together with a jumbo rubber band. Phew. And Georgiana was so busy acknowledging her other fans that she hadn't even noticed.

"Sorry," Parker said to Professor Bell. She brushed him away like an annoying bug and tried to hustle Georgiana down the center aisle toward the front of the room, where Dorothy—and Carrie, who had run up there like a shot—were ready to start the meeting.

But Georgiana didn't budge. Her attention was glued to the giant photo of Lorella on an easel near the first buffet. It was Dorothy's idea, and Jennifer had blown up the librarian's dated, blurry obituary photo.

"That's her?" Georgiana asked Summer loudly, over her shoulder. She looked confused, and a little shocked, maybe. "The one who got murdered in this place?"

For a second or two, the Events Room went dead quiet—except for the sound of Jennifer popping another cork. Yep, she was probably ready to start drinking on the job now.

And yikes, poor Juliette-Margot, hearing that. Summer tightened her grip on the little girl's hand, but she wasn't acting scared. She seemed just as morbidly fascinated as everyone else. Jeez, where was Dash?

She spotted her friend near the drinks table, looking as frozen as the two strawberry daiquiris he'd been transporting. It had to be tough having Georgiana for a mom. GH Hamel might be a famous mystery writer, but she wasn't exactly the queen of tact.

She might even be more embarrassing than Harmony Smythe-Sloan.

A buzz began to rise from the crowd, as if the Magnolia Events Room had been invaded by a swarm of killer bees. Summer frowned. Everyone at Hibiscus Pointe had to know already that Lorella was murdered. Gladys Rumway had probably made sure of that by now, if the residents hadn't figured things out themselves, with all the cops and crime tape and extra security.

Not to mention the media. It was Felicia Hernandez's lucky day—she and her news team would get two stories for the price of one. GH Hamel—no way could they really be here for Carrie—and the murder at fancy Hibiscus Pointe.

The media might not be able to get much out of Jennifer, but someone else would blab. Gladys, for sure, but there were plenty of others who'd want their fifteen seconds of fame, too.

Dorothy tapped on the microphone. "We're going to start, everyone." Her voice came out a little muffled and wobbly, but she leaned forward and raised her voice. "Quiet, please."

The buzzing immediately stopped. Wow, Summer thought. Impressive. But then, everyone always listened to Dorothy Westin.

Even her.

"I'd like to welcome you all to the very first meeting of our new Hibiscus Pointe Book Club," Dorothy said. "It is my honor to dedicate this event—and the club itself—to the memory of its founder, Lorella Rose Caldwell. Let's take a moment of silence to remember Lorella, and continue to keep her in our thoughts and prayers."

And solve her murder quick, Summer added to herself, glancing at Professor Bell in the last row of seats. He was staring straight at Georgiana, his man bag on his lap. No way would she let him out of her sight—or near Dash's mom, even if she was one scary lady. There was something really sneaky and shady about the professor. Not to mention, he was one of their top suspects. Had he realized the gold bookend in his office—the possible mate to the murder-y one—was missing?

"Thank you, member and guests," Dorothy said, after what seemed to Summer like an eternity. "To start our meeting off on an extra-special note, I'd like to thank the two wonderful author guests who graciously agreed to join us." She turned and smiled at Georgiana and Carrie, who sat next to each other in the velvet-cushioned Events Room chairs. "GH Hamel, of course, whose best-selling works of romantic suspense I'm sure many of you have already read. And I'd also like to introduce an up-and-coming young author, Carrie Dunbar."

"I'm on my second book, actually," Carrie broke in, with an apologetic little wave to the audience. "But I feel like it's kind of my debut, since this is my first author tour. I'm so excited to meet you all, and thrilled to be sitting here next to Georgiana. I've been reading her books since I was twelve. She's just one of my biggest idols."

The idol didn't appreciate the backhanded compliment, Summer noticed. Georgiana looked ready to laser Carrie through her Lucille Ball fake eyelashes.

"Georgiana, as our guest of honor, would you like to come up now and get us started?" Dorothy said quickly.

Parker went over and said something into her ear. "Oh," Dorothy said. "It seems our authors would prefer to wait until we finish our book club business, and after they speak the refreshment tables will reopen for the reception."

"Hear, hear," Gladys called out. "Let's open those tables back up now." A few people applauded.

Dorothy ignored that, and picked up a pile of pages from in front of her on the podium. "I trust you all took the handouts by the door—just some general guidelines and book suggestions—but why don't we go over a few ground rules before we discuss them?"

Ugh. This was exactly like school.

"Oh, and one more thing." Parker hurried back over and leaned into the mic. "Carrie and Georgiana have some fantastic author events coming up very soon, since they're both in town. We're still working on the details, but tomorrow night we'd love for you to join us at Milano Book & Bar for a cocktail party and author signing. Jennifer, your Resident Services director, is making arrangements for Hibiscus Pointe shuttle transportation. Hope to see you there!"

"We're meeting at 7:00 p.m. in the main lobby," Jennifer added, over the enthusiastic chatter.

"Thank you, ladies," Dorothy said. "That does sound like fun. We'll all look forward to that. So let's get back to our discussion, shall we?"

Wow. Dorothy was smooth.

Summer tuned out temporarily to watch Professor Bell as her friend outlined the way the club would work. Two meetings a month. One to discuss a short story and the other a whole book. Rules for how the discussions would work, and being polite. Blah, blah.

The professor wasn't paying much attention to Dorothy, either, Summer could tell. He frowned in concentration, making a bunch of notes in a little black notebook he'd taken from his man bag. It looked like some kind of journal.

How could she get a look at whatever he was writing? Maybe if she snuck over and distracted him...

Dash and Juliette-Margot, her nose in her *Eloise* book, were sitting in the same row. The perfect cover. Summer could pretend she was joining them.

"So now that you've all had a chance to look over the title suggestions, what do you think?" Dorothy was saying as Summer picked up a pre-poured piña colada from one of the drinks tables and moved as nonchalantly as she could toward the back of the room. "What type of books would you like to read first? I've already had some requests for mysteries and thrillers."

"Police procedural!" Peggy Donovan called.

"Private investigator!" Gladys shouted over her. "The more hard-boiled, the better."

"I like a good spy thriller myself," Ernie said. "You know, like Tom Clancy. Or Robert Ludlum. Lots of action."

Helen Murphy shuddered. "No, thank you. I abhor violence. I'm sure most of the ladies here would prefer to read something a little more romantic."

Gladys snorted. "You mean, like Angelina St. Rose? Puh-*leez*."

Guess there was no point in suggesting any *Citizen's Arrest* books, Summer told herself. Too bad. They probably could have done a viewing party instead of a discussion for the next meeting.

Dorothy cleared her throat. "Well, I'd like to make another suggestion, if I may. How about GH Hamel's latest title, *Good Night, Sweetheart*? Since so many of us have already read it, and Georgiana is here to give us some insights into the story, it seems like a wonderful choice for our first discussion."

Everyone seemed okay with that idea. Georgiana actually smiled out at the audience, and Professor Bell glanced up from his notebook, all attention now. Good, Summer told herself. He wasn't going anywhere before she got over there.

The only person who wasn't happy about Dorothy's suggestion was Carrie. She'd bust out bawling any second.

"And, of course, we can read Carrie's new book for the next meeting." Dorothy's voice was soothing but perky at the same time.

The younger author instantly brightened, her face as pink as her way-tight, moth-eaten velvet dress. "*A Killing Fog*," she threw out, for anyone who cared. "But don't forget about *Debut for Death*, too." She smiled at Dorothy. "I can come back for the meeting."

Pathetic. Summer had just made it to the back of the room, and was about to start up the center aisle toward the professor, when she noticed a woman stop by the door in an obvious, Party-Hearty store black wig. And those wraparound glasses people wore after they had eye surgery.

The woman bent down toward the box of beat-up and duplicate library discard books Dorothy was hoping people would take on their way out. There was no disguising the curvy figure under that oversize black sweatshirt and denim leggings.

Summer had to hand it to Trixie Quattrochi. The woman had guts, showing up here. Or else she was just begging to get nabbed.

Trixie had to know by now the police wanted to talk to her. Not to mention Summer and Dorothy. Oh, and Jennifer, about those skipped rent payments. She wasn't here for the book club launch, or to pay her respects to Lorella, for sure. What did she want so badly that was worth the risk of anyone recognizing her?

This time, Summer decided, she wasn't going to scare Trixie off by letting her know she'd spotted her. She needed to know what Trixie was up to first. She'd just sit casually down at the end of Dash and Professor Bell's row, and then turn her head very casually...

Too late.

Trixie had already disappeared from the doorway.

Summer jumped up and tore out of the Events Room, running smack into the WMLO cameraman on her way.

The hall was empty. Summer ran toward the elevators and checked above the doors to see which floor Trixie was on by now. One elevator was heading up, but the other was stopped at 7.

She was way faster than the elevator. If she took the emergency stairs, she could beat Trixie downstairs to the lobby of Tower B and intercept her suspect before Dorothy finished the book club meeting. She could drag Trixie back with her until the cops got there and keep an eye on Professor Bell at the same time.

Piece of cake.

Summer pushed through the exit at the end of the hall, hopping a little as she removed her huarache sandals. Trixie would be in for a Texas-sized surprise.

TWELVE

"SUMMER, PLEASE," DOROTHY said as her friend sprawled miserably in Dorothy's comfy chair. "Stop blaming yourself. It wasn't your fault. You did the best you could."

"I should have taken the stupid elevator. Aargh!" Summer hugged a crocheted pillow. "I can't believe I lost Trixie. Twice. No, three times, if you count the RV."

"And I can't believe those emergency doors were blocked at the ground floor," Dorothy said, frowning. "That is a very serious safety violation. We need to talk to Jennifer about that."

"Trixie probably did it somehow," Summer said. "I wouldn't put it past her. Maybe she saw that the elevator wasn't leaving the top floor. But I really don't think she knew I saw her, so she couldn't have known I was following her."

"Well, so far Trixie has proved to be very observant," Dorothy said. "It would be a mistake to underestimate her."

Summer sighed. "I guess. And Detective Donovan was supposedly 'out' again when I called. Yeah, right. And even Merle didn't believe me when I said I'd seen Trixie at the book club meeting, I could tell."

The girl pouted just like Maddie had when she was frustrated by something—usually, when she felt she wasn't being taken seriously. Or her feelings were hurt.

Dorothy had seen that expression many times, from both her friend and her daughter. "I'm sure you're reading a little too much into things, dear," she said gently.

"No, I'm not." Summer just sounded stubborn now. "I mean, isn't Detective Donovan ever at the station anymore? Or maybe he's just not taking my calls, because he doesn't want us working on the case. Or it might be because of Jennifer..."

What on earth? "Wait," Dorothy broke in. "Jennifer? What does she have to do with any of this?"

Summer studied her manicure. "Oh, nothing. But either way, it wouldn't be very professional of him to ignore me, or any important stuff for the case."

"Summer," Dorothy said, with a frown, "if there's one thing we do know, it's that Detective Donovan always conducts himself professionally. He's very serious about his work."

"Then he should listen to us," Summer said. "Hey, quit it!" she added to Mr. Bitey, waving the chair pillow at him.

Gracious. Now Dorothy's ill-behaved cat was trying to bat at Guinevere from behind her friend's ankle. She clapped her hands at Mr. Bitey. "No, no," she told him. "You're being very rude to our guest."

"I don't think he cares much," Summer said, with a glance at the badly gouged powder room door.

"No, he doesn't. I shouldn't have let Guinevere out yet." Dorothy scooped up the protesting tomcat and carried him firmly toward the powder room. "Now it's his turn in kitty jail."

She had to find a home for poor Guinevere soon. Right after her owner's murder was solved. That was the most pressing thing at the moment. A bit inconvenient for both her and the little gray cat, perhaps, but so be it.

"So, what do you think Trixie wants?" Summer said as Dorothy returned to the couch and rubbed her ankles. She'd been on her feet the entire day, and they were throbbing mercilessly. "I mean, if she's on the run, why doesn't she just leave town for good? Especially if she's the one who killed Lorella."

"An excellent question. It doesn't make much sense, does it?" Holding her peach skirt in place, Dorothy lifted first one leg, then the other, up onto the couch. Now she was sitting almost the same way as Summer. It felt rather comfortable.

"Remember what Trixie said in her letter to Lorella, about the rat-killing thing?" Summer said. "I did a search on the internet, and she wasn't talking about killing a bunch of vermin. 'Rat killing' is some Texas expression that means, like, taking care of business."

"Well, that's interesting," Dorothy said. "I hope she didn't mean killing Lorella."

"Exactly," Summer said. "But we still can't forget about Professor Bell. What happened with him after I left?"

Dorothy sighed. "He tried to pester Georgiana again, at the reception. It seemed he had a manuscript he wanted her to read. A very long one, I might add. The package looked quite bulky."

"That makes sense," Summer said. "He's writing a romance, I think. Can you believe that? He's not bad-looking, but he's, like, the least romantic guy on earth. Sooo boring. What did Georgiana say?"

"Well, she was so mobbed by fans after she and Carrie gave their talks, it was difficult to hear," Dorothy said. "Georgiana didn't look very happy, it's true, but she told him to bring it to the author signing at Milano Book & Bar tomorrow night."

"So Professor Bell was pretending he just came to the meeting to get Georgiana to look at his book," Summer said. "That guy is such a sneaky stalker. And probably a murderer, too. I don't know how he'd tie in with Trixie, though."

"True," Dorothy said. "And we need a bit more evidence before we bring him up to Detective Donovan as a serious suspect. We have that possible matching murder weapon, of course, but as the professor pointed out to you, those bookends are quite popular."

"I hate to say this," Summer said, slowly, "but there's another person we might want to think about as a suspect, too. Ol' GH Hamel. Even if she's Dash's mom."

"Georgiana?" Dorothy sat up straighter on the couch. "You can't be serious. Why, she just arrived in town. And she didn't know Lorella."

"She might have," Summer pointed out. "Remember, when we almost had breakfast yesterday at the crepe place, we found out they went to the same college? Wellsburg, or whatever it was."

"Wellsmount," Dorothy murmured. It was true, that odd coincidence had slipped her mind. She'd meant to ask Georgiana about it. But right now she was tired. And hungry. She'd been so busy running the meeting and speaking with everyone afterward that she hadn't had a single bite to eat at the reception.

"Remember when Georgiana saw Lorella's picture on the easel when she was walking into the Events Room?" Summer said. "She stopped in the aisle and made a big deal of asking if that was the person who got murdered. She acted really surprised. Maybe she was faking so everyone would *think* she didn't know Lorella."

"That might be reaching a bit," Dorothy said. "What kind of motive for murder could Georgiana possibly have, supposing she was even acquainted with Lorella?"

"Well, she knows how to get away with a crime," Summer said. "She has to be sneaky in her books, right? Or her characters do, anyway."

"But Georgiana arrived in town after Lorella was murdered," Dorothy pointed out.

"Actually, we don't know that," Summer said. "Remember, Dash said she came down here a few days early? Maybe she didn't really go to that bookstore when she got off the plane. Or maybe she did, but her flight got in superearly that morning."

Dorothy's head was beginning to spin. A revered author like GH Hamel would never be involved in a terrible crime like murder. That idea was just impossible. Lorella had been a professor—and a librarian, too. Both women obviously shared a love of literature. Preposterous.

"There's another thing, too. Georgiana and Lorella both had that same bloodstone ring." Summer took a deep breath. "I'm sorry I didn't tell you this earlier, Dorothy. But I kind of borrowed Lorella's ring from her jewelry box. You know, to give to the police later."

Dorothy frowned. "Why didn't you mention that, dear? It could be important to the investigation, somehow."

"I know." Summer's voice sounded very small. "I guess maybe I was thinking the rings might be like the bookends, or something. A dime a dozen, so it would be okay to keep it myself for a while."

Goodness. Dorothy's young friend was like a magpie with a shiny bauble. But no harm done, Dorothy supposed. "Where is the ring now?"

"In my undies drawer," Summer said. "It's really safe there, I promise."

"Mmm," Dorothy said.

Summer checked her phone. "It's almost five," she said, clearly eager to change the subject. "Are you going to dinner in the dining room tonight?"

"I suppose," Dorothy said, with a sigh. She didn't have much choice, because there wasn't a single food item in her fridge again. She'd skipped the last shuttle bus to Publix. The idea of mingling with a crowd again so soon was not terribly appealing. No doubt some people would want to discuss today's book club meeting— or worse, argue about the title choices again.

"Well, I have an idea," Summer said. "My friend Esmé—you remember her from Chameleon, right? — picked up a second job at La Volpe downtown. She just texted me that it's really dead there right now, and we might be able to get a free dinner if we go superearly. What do you think?"

"I think that sounds marvelous," Dorothy said, standing up. "Just let me grab a light jacket."

She felt miraculously better already.

ESMÉ HADN'T BEEN kidding about this place being dead, Summer told herself as she and Dorothy waited for service at a marble-topped table for two near the tiny bar area of La Volpe. The bartender, a good-looking Italian-American guy a year or two younger than her—okay, maybe five or six—had thrown them a smile when they walked in, and then disappeared for good.

Jeez. It sure was dark in here. Kind of gloomy, actually. A lot of wooden paneling and marble, with a bunch of creepy-looking busts of old guys with beards. Good wine list, though, and there was a candle and a single red rose in a bottle on every table.

Where was Esmé, anyway? Or, more like, where was anyone?

"I don't understand it. This restaurant was once very popular," Dorothy said. "Harlan used to bring me here, years ago, and it's one of Ernie's favorites, too."

"Huh," Summer said. "Maybe it's more of a guy place. You know, lots of spaghetti and meatballs and stuff. I bet a lot of couples used to get engaged here, with all the roses and opera music."

"Yes, it did have atmosphere." Dorothy looked a little sad.

"Hi, guys." Esmé appeared at their table, a little out of breath, and handed them each a menu. "Sorry about the wait. I just finished up at Chameleon, and got over here as fast as I could. Matteo was supposed to cover for me till I got here, the rat. His parents own the place, and they're on vacation."

"How nice to see you, Esmé," Dorothy said. "You look lovely."

"You do," Summer agreed. "That's a great outfit under there."

Esmé grinned and pulled aside her long white waitress apron to strike a pretend model's pose in her form-fitting black dress, glittering gold earrings, and designer pumps. Her long dark curls, which she usually wore braided or tied back in a scarf or butterfly clips, were semitamed by a wide black headband. "Thanks. It's my new, classy look. Had to step up my game to work at this place. Plus, I have a hot date later."

Personally, Summer liked Esmé's usual funky style a tiny bit better—her friend was a part-time design student with the coolest clothes—but she would never say that. "So, what's good to eat here?" she asked.

Esmé shrugged. "I'd stick with the lasagna. The seafood's supposed to be fresh, but it seems a little nasty, until they dump all the sauces over it."

"Oh." Dorothy shuddered, just a little. "How about the Italian salad?"

"Good choice," Esmé said. "And the bread is always good. How about some wine first? There's a pretty good bottle of Shiraz open that'd go with the lasagna."

"Great," Summer and Dorothy both answered, at the same time.

"So you never really told me how the rest of the book club party went, and I haven't heard anything from Dash," Summer said when Esmé had left. "Was Georgiana a big hit with the crowd? And what about, uh, Carrie?"

"I thought things went rather well," Dorothy said. "Better than I expected, in fact. Georgiana enthralled everyone with the most fascinating stories about her research trips to all kinds of exotic locales, and Carrie also held people's interest, I think."

"What did she talk about?" Summer asked.

"A little bit of everything," Dorothy said. "Her books, her long, difficult journey to becoming a published writer, her plans for the future. I felt a bit sorry for her, I have to say. She had a tough time breaking into the book business, but hopefully, she's on her way now."

"Why didn't she publish her books herself?" Summer said. "A lot of people do that now."

"I'm not sure," Dorothy said. "But if you don't mind dear, I'm afraid I'm feeling a little book-clubbed out. Do you mind if we talk about it later?"

"Oh, sorry," Summer said. Her friend did look tired. "Fine with me."

Esmé brought over a basket of warm Italian bread, rosemary focaccia, and garlic bread sticks, along with small white plates, three glasses of Shiraz, and an extra bottle. "Mind if I join you for a couple of minutes?" she asked. "If I get any customers, it'll be later, after the Milano Playhouse lets out, and Matteo actually did a good job setting things up."

"Sure," Summer said.

"I wanted to talk to you two anyway," Esmé said, unloading her tray. "It's about that lady who got murdered over at your complex. You know, the librarian?"

Dorothy's eyebrows shot up. She looked a lot more alert now. "You and Lorella were acquainted?"

"No," Esmé said. "Summer and Dash were telling me about her when the three of us were out last night." She placed the tray on a nearby table and drew up a wrought-iron chair. "But I saw the lady's pic in the newspaper rack at the Green Caffeine this morning, and I recognized her right away. She and some guy used to come in here all the time."

"What did he look like?" Summer had a feeling she already knew the answer.

Esmé shrugged. "Well, he was maybe about ten years younger than her. Good hair, not too gray, kind of long. Always wore a navy blue jacket. Lousy tipper.

The woman always slipped me a few extra bucks on her way out. And the guy always smelled like..."

"Pipe smoke?" Summer finished.

"Yeah, that was it. I was going to say burned wood. He was a little snotty. And the lady—Lorella never said much to me, either, but she seemed nicer. Just really quiet."

Summer and Dorothy exchanged glances. Yep, that was a perfect description of Professor Bell. Better than the ones the detectives usually got out of eyewitnesses on *Citizen's Arrest*.

"Did you ever catch anything of their conversations?" Dorothy asked.

"Not really," Esmé said. "They had their heads pretty close together most of the time."

"So maybe the professor wasn't really a stalker," Summer said to Dorothy. "Or he didn't turn into one until later, at least."

Dorothy added a few drops of balsamic vinegar to the oil on her plate and swirled it with a bread stick. "It definitely sounds as if they had a romantic relationship, then."

"Those two didn't seem that chummy to me, actually," Esmé said. "Lorella always looked as if she was sort of mad at him, or something. I think they were working on some big project together, because the guy wrote down a lot of stuff in a notebook."

Summer sighed. "I really, really wish we could get a look at that notebook. He had it at the book club meeting today," she added to Dorothy.

Esmé refilled her wine. "Wait, you know this guy, too?"

"We've met," Summer said. "Unfortunately. He's

one of the people Dorothy and I think may have murdered Lorella."

Behind Esmé, Dorothy shook her head, warning her to shut up. Oops. But it was true, right? And maybe her friend could help them.

"Well, that isn't good," Esmé said. "I hope he didn't kill her, because the thing is, he comes in here all the time, with a lot of different women. Not just Lorella. And they're definitely dates."

"Wow," Summer said. "I bet Lorella was ticked off at the professor for cheating on her, then. So maybe she confronted him and boom! He kills her."

"Oh dear," Dorothy said. "If that's true, which I hope it isn't, other women may be in terrible danger."

"I don't know, he seemed like a wimp to me," Esmé said. She was really warming up now, with all the wine. "But I can tell you one thing. He has all those dates because he strikes out every time. I've never seen him with the same woman twice. Except Lorella."

Well, no shock there, Summer thought. Professor Bell was definitely a loser. "I wonder how he manages to get all those dates," she said. "Do you think he…um, pays them?" Ick.

"Nope," Esmé said. "Have you guys ever heard of Silver Sweethearts?"

"I have," Dorothy said. "It's an online dating service for seniors. Rather upscale, I believe. Several of the ladies at Hibiscus Pointe have tried it. Not as many of the gentlemen, I'm afraid. Since there are fewer older men than women down here in Florida, they have plenty of opportunities to meet romantic interests in person."

"You can always tell it's a blind hookup"—Esmé glanced at Dorothy—"I mean, *date*, because the woman puts a single red rose on the table so the guy will know it's her. They sell them on the corner, at Fleurs de Paris. That's where we get ours for the restaurant."

"Imagine dating someone you had only met online," Dorothy said. "I don't approve of that at all. Much too dangerous."

"Oh, it's not so bad," Summer said. "I mean, I've never done it or anything. But I know plenty of couples who got together that way."

Like her sister Joy and that insurance guy Toby. The relationship hadn't lasted that long, though. Her uptight sister had sent the guy packing even faster than she'd gotten rid of her.

"Well, your professor buddy doesn't have much luck with the ladies," Esmé said. "Only one woman, other than Lorella, has ever come back. And that was just to toss a carafe of house merlot at him."

"Order's up!" someone yelled from the kitchen, over the opera music.

"I'll be right back," Esmé said. "Luigi gets a little impatient if his creations get cold."

"Summer, I think we should go back to Santa Teresa to question Professor Bell directly," Dorothy said. "Perhaps this time you could tell him you'd signed up to audit one of his classes."

Ugh. He probably wouldn't buy that, and she really, really didn't want to go back to that campus. "Shouldn't we talk to him somewhere else?" Summer said. "You know, to throw him out of his comfort zone. He's coming to Milano Book & Bar tomorrow night for the author signing, remember?"

"Well, that's true."

Good. Dorothy seemed fine with that plan. Unless… "You know what?" Summer said. "I may have an even better idea. Just let me work a few things out first, okay?"

"All right, dear." Dorothy was leaning over to smell the pretty red rose in the little wine bottle vase.

"Hey, say mozzarella cheese!" Summer held up her cell phone. "This'll make *such* a cute pic."

She quickly snapped the photo, and Dorothy blinked, startled, as the flash lit up La Volpe. Perfect.

THIRTEEN

EARLY THE NEXT MORNING, after spending a bit of separate-but-equal quality time with the cats, Dorothy pulled on a tailored denim shirt over a pair of dark blue slacks and headed straight to the Hibiscus Pointe Library.

She didn't relish the idea of returning to the spot where Lorella had lost her life, but it was time to get serious about putting things in order. Lorella would surely be distressed if she knew the place was untidy.

And hopefully, once all the GH Hamel and Carrie hoopla died down, they could hold regular book club meetings there, as Lorella had intended.

The library was eerily quiet, and Dorothy felt a bit unnerved, even with the morning sun streaming under the door from the hallway window beyond it. Perhaps she should have left the door open, but she thought it best that no passersby would be reminded of the sad state of the library until she had remedied the chaos as best she could.

At least the cleaning staff had removed those awful, telltale bloodstains from the carpet and the floor. And someone had replaced Lorella's broken chair with one of the elegant guest chairs from Jennifer's office.

She and Harlan had sat in those very chairs on their first visit to Hibiscus Pointe, and signed the papers with their intent to buy a condo. Initially, she'd been hesitant, but Harlan had insisted they move to a senior community. It would be so much easier on her, he'd gently pointed out. Better for her health, with all kinds of amenities.

And fewer memories of Maddie.

Sometimes, when she was alone in quiet places, she felt they both were with her. And this time, she also sensed the presence of someone else. Lorella Caldwell, silently compelling her to make things right—and bring her killer to justice.

The police had already removed the papers and clutter from the librarian's desk. All that remained was a single, folded piece of paper. How odd. They couldn't possibly have missed it.

Frowning, Dorothy approached the desk with a soft cloth and a spray cleaner.

It was a note. And it was addressed to Dorothy Westin.

Angels of mercy, as her mother used to say. Had Lorella left her a message, before she died? A task she needed done in the library, perhaps? A clue to her killer? Or…please no…maybe even a note from the murderer him—or herself?

Dorothy tried to ignore the sudden, erratic pulsing in the center of her chest. Carefully, she placed the spray bottle down on the desk and slowly unfolded the page.

The first thing she noticed was the proliferation of exclamation points. So very many of them, embellished with small, fat circles at the base of each. And a heart, and a smiley face.

Neither Lorella nor a coldhearted killer seemed likely to use that type of personal expression.

Hey, Dorothy!!
Can't wait for tonight at Milano Book & Bar!!
Guess what? WMLO is coming back to do a seg-

ment for the 11 o'clock news!!! Amazing press for
the book club, huh? (And me and Georgiana!!)
See you there!!!!!!!!
Hugs, Carrie

Dorothy dropped down into Jennifer's spare chair.
Her heart was still pounding, but this time in anger.
How had Carrie gotten into the library? As far as she
knew, only she and Jennifer were supposed to have
keys—although a locked door never stopped some people. Like Summer, for instance, with her plastic card.

She'd have to talk to Security about changing that
lock.

The door opened, startling Dorothy yet again. It was
just Parker, which made her feel a little silly. She really was extra jumpy, after finding poor Lorella the
other day.

"Oh, hi, Dorothy." Carrie's publicist seemed surprised to see her, too. "I didn't think anyone would be
in here so soon. After what happened, I mean. I was
just on my way to the pool, and I thought I'd pick up a
good beach read."

"Hello, Parker," Dorothy said. The svelte young
woman indeed seemed ready for a dip, judging from the
lacy black pool cover-up she wore over her emerald-blue
maillot. "I'm sure we have something that might fit the
bill." She nodded toward an assortment of paperbacks in
the large wicker basket near the door. "You might look
through that first. There's women's fiction, romances,
cozy mysteries, and even a Western or two, I believe.
Feel free to take a few. No need to check them out."

"Thanks." Parker headed toward the basket. "I usually read on my phone, but I left it back at the condo,

right on the counter, so Carrie couldn't reach me. I definitely need something to get rid of stress."

"Ah," Dorothy said. "I've noticed that you are quite a busy young woman."

Parker quickly selected a thick paperback of either fantasy or science fiction—*Game of Drones*, Dorothy noted, so it was difficult to tell—and tucked it into her designer tote. "Oh, it's not the work I mind," she said. "It's Carrie. She's the craziest, most demanding client I've ever had, and you know what? Between you and me, I'm not really a big fan. Of her *or* her book."

Goodness, Dorothy thought. She'd never heard Parker say very much, and she certainly hadn't expected *that* information. "My, that's a shame," she said carefully. "Is Carrie aware of how you feel?"

Parker shrugged. "I doubt it. And I really don't care, to tell you the truth. I'd quit, but we have a contract, and I don't have any other jobs lined up yet. Carrie paid me extra to work with her exclusively for three months. But I didn't mean twenty-four-seven. It's a nightmare."

"Perhaps if you spoke to her about a few ways to improve your professional relationship so it works better for you…" Dorothy let her voice trail off delicately.

"Maybe," Parker said, with a sigh. "I hate to bring up the whole thing and risk setting her off, especially since we're roomies right now. I just have to deal with it. But I swear, I could just kill that girl." She headed for the door.

"Have a nice morning at the pool, dear," Dorothy called after her. Perhaps the publicist was being overly dramatic, but Dorothy understood Parker's frustration. In all truthfulness, Carrie Dunbar *was* a bit much to take, even in small doses—with Tylenol, every four hours.

Dorothy turned her attention back to tidying the librarian's desk. With luck, she could get to the pool herself, in an hour or two, and do a few laps. She usually preferred an early-morning swim, but with so much to do over the last few days, she'd sadly neglected her workout routine.

Chair yoga was listed for that afternoon on the daily activities board in the main lobby, but really, she might better spend her time on a cut-and-style in the Hibiscus Pointe Salon. And maybe a nap.

Dorothy had just finished flipping the page to the correct date on Lorella's quote-a-day desk calendar when she suddenly identified the light, not entirely unpleasant lingering scent beneath the pungent tone of vanilla air freshener.

Pipe tobacco.

Several gentlemen at Hibiscus Pointe smoked pipes, of course. But this particular blend was quite distinctive, with not so subtle tones of pine, leather, and something else. Chocolate, perhaps.

Hadn't she noticed a touch of that very same scent just yesterday, at the book club reception?

Yes, when she'd been chatting with Georgiana, and Professor Charles Bell had scurried up and tried to give the author a bulky manila package.

How recently had he visited the Hibiscus Pointe Library—and why?

SUMMER TRIED TO hold the dry cleaning bag with her fuchsia tube dress inside as far as possible from her body as she hurried along Fourth Avenue downtown. She was already half-drenched from the extra-intense noon heat and she didn't need her outfit for the book signing party tonight getting all glommed up, too.

Too bad the Fresh in a Flash Dry Cleaners had refused to deliver overnight. Their name was totally false advertising. In LA, round-the-clock service was never a problem. Here in Milano, it seemed like any kind of service was a problem.

Summer stopped short at the Decker & Meyers store. She hardly ever gave the place a second look, since mostly older ladies shopped there. But every once in a while they had something cool. For the visiting granddaughters, maybe.

Plus, she'd applied online for a job two weeks ago. Working retail had its advantages, since it usually involved an employee discount. But she'd never heard back.

Right now, though, the cutest pair of hot-pink retro stilettos—on sale—were calling to her from the window. She had other pink shoes, of course, but it just so happened she'd spilled red wine on the satin pair she'd planned to wear tonight.

She stepped toward the door and a tanned, muscled arm reached in front of her to open it.

"Looks like you have your hands full."

Detective Donovan, of all people. And right behind him, his sharp-eyed, red-haired grandma in her wheelchair. Fabulous.

"Yeah, lots of errands," she said. Should she just turn around and leave now? She really didn't want to shop for pricey-even-with-the-discount shoes in front of him. Or his grandma. "Guess we had the same idea."

Well, that sounded stupid. Obviously, the guy wasn't

shopping for women's shoes. But he had to know what she meant.

"You'll need to check that bag, Ms. Sloan." Olga, the pointy-nosed guest services coordinator, came up and held out her arms as the three of them entered the store.

So okay, she'd stopped by here once to sign up for the personal shopper service, before she realized this wasn't a very happening store. She always used her other last name—her dad's—for stuff like that. It saved a lot of time. And money.

"Guess you're a regular here." Detective Donovan grinned at Summer.

For some reason, he seemed to find the shopper service deal amusing. His grandma obviously didn't. She was scowling in her wheelchair, which had several bags draped over the back.

Summer held her sticky dry cleaning bag to her chest. "Oh, thanks, but I'm not shopping," she informed Olga, trying not to notice as Detective Donovan raised one eyebrow. "But you can take Mrs. Donovan's stuff here. Just put it under my name."

"Maybe you can give my grandma here a few pointers," the detective said, unhooking the bags for Olga before the concierge took off. "We've been to every shoe store in Milano this morning." He wheeled the chair to the side as a trio of chattering ladies came in behind them.

"I am perfectly capable of doing my own shopping, thank you very much," Peggy said, throwing both Summer and her grandson a dirty look and wheeling off toward the clearance section.

Jeez. What was her problem? Mrs. Donovan really,

really hated her. Maybe she was still mad about her wrecking that tennis game.

Detective Donovan looked superuncomfortable. Summer wasn't sure if it was because his grandma was so rude or he hated being stuck in a women's shoe store. Maybe both.

"So, what's the latest on the Caldwell case?" she asked him, stuffing the dry cleaning bag under her arm more to get it out the way. So much for no wrinkles. Now she'd have to steam it in the shower when she got home. "Anything new?"

"Not much." He ran a hand through his dark brush cut. "It'll be a while before we get all the lab results back. This isn't a high-profile case, I'm afraid."

Summer frowned. "What do you mean? Are you saying Lorella's murder isn't important?"

"No, of course not." The detective shrugged. "The forensics lab is always backed up. The best we could hope for in rush situations is maybe a week or so. And this particular murder just isn't a rush. It's not like the DA or the media is breathing down anyone's necks."

"Well, I think that's pretty sad," Summer said. Apparently, no one else in Milano besides her and Dorothy— and maybe Jennifer, and all the residents at Hibiscus Pointe who were worried about a killer on the loose— thought a quiet librarian with no family getting murdered was a very big deal.

Even Felicia Hernandez and her WMLO news crew seemed more interested in covering the great GH Hamel's visit than Lorella's death.

"I know, it's really too bad, but unfortunately, I don't get to call the shots," Detective Donovan said. "There's a lot of crime out there, I'm afraid."

Maybe, Summer thought, shifting her dry cleaning bag. But once again—this time in a good way—Milano wasn't exactly LA. How many murders did this place have in a week?

"So, are you looking forward to the author party tonight?"

Was he trying to be social? Or just changing the subject?

"Yeah, it should be fun," Summer said. "Are you going? For the case, I mean."

He smiled, displaying the cute, tiny dimple that always made him seem a little less like a tough guy. "I thought I might attend in more of a social capacity."

"Oh." The way he was looking at her right now—still smiling, but kind of hesitating underneath—was he actually hinting around at asking her out?

Or...was this his way of letting her know he was bringing Jennifer on a date? Yep, that was probably more like it.

"Yeah, it should be a good time," Summer said carefully. "So, are you planning to—"

"Uh-oh," Detective Donovan broke in, gazing over her shoulder. "Sorry. Looks as if my grandma has a situation over there."

Summer turned around. Peggy and another lady were arguing over the last pair of same-sized shoes from the sale rack.

"I'd better go see if I can help work things out," the detective said. "Otherwise it could get ugly. See you later, okay?"

"Um, sure," Summer said. No way was she sticking around for whatever happened next. "I'll look for you at the party, I guess."

It didn't seem as if he'd heard her. The detective was already halfway to the clearance section, as other shoppers around Peggy and her shoe nemesis entered the fray.

Well, fine. If he was bringing Jennifer to Milano Book & Bar as his date, she'd find out soon enough. She didn't care that much anyway. Her main focus had to be on solving Lorella Caldwell's murder.

Someone had to. And with the lab and the Milano PD taking their sweet time, it might as well be her and Dorothy.

Summer was halfway down the last side street off Fourth Avenue to her car—oh, rats, had she forgotten to feed the meter again?—when she spotted Trixie Quattrochi. Again.

White-blond hair, pulled into a long ponytail this time, under a large-brimmed black sunhat. Denim leggings, curvy figure, red cowboy boots that came up to the ankle, lots of bracelets.

Her slippery suspect was just passing the Tiny Bubbles Laundromat, lugging a giant bag of clean laundry. Well, that made sense, sort of. If Trixie was hiding out in town, she had to do something about her dirty clothes, right?

Tiny Bubbles was kind of off the beaten track. Plus, they served champagne. The place had a funky little bar at the back, in an attempt to make doing your laundry trendy and fun.

Huh. Trixie seemed like more of a Jack Daniel's girl than a champagne aficionado. But still.

Summer dumped her bag and her dry cleaning on the sidewalk and snuck up on Trixie like Mr. Bitey stalking Guinevere. And then, before the woman could react, she pounced on her prey and tackled Trixie to the ground.

FOURTEEN

EXCEPT IT WASN'T TRIXIE.

The middle-aged woman Summer had just pinned down on the sidewalk let out a muffled scream. Her blue eyes looked...beyond terrified.

"Oh my gosh, are you okay?" Summer quickly disentangled herself and leaned back on her heels to assess any possible damage. Luckily, Fake Trixie had fallen on top of her overstuffed laundry bag after she spun them both to the concrete. But still... "I'm so, soooo sorry, I made a really big mistake."

"You can say that again," the blond woman said, giving her an angry kick with the toe of her cowboy bootie.

Guess she deserved that.

"Have you been drinking?" the woman demanded. "I knew it was a mistake for that Laundromat to start serving alcohol. It's ruining the neighborhood."

Summer helped her mistaken suspect to her feet and retrieved the woman's sunhat, which had landed near a doggy waste removal station. "Don't worry, I'm not drunk. I swear."

"Well, you're just a crazy person, then," the woman muttered, rubbing her elbow. "You're lucky I'm okay and I am also going through an exhausting divorce right now, or I'd sue your tail off for assault."

"I thought you were someone else," Summer tried to

explain. "I'm, uh, on the neighborhood watch here and the person I was after is a real troublemaker."

"Wait a minute. I'm one of the heads of our neighborhood watch on this block and I don't remember you at all."

"Hey, is there anything I can do for you?" Summer asked quickly. "If you give me your address I'll send you—"

"I'm not telling you where I live," the woman said. "And if you don't mind, I'd rather you just went away."

Well, that was fine and dandy with her. Summer apologized again and hurried toward her car, after scooping up her shoulder bag and the totally messed up dress. She should have known she wasn't going to just see Trixie out of the blue again like that. Trixie and Ray had managed to elude both her and Dorothy and the cops so far.

Those two were definitely pros.

She had one more stop to make on the way home: the Majesty Golf & Tennis Club. She needed to see if the cute head tennis pro over there, Garrett something, might take her up on a last-minute date invite for the book party tonight. For Jennifer, not her, of course—but there was no need to spell all that out right away. Just in case Jennifer already had a date—with Detective Donovan.

Jennifer and Garrett would be perfect for each other. From what she'd seen of the guy from a distance at the intercommunity tennis tournaments, he seemed nice and he was pretty clean cut. Not to mention he had very ripped arms.

He and Detective Donovan actually had a lot in common.

Plus, if the tennis pro and her friend hit it off, then she might have a chance to spend a little extra-quality time with the detective. He had to know more than he was letting on, she was sure, no matter what kind of excuses he made up about lab delays or that she and Dorothy weren't supposed to be working on the case, or whatever.

The tony pro shop at Majesty Golf & Tennis was jammed with members, most of them dressed in tennis clothes with racquet bags over their shoulders. A group of men were talking about some critter or something over at the golf course. Another gator, probably.

Garrett and another guy in a polo shirt with the MGT crown logo were swamped at the members counter, with members demanding a court or doubles partners. Stat.

Jeez. Now even more people had shown up and were getting in line behind her. Apparently, the golf course was temporarily closed, so they were trying to make other plans.

"I'd much rather have a lesson with Garrett," she heard a woman tell the younger guy with the clipboard. "But if Judy is all you've got…"

Aargh. She didn't have time to come back later. And she needed to get this over with. It had been a while since she asked anyone out—maybe for one of those girls-ask-the-guys dances in junior high—but hopefully, by the time she got to the counter, she'd have a plan.

"Hi there," she said to Garrett, flashing him a big smile before the kid with the clipboard could intercept her. "I'm Summer Smythe, from over at Hibiscus Pointe. I don't need to book anything."

The tennis pro's melted-Hershey's eyes, which perfectly matched his smooth, flawless skin tone, were filled with confusion. And maybe a tiny hint of impatience. "All right, then. How can I help you, Summer?"

Whoa. British accent. Very hot. Jennifer was going to love this guy. Plus, he coached wheelchair tennis. He had to be cool.

"Well, uh, I have a really big favor to ask. I'm a friend of one of your wheelchair players—Peggy Donovan?" Summer tried to ignore the annoyed vibes behind her in line. "She and I are attending a sort of charity party"—well, that was stretching things, but book clubs *did* promote literacy, right?—"tonight at Milano Book & Bar. She and another friend of mine were hoping you might stop by to represent Majesty Golf & Tennis and help benefit a reading program for, uh, at-risk seniors."

Oops, was that even a thing? Maybe she was pushing it. But Garrett had stopped frowning, at least. "And kids," she added quickly. "They read together."

"Come on, young lady, wrap it up," a man behind her called.

Summer ignored the crabby guy and kept her eyes on her mark. "So, what do you think? It would mean so much to Peggy and the kids. You could be my date, if you wanted. Just for the evening, I mean."

"Okay, sure. If it's for a worthy cause, I guess," the tennis pro said.

"Awesome," Summer said. "So seven o'clock at Milano Book & Bar, okay? I'll meet you there."

She handed him her social card—the one with a fake number, because it was all she had on hand at the moment—and beat it out of the pro shop before Garrett could change his mind.

The valet at the bottom of the front steps was superefficient and she handed him her last five bucks when he brought up the MINI. He didn't seem that impressed with the tip, but Summer couldn't worry about that now.

With luck, she could get in a little pool time before she had to get ready for the author signing—and her fake charity date.

Summer had the Majesty Golf & Tennis guardhouse in sight—why did they have to check people on their way out, anyway?—when a windowless white van pulled out in front of her. She honked and the driver made an obscene gesture in her direction.

It didn't matter how many fingers he held up, or which one. Because the guy had a long snake tattoo down the side of his left arm.

Ray. The Snake himself. What was he doing at a fancy-schmantzy golf and tennis club?

The van made a sudden left turn onto what looked like a cart path and Summer hit the brakes just as she reached the gatehouse. She tried to back up so she could pull a U-ie, but the security guard came out and blocked her way.

"Hold it, miss," he said, holding up one hand. "You can't turn around here."

"I need to follow that van." Summer pointed toward the clunky vehicle, which was already speeding away.

"Sorry. You'll have to go through the gate and come around again."

Summer tried not to let her irritation show. "Okay," she said. "Would you mind moving a little so I don't—"

"You were traveling at an excessive speed, by the way," the chunky man broke in, adjusting his Majesty Golf & Tennis cap. "We have a fifteen-mile-per-hour limit on our main road here. Ten in the subdivisions."

"Got it." Summer sighed. By now Ray was out of sight.

She followed the man's instructions, but as she went

through the gate on the other side and turned right toward the cart path, another security guard came up and cut her off. "No cars on the cart path," he said.

"But I'm following someone else." Summer pointed at the lingering MINI storm of sand and dust Ray had left in his wake.

"Sorry. Club rules. If you go out by the gatehouse behind you, you'll meet up where the path lets out, on Majesty Boulevard."

Well, that was just perfect. Summer had no choice but to turn around, one more time. The gatehouse guard gave her a jaunty wave on the way out.

Ray was a snake, all right. Just as slippery as his girlfriend. But at least she could report the suspect sighting to Detective Donovan tonight.

DOROTHY HAD HAD a lovely afternoon. She'd managed a refreshing nap after her cleanup session in the library, and she'd even had her hair done in the Hibiscus Pointe Salon. Best of all, she'd been lucky enough to just miss Gladys Rumway.

She wasn't quite as fortunate to avoid Carrie Dunbar. Or at least the eager young author's voice on her message machine. Carrie had made four calls.

Dorothy skipped through to the most recent one.

"Hi, Dorothy! Would you and Summer like a ride downtown for the signing party? I've got this brandnew idea for our next book club event…"

Dorothy shuddered and stabbed at the delete button with her finger. It was easy to see why Parker found her employer so exhausting. Hadn't one of them mentioned at Dash's dinner party that Carrie only needed four hours of sleep per night?

She probably spent all that extra time dreaming up new promotional ideas. It was a wonder she found any spare time to actually write.

Dorothy shook her mind free of Carrie and headed to the spare bedroom to free Guinevere. "Here, kitty, kitty," she called softly, with a quick glance over her shoulder. Where was Mr. Bitey? He hadn't come bounding out to greet her as usual.

Oh dear. A thin gray tail stuck out from beneath the bed skirt of the far twin bed, twitching slightly. And the bowl of kibble she'd left for the small kitty was overturned on the pale blue carpet—completely empty.

Guinevere was not a messy eater. But someone else was.

After a quick glance around the guest room, Dorothy marched to the closet and pulled open the accordion door. Sure enough, Mr. Bitey sat up tall on top of a houndstooth suitcase, looking quite pleased with himself.

"Shame on you," Dorothy scolded. "How did you get in here, you greedy rascal?"

In answer, the orange tomcat brushed past her and scurried out toward his scratching post in the living room. Not quite as quickly as usual, because of an overloaded tummy.

"You poor thing," she said to the small gray cat, who had disentangled herself from the bed skirt and come over to wind around Dorothy's ankles. "I'll get you a new dinner right away. And Mr. Bitey is going on a strict diet."

The sooner she found a proper home for Guinevere, the better. Perhaps she could make some queries this evening at the party. How very sad that Lorella's beloved pet had been forced into foster care with a jealous bully.

Surely Guinevere was mourning her late owner. Did anyone else miss Lorella? Somehow it didn't appear that way. She had died alone, no doubt in fear. And that was the saddest thing of all.

The least Dorothy could do for both of them was to find the lightly lamented librarian's killer.

At six forty-five sharp, Dash pulled the Mercedes up to the side door of Hibiscus Gardens and jumped out to help Dorothy into the backseat. Summer was already there, all dressed up and her hair wet-combed from her post-swim shower.

She was wearing Lorella's ring, Dorothy noticed. Perhaps her friend planned to give it to Detective Donovan tonight. She hoped so, anyway.

"Hello, Dorothy." Georgiana twisted around from the front, her face partially hidden by tinted glasses and a red chiffon driving scarf that went over her head and around her neck. "I was just telling Dashiell and Summer that I'm so glad to have company on the way to this shindig. It could be a mob scene."

"Yes, I'm sure," Dorothy agreed politely. Nothing, she suspected, would please Georgiana more, no matter how much the author denied it.

"I added one more," Summer said, bringing a compact and lipstick from her bag. "His name is Garrett and he's the head tennis pro over at Majesty Golf & Tennis. You'll like him, I think."

"I haven't met this guy yet," Dash said as he navigated the speed bumps out of Hibiscus Pointe. "Don't I get to approve him first?"

"Oh, it's not a date, really. Not for me, anyway."

Dorothy readjusted her new Designer Shoe Hut purse on her knees. Sometimes she didn't quite understand how young people operated these days on the romance front. But her friend seemed to be happy with whatever path she was following.

It did surprise her, though, that Summer might be interested in someone other than Detective Donovan. She'd been so sure there had been sparks between those two earlier. But really, it wasn't any of her business.

She'd learned her lesson long ago with Maddie.

"You know, I must tell you all, I am quite enjoying my stay in Milano so far," Georgiana remarked as they turned onto Majesty Boulevard. "More than I expected, in fact. Not that I don't always enjoy a visit with my son and his family," she added quickly. "When I'm invited."

Dash kept his eyes on the road as he changed lanes to avoid a slow-moving Cadillac. "We all love having you, Mother. And you're always invited. You know that."

"Yes, well." Dorothy could hear Georgiana's nails tapping the seat divider. "I'm seriously thinking of buying a place down here—or, at the very least, establishing a more frequent presence in the Hamel-LeBlanc household."

Summer snapped her compact shut, seemingly by accident, and Dorothy saw the side of Dash's face turn whiter than the exterior of the Mercedes.

This would be an excellent time to change the subject, Dorothy told herself. She needed to ask Georgiana something that had been bothering her, and it might as well be now. A direct approach might be best.

And perhaps, if she asked in a very casual tone, with others in the car, it would seem less important. The silence in the air was already quite awkward.

"Tell me, Georgiana," Dorothy spoke up, "is it possible that you were ever acquainted with Lorella Caldwell? That old photo of her on the easel at the book club kickoff…did it by any chance look familiar? I know you both attended Wellsmount College around the same time, and I thought, by your reaction yesterday, that maybe you had recognized…" She let her voice trail away delicately.

Oh dear. She'd made a terrible mistake, Dorothy realized. The silence in the car had become even more ominous. But it was too late to withdraw the words now.

"It's possible," Georgiana answered finally, with a shrug from the front seat. She didn't turn around this time. "I did take a second look at that photograph. Blurry, and quite dated. But, you see, I am probably quite a bit younger than Lorella."

Dash cleared his throat, and Summer bit her freshly-geranium-pinked lip as she shot Dorothy a dubious look.

"Oh yes, of course," Dorothy said. "How silly of me."

"Darling, where is the lighter in this fancy car?" Georgiana asked her son. "My e-cigarette is out of juice, and I need to recharge."

"We don't have one, Mother," Dash said. "I'm afraid you'll have to wait."

"Hmmph," Georgiana said, looking quite put out. "Well, fine. If you don't mind, everyone, I need a few moments to think about my off-the-cuff remarks for this evening."

Clearly, that was the end of the conversation regarding Lorella. For now, anyway. Dorothy knew she'd need to find some other way of bringing up the subject later. Georgiana was obviously being evasive about her fellow alumna—but why?

FIFTEEN

SUMMER WAS RELIEVED that the rest of the drive downtown to Milano Book & Bar had been quick and relatively painless, with everyone lost in their own thoughts.

She was starting to feel a little nervous about the whole deal with Garrett. It was a stupid idea to try to set him and Jennifer up, she realized now. Even for something as tame as this, a book signing party. At least nobody thought of bookstores, even cool ones with a bar like this one, as big hook up places. Totally safe, no pressure.

So hopefully, Jennifer wouldn't be mad at her, and with luck maybe Garrett wouldn't even realize she'd invited him here under false pretenses. But she did need to talk to Detective Donovan alone tonight about seeing Ray near the golf course.

As they all got out of the car, Dash quizzed the valet on exactly how and where he planned to park the Mercedes. The kid pointed to a supertight spot, just a few feet away from the bookstore entrance.

Sometimes Milano was a lot like LA, after all.

"Do you think there will be anything to eat at this thing?" she whispered to Dorothy as they stepped through the heavy oak door. Dash and Georgiana were still outside, getting ready for another one of her big entrances.

She was starting to get a really good idea of why Dash was always so annoyed by his mom.

"I imagine there will be something," Dorothy said. "Hors d'oeuvres, at least, since they're serving cocktails. There should be a large group of us for dinner at the New Algonquin afterward. I believe that's what Parker mentioned, anyway."

"Never heard of the place," Summer said. "But at least it'll be a chance for us to dig up more dirt for the case, I guess."

"Yes, it may be more of a challenge than we'd expected here at the signing," Dorothy said. "Just look at all these people."

"Wow, you're right," Summer said. Milano Book & Bar was packed, and not just in the bar section. It wasn't the biggest space in the world, but the bookstore part probably hadn't seen this many people in years. Maybe ever.

She spotted Garrett just after Dorothy excused herself to find the powder room. He was waiting right by the sign that said Welcome, Authors and Guests. Signing Today: Georgiana Hamel, Bestselling Author of *Murder in the Mist*. Below it, in smaller letters, a bookstore employee had tacked a large green sticky note that said And Carrie Dunbar.

Ouch.

"Hey." Summer gave Garrett a grin as she went up to him, but not a really big one so he wouldn't get the wrong idea.

"You look really nice," he said, smiling back.

So did he, in his casual blue-toned madras sport jacket, pale blue polo, and khaki pants. But she wasn't even paying attention to that, really. Where were Detective Donovan and Jennifer? They hadn't gotten here yet, unless she was missing them in the crowd.

She didn't recognize a lot of these people. Not many of them were Hibiscus Pointers, that was for sure. At least, not so far. Carrie was already up there in the roped-off authors' area with Parker.

A long, velvet-skirted table was set up toward the back of a parquet dance-floor-type space. It held two microphones, piles of books for signing, and two brass holders. This time there were cards printed with both authors' names. At least Carrie was getting equal billing this time.

The sort-of debut author did look pretty happy as she stood there in a bright green retro dress with a swirly circle skirt, smiling out at the crowd. Every now and then, she gave a little wave and an even bigger grin.

Summer looked around. Who was Carrie waving to? No one, she realized. The newbie was totally faking it, trying to make it seem like people knew who she was. Jeez.

Behind the table, Parker—wearing all black, as usual—seemed too busy to look up. She was laying out postcards for people to take in front of Carrie's book pile and placing bookmarks inside each title.

"So, what exactly is this event, again?" Garrett asked. "I think I see a few Majesty members here. I'm sure they'd be happy to make some big donations, since your charity is such a great cause. Do you want me to introduce you?"

Yikes. "Um, no, thanks," Summer said. "We don't want to hit them up right away. You know, before the authors speak. That would be really rude, I think."

Where was Georgiana, anyway? She and Dash sure

were taking their sweet time. "How about a drink?" Summer said. "It'll take forever for the servers to get to us, but we could grab something at the bar. Oh, and I see a good friend of mine right near it. Let's go."

She'd never been so glad to see Ernie. By the time she and Garrett joined him, Dorothy was also headed their way. Good. Now she and Garrett wouldn't have to chat about nothing. Or worse, charity donations.

"Nice to meet you, Garrett," Ernie said, after she had introduced them and the guys had shaken hands. "Looks like our girl Summer here is taking a step up in the date department."

Summer felt her face grow hot as a fireball shot. What was *that* supposed to mean? Now she was probably the same shade as her bright pink dress.

"Ernie!" Dorothy scolded as she reached their group. "Summer and this nice young man have just met, I believe. I'm Dorothy Westin," she added to Garrett. "It's lovely to meet you. Are you a fan of Georgiana Hamel's?"

"Not really, I'm afraid," Garrett said. "I guess I'm just a fan of my gorgeous date here."

Ooooh. This was not good. Maybe she could talk Dash into playing the fake jealous ex-boyfriend. If he ever showed up. "How about that drink?" she asked Garrett. "I'd love a mojito with an extra stick of cane sugar."

"Sure," Garrett said. "Anyone else?"

"Chardonnay would be lovely, thank you," Dorothy said.

"I'll step over to the bar with you, son," Ernie said quickly. "I could do with another Scotch myself. What do you drink?"

The tennis pro shrugged his wide shoulders. "Pellegrino, mostly. I'm pretty much in training year-round."

Ugh, Summer thought. She and Garrett were complete opposites, she could already tell. She was all for being healthy and everything, but… Where was Jennifer, for cripes' sake? And Detective Donovan? Those were the two biggest straight arrows she knew.

But at least she and the detective had a few things in common. They both solved murders. Donovan had a sense of humor, at least, underneath that sharp suit he always wore. Along with the ripped bod.

"Oh, look, Georgiana just walked in," Dorothy said.

"Good." Summer glanced over at the authors' area. "Looks as if Parker's got everything set up, so maybe they'll start soon."

"If Georgiana isn't waylaid," Dorothy said. "Look who else is here."

Summer turned back toward the door. Professor Bell had just stepped out from behind a pillar near the book display at the front. He had his man bag over his shoulder again and it looked as if the buckles were going to burst on that thing. "I think he's written even more pages of that manuscript he's dying for Georgiana to read. Should I go over and rescue her?"

"Oh, I bet Georgiana can handle him on her own," Dorothy said, just as the famous author stiff-armed the professor and swept past him with a haughty glare.

Dash and Georgiana didn't make their way to the authors' area right away. Instead the two of them headed straight toward the bar. The crowd quickly let them through after the author made it clear with a few head shakes that she wouldn't sign autographs until later.

"It's like they're royalty or something," Summer said.

"Well, Georgiana has often been called the queen of mystery." Dorothy smiled at Ernie as he handed her a very full glass of white wine with a Book & Bar cocktail napkin.

Garrett was right behind him, with his water and her mojito. "Thanks," she said, taking a huge sip. Yum. Nice and sweet. So what would they talk about now?

Luckily, Ernie started talking about some spy thriller he'd just finished, which Garrett's dad thought was awesome, too, and Dorothy joined in, so Summer didn't have to say much.

As she stirred her drink with the little sugarcane stick, watching Dash try to get an order with the harried bartender, Georgiana came up beside her.

"Striking ring," the tall woman said in a low voice as she readjusted her red scarf over her shoulder. "I noticed it in the car."

Oh. Summer had almost forgotten she was wearing it. Neither Dorothy nor Georgiana had mentioned it earlier. "Uh, thanks. It was my grandma's."

No way would Grandma Sloan have worn anything that expensive. She'd been pretty cheap, from what Summer could tell. And she'd never even met her other grandma, Harmony's mom. She'd probably been an unmaterialistic hippie.

"I'd love to have a closer look at it," Georgiana said.

It didn't sound as if Dash's mom would take no for an answer. Why had she worn the stupid thing tonight? She'd grabbed it from her drawer as she was getting dressed and it had looked kind of cool. She didn't think anyone would notice it, really. She only wore big jewelry when she was getting super dressed up.

Summer switched the mojito to the other hand,

twisted the ring off her finger—it was a little tight—
and handed it over to Georgiana.

The author held the bloodstone ring up to the light,
compared Lorella's to her own, then turned it around
and peered at the gold band. "Lovely," she murmured,
returning it to Summer with a deep frown.

Dash returned then with his mom's drink, and Parker
started tapping on Carrie's microphone. "Georgiana,
shall we get started?" she called.

Georgiana swept toward the authors' area without
another word, drink in hand, and Summer breathed a
sigh of relief.

Obviously, Dash's mom didn't like anyone to copy
her, she thought. Okay, so maybe she shouldn't have
worn the ring tonight.

But Georgiana needed to get over herself.

DOROTHY ALLOWED HER mind to wander a bit as Parker
introduced GH Hamel and Carrie to the crowd. Milano
Book & Bar had been the perfect choice of venues for
the signing event and, judging by the expressions on
their faces, the staff was clearly thrilled by the turnout
this evening.

The bookstore was simply lovely. Why hadn't she
been here more often? Too many trips to the library, she
supposed. The rich feel of the mahogany bookshelves,
Oriental rugs over shining wooden floors, and just the
right amount of lighting gave the place a cozy, highly
literary feel.

Too bad the WMLO news crew Carrie had been so
excited about in that note she'd left her in the library
hadn't materialized.

"So our signings will take place directly following

a few short readings by the authors from their latest books," Parker was saying. "Please hold any comments or questions until afterward, because we'll be having a brief Q&A session, as well."

Dorothy couldn't help feeling relieved and grateful that Parker was acting as mistress of ceremonies this evening. Hopefully, once the book club activities were scaled down after the guest authors' departures, she wouldn't be quite as nervous leading meetings.

Perhaps the members could even take turns running the show. She doubted that that idea would fly, though—everyone always seemed too busy to fully commit to things, and besides that, the Hibiscus Pointe Book Club seemed to attract the most argumentative individuals.

Dorothy tried to move, slowly and casually, closer to Professor Bell. He was leaning back against a pillar now, his brow furrowed and his arms crossed against his chest, as Georgiana and Carrie presented their opening remarks.

She imagined he looked much the way his students did as they listened to his lectures. Half listening, with a hint of bored resignation.

She hoped she wasn't giving that impression herself right now. And heavens, had Charles Bell actually noticed the way she was rudely staring at him?

To her horror, he smiled and actually winked at her. A very quick flutter, but most definitely a wink. Oh dear.

Dorothy immediately focused her full attention on the authors at the table, who were now taking turns reading from their works. In public, Georgiana was gracious and charming, and Carrie played the starstruck fan and ingénue to the hilt.

Dorothy was familiar with GH Hamel's highly polished books, of course, but she had to admit that she was pleasantly surprised by Carrie. It was entirely possible she hadn't given her enough credit.

The younger author read steadily and lightly, pausing in all the right places, and the story line of her first book, *Debut for Death*, didn't sound half bad. A beautiful debutante murdered at her own coming-out ball, leaving behind a grieving twin sister and a heartbroken suitor to solve the crime together.

The crowd loved it. Even Georgiana applauded lightly when Carrie had finished reading. Perhaps she would purchase the book tonight, Dorothy told herself, instead of waiting for it to appear in the library or in paperback.

Her to-be-read pile on her nightstand was already almost as tall as the lamp, of course. But she should buy *Debut for Death* anyway, as the new head of the Hibiscus Pointe Book Club—and no doubt it would make Carrie very happy.

There were plenty of questions for both authors during the Q&A. Dorothy took that opportunity to edge her way back closer to the bar area, where Ernie, Dash, Summer, and her date—what was his name again?—were still gathered. Sadly, but perhaps not unsurprisingly, the three men and her sleuthing partner all looked rather out of their elements.

Dorothy wasn't about to risk glancing back over her shoulder at Professor Bell, but she did stop for a moment in the crowd to listen as Georgiana answered a few questions about how she'd gotten her start and where she got her stories.

Could the reigning queen of mystery have been involved somehow in Lorella Caldwell's death?

It was almost ridiculous to even speculate on that, of course. Georgiana was a successful career author who had seemingly nothing in common with shy Lorella other than a possible, long-ago college connection. Besides, she lived nearly fifteen hundred miles away in New York City.

Surely it had to be just a coincidence that Georgiana had shown up in Milano on the exact day of Lorella's murder. But still...something wasn't right.

SIXTEEN

SUMMER HAD PRETTY much written off Jennifer and Detective Donovan as no-shows for the book signing party when the two of them finally showed up, along with his grandmother.

She needed to make her move quick. Peggy had just wheeled off toward the signing line, clutching the GH Hamel book she'd brought from home.

"I'll be right back," she told Ernie, Dash, and her fake date. "Some friends just came in I want Garrett to meet, so I'll go get them."

The guys hardly noticed, which was fine with her. They were talking about Florida State basketball or something, which was even more boring than listening to Georgiana and Carrie go on and on about themselves and their books.

At least it was easier to push through the crowd now that everyone, including Dorothy, had lined up to buy books from the employees at a side register and to get them signed by the authors.

A sudden burst of sharp, high-pitched barks rose above the noise of the crowd, hurting Summer's eardrums. Was there actually a *dog* in here?

Yep. And it wasn't a service dog. Her mouth dropped open in disbelief as Carrie reached under the skirted table and brought up a small canvas boat bag custom-printed with the cover of *Debut for Death*. Two little brown ears and a pink hair ribbon stuck out of the top as the sides of the bag jiggled and lurched.

People oohed and aahed at the tiny dog and started flooding toward Carrie's table like rats. She took it out and set it on the table, right next to where she was signing. Georgiana, Summer noticed, was definitely not amused.

"It's a teacup half Yorkie, half Chihuahua—a Yorki-huahua," Carrie told everyone as they handed over their quickly purchased books. "Adorable, huh? So who do you want me to make this out to?"

Summer was pretty sure that dog belonged to Helen Murphy. She'd seen and heard it yapping in the Residents Board president's pool bag a few times. Carrie probably paid her to borrow it. Yep, there was ol' Helen, standing at one end of the table, giving all the gushing book buyers a plastic dog-pimp smile. Pathetic.

"Hey, sorry we're late." Detective Donovan was standing beside her, with Jennifer just behind him. Were they together-together? She couldn't tell. "Did we miss much?"

"Not really," Summer said. His sharp blue eyes looked a tiny bit softer tonight. Was he just tired? Or maybe it was the lighting in this place.

"Shane had to work later than he expected," Jennifer put in. "Peggy and I picked him up at the police department. It's really close to here."

"I know," Summer said. She'd spent some time down there on her and Dorothy's last case. Mostly as a murder suspect.

So why hadn't Jennifer just brought Peggy to the book signing first and gotten *Shane* later? Maybe she'd spent the extra time getting ready. She looked really put together in a splashy orange tropical print dress that showed off her glowing tan and dark hair. She was wearing flats again—white ones, and it looked like the Pilgrim buckles were finally gone for good. She'd even added some extra eyeliner, which gave her a cool sixties look.

Obviously, Jennifer had made a special effort tonight.

"So, did something come up on the Caldwell case?" Summer asked Detective Donovan.

"Not really," he said. "Just paperwork, mostly. I was out at Majesty Golf & Tennis this afternoon, investigating an incident, and—"

"Hey, I was there, too, around three-thirty," Summer broke in. "And guess what? So was Ray. He was driving that white van and he cut right in front of me. I lost him on a cart path."

The detective's eyebrows shot up. Good, he was taking her information seriously for once.

"I don't think Trixie was with him," she added. "But it's possible."

"You mean Trixie Quattrochi?" Jennifer asked. "I really need to talk to her about some Hibiscus Pointe business."

Probably all her unpaid rent, Summer told herself. Nothing to do with Lorella's murder. But it looked as if all three of them wanted to get a hold of the Texas Tornado.

"Hey, Summer, I finally found you." Garrett came up and handed her another mojito. "Are these the friends you wanted me to meet?"

Trapped. And just when she'd had a chance to chat about the case with Detective Donovan. She forced herself to smile. "Uh, yeah. Jennifer and Detective—I mean, Shane—this is Garrett."

Was it her imagination, or did the detective look the teensiest bit annoyed? Or even…jealous? For half a second, anyway. "Nice to meet you," he said to Garrett, shaking hands.

"We've met," Jennifer said. "Hi again, Garrett. Remember me from the Tee for Two tournament at Hibiscus about a month ago?"

"Ah, right. Sorry, I'm afraid I didn't recognize you at first." Garrett poured on the cool British accent. "How are things over at Hibiscus?"

"Oh, wonderful as always," Jennifer said, with a smile.

Was she serious? Or being sarcastic? Summer wasn't sure.

As Garrett and Jennifer began trading heartwarming club stories, Detective Donovan scanned the room. "Excuse me," he said, to the three of them, "but I think my grandmother may need some help with all those books she's snapping up."

"Talk to you later," Summer called after him as he walked away, but he didn't seem to hear her. Oh well. At least Jennifer and Garrett seemed to be hitting things off. They were chatting away as if they'd known each other forever.

Hopefully, that wasn't what the detective was ticked off about.

As Summer was considering that, Parker passed by with a glass of wine in one hand and an extra-large glass of bourbon in the other. For Georgiana, probably.

"Great ring," she said to Summer, stopping to nod

toward the bloodstone. "I love vintage jewelry. Where did you get such a great piece?"

"Oh, this?" Summer said, with a shrug. "It was left to me. By, uh…a family friend."

"Lucky you," Parker said, moving on toward the authors' area. Georgiana was looking very thirsty. Carrie was busy signing books.

Jeez, what was it with the ring? Summer wondered. It was awesome enough, she supposed, but it was weird it got so much attention. Where would Lorella have worn it, anyway?

Summer and Dorothy had no proof Georgiana had anything to do with the librarian's murder, so there was no point in giving it to Detective Donovan yet. In fact, she should probably just put it back in the dead woman's condo, even though it meant the ring would probably get carted off with all her other things. Lorella had no family to give it to, so it might even be thrown away, like Trixie's junk.

That would be a major waste, Summer told herself. And what if it did turn out to be some kind of evidence? She'd keep the ring for now.

THE NEW ALGONQUIN CLUB was impressively decorated, much like Milano Book & Bar, but a bit stuffy, for Dorothy's taste.

Everyone seemed to be having a fine time at the sit-down dinner, though Summer's date apparently had to leave early. Her friend looked miserable sitting between Jennifer, who looked very pretty and seemed a tad more relaxed than usual, and an even quieter than usual Detective Donovan.

It was a smaller after-party group from the bookstore—Georgiana and Carrie's publisher, Maxwell & Perkins, was footing the bill, thanks to Parker's request—but the core Hibiscus Pointe Book Club members were in attendance.

Fortunately, most of them were seated at another table. Dorothy could hear Gladys and Peggy trying to top each other with police knowledge. Professor Bell was seated with that group as well, thank goodness. He didn't seem to be saying much, but Dorothy refused to glance his way.

Perhaps that had been a tic, not a wink. She hadn't noticed earlier that the professor suffered from that affliction, but she certainly wasn't going to encourage any flirty behavior from that ridiculous man—who might even be a cold-blooded killer.

She and Summer definitely needed to stay on guard around him.

Georgiana had been holding court at their own table, with Carrie breaking in whenever the older author came to a dramatic pause—or took time to sip her drink. That was fine with Dorothy. It rather took the pressure off, really, for polite conversation.

"Excuse me, Ms. Hamel." A distinguished-looking man in a tuxedo, who had seated them in the dining room, appeared at the author's left shoulder. "Would you allow a picture to be taken for our Distinguished Authors wall?" He indicated another man behind him, holding a fancy-looking camera.

Dorothy had seen the large collection of framed portraits, autographed photos, and book covers on their way in. Almost all of the literary glitterati who'd dined at the members-only club were male, she'd noted.

"No, photos, thank you," Georgiana answered, holding up a hand. "However, I might happen to have one or two with me in my bag. Dashiell, darling, would you be a lamb and get that out for me?"

Her son complied, and Dorothy wasn't terribly surprised to see that the photo was both highly glamorous and considerably dated. "Just put it right at the top of all those boring, old men authors," Georgiana instructed.

The man in the tuxedo and his photographer companion beat a hasty retreat with the glossy promotional photo, and Georgiana smiled in satisfaction.

Carrie, though, looked glum. "They didn't want my picture for their wall," she said, with a slight pout.

"Hey, no big deal," Summer assured her. "Most of those author guys are dead by now anyway."

Georgiana sputtered her drink, and Dash quickly patted her on the back.

"Oh, give it a break, Carrie." Parker looked completely exasperated. "You've got all kinds of other promotional stuff to be grateful for. I just booked both you and Georgiana for a live TV interview with Felicia Hernandez at WMLO on Monday, because she felt really bad she had to leave early tonight."

"Yeah, she was covering something down by the marina," Ernie said. "I saw a clip on my phone when I was checking the sports headlines about an hour ago. A fire, looked like."

Parker didn't seem to hear him, she was so worked up. "And I'm finalizing details for a beachfront reception at Tangerine du Sol, courtesy once again of Maxwell & Perkins," she went on, throwing her Algonquin Club—monogrammed napkin down on the table cloth. "What more do you want from me, Carrie? Blood?"

Everyone, including Dorothy, looked on in shock

as the slender publicist grabbed her bag and flounced off toward the bar, where she would no doubt console herself with her smartphone and another pomegranate cosmo.

"Wow." Ernie gave a low whistle, and Dorothy shook her head at him, very slightly.

For once, Carrie had nothing to say.

When Georgiana stood up from the table, looking highly amused, and excused herself for the powder room, Dorothy quickly followed. She needed to talk to her, and there was no point in putting things off.

The author was powdering her nose when Dorothy pushed open the heavy oak door of the ornate ladies' lounge. "Georgiana," Dorothy said, placing her purse on the marble counter, "I couldn't help but sense there was something you weren't telling me earlier. About Lorella Caldwell. You did know her back at Wellsmount, didn't you?"

Georgiana glanced at her briefly in the mirror. "What makes you think that?"

"Georgiana." Dorothy crossed her arms. "I took it upon myself to do a bit of yearbook research," she fibbed. "And I know full well that you're not younger than Lorella. In fact, you're nearly four years her senior."

The author sighed heavily and pointed to a floral satin love seat behind them. "Take a seat," she said.

SEVENTEEN

"You're right, Dorothy," Georgiana said, taking her e-cigarette holder from her fringed black-and-red clutch. "I don't know how you managed to get a hold of those yearbooks, but it's true. I did once know Lorella—at least, as well as anyone could."

Dorothy nodded from her perch on the edge of the love seat, relieved but not surprised that her suspicions had proved correct. Probably better to say nothing yet, and let the woman talk.

"Lorella was always something of a recluse," Georgina said, sweeping over to a chair across from Dorothy. "A mousy, tweedy little thing, really. But smart. She might have been the most dedicated young woman at Wellsmount, in fact. Other than me, of course. She spent most of her time in the bowels of the library, and we struck up an acquaintance while I was researching my thesis. Lorella worked night and day as assistant to an older, very well regarded professor."

"Interesting," Dorothy murmured. How odd that she had become a professor's assistant again, later in life.

"At the time," Georgiana went on, "I even thought the two of them were having an affair, despite the difference in their ages. But the professor was married, with a son. The wife objected to him and Lorella spending so much time together—they had a mutual interest in romantic poets—and that was the end of it. Or so she said."

"But Lorella taught at Wellsmount later," Dorothy said. "Did she and her lover—or mentor, should I say— serve on the faculty at the same time?"

"That was much later," Georgiana said, with a wave. "They kept up a limited friendship and correspondence of sorts while she was in graduate school. Until he died of a heart attack, alone in his office. On New Year's Eve. Intriguing, wouldn't you say?"

Was she implying the professor hadn't been alone after all? Or that Lorella was somehow involved in his death? Dorothy wondered.

"But here's the kicker." Georgiana slapped her silk-covered knee. "He left a fair amount of money to his former assistant. His wife was furious."

This was beginning to sound rather like one of the highly dramatic author's books, Dorothy told herself, annoyed. And what did this story have to do with Georgiana herself? "So," she said, treading carefully, "did Lorella confide in you, then, in any way?"

"Not really." Georgiana shrugged. "I pieced all of this together. More or less. The year I graduated—summa cum laude, naturally—she was a lowly freshman."

Somehow Dorothy did not feel confident about many of these details. Much of her story sounded like pure speculation. "Georgiana," she said, with a frown, "why didn't you mention any of this earlier? And in light of... what happened...you really do need to tell Detective Donovan everything you know about Lorella. Any detail, no matter how small or long ago, might prove helpful for the investigation."

The author drummed her long red nails on the arms of her chair. "I suppose."

Georgiana was still hiding something, Dorothy was

sure of it. She might even know something about Lorella's murder. In fact, at this point the famous mystery author herself could very well be the guilty party.

Dorothy eyed the hand-fired, heavy-looking vase on
the small coffee table between them—and the distance
to the door, just in case. At this point, she wasn't going
to question Georgiana's change of travel plans to arrive
the day of Lorella's death.

It would be foolish to completely tip her hand regarding her suspicions right now. Not to mention, possibly
dangerous. She might be quicker than Georgiana, but
the author was probably stronger.

"Whether or not you and Lorella were close, Georgiana, you owe it to her to help find her killer, don't you
think? We all do."

Georgiana's eyes blazed. "Of course I want justice for
Lorella," she said. "She was a good woman. And solving murders is what I do, fictionally speaking. But..."

"But what, Georgiana?" Dorothy prodded gently.

The queen of mystery suddenly looked a lot smaller.
"I suppose, since Lorella is gone now, it won't matter so
much if I break my vow of secrecy. But I suspect she'd
expect me to keep it beyond the grave. She'll come back
and haunt me now, I'm sure."

"Perhaps if she knew the circumstances," Dorothy
pointed out. Goodness, this was a ridiculous train of
reasoning.

Georgiana sighed. "You are a persistent woman, Dorothy Westin. So here it is: Lorella was also an author at
Maxwell & Perkins. I'm sure you've heard of her. She
was the fabulous, somewhat risqué, and famously se-
cretive romance writer—"

"Don't tell me," Dorothy said. "Angelina St. Rose."

SUMMER DIDN'T CARE that Detective Donovan and Jennifer had said an early good-night to take his slightly tipsy grandma back to Hibiscus Pointe. Not one single bit.

Why did Peggy always wreck things for her? Now here she was, stuck on a Saturday night, sitting by herself at a table in the middle of a bunch of dirty dishes.

Dorothy and Georgiana had gone off to the ladies' room—they'd been gone forever—Ernie had joined a poker game off the grill room with a bunch of guys, Parker was still at the bar, and Carrie was circulating at the other tables, offering people coupons for her next book.

Professor Bell had disappeared somewhere, too. Probably lurking somewhere outside the ladies' room, waiting to pounce on Georgiana with his manuscript. Dash's mom would be lucky if he didn't try to slip it under the stall door.

She should have kept a better eye on him. Maybe she should go track him down right now, just in case he was up to something. She'd been distracted by the whole Jennifer-Garrett-Donovan thing. That was stupid.

"Oh, Summer, I am soooo exhausted." Carrie plopped herself down back at the table, right next to her. "Think I need to take off my shoes. But everyone's been dying to talk to me about *Debut for Death*, so it's worth it, I guess."

Summer's Saturday night had just gotten worse. Much, much worse. She didn't need company that badly.

"Is there any more water left here? My voice keeps going hoarse."

"Sure, here you go." Summer reached for the pitcher of ice water in the middle of the table and placed it in front of Carrie. The girl was like one of those old-school dolls where you pulled the string and they blabbed and blabbed. Chatty Carrie needed to promote herself more online. That way, at least she'd never know when people shut her off.

Hopefully, Dash had gone to get the valet. She didn't even feel like going out later. She'd spilled tomato sauce on her dress, anyway.

"So, where did you get that amazing ring?" Carrie asked, pointing, as Summer reached for her phone to text him. "Can I try it on?"

What was it about the stupid ring? This was really weirding her out now. Or maybe she was just feeling guilty about borrowing it from Lorella's condo. She should have put it in her purse when everyone started noticing it.

"Hey, you know what? I forgot, I was supposed to meet Dash in the bar, like, ten minutes ago. I'll be back, okay?" Summer pushed back her chair and made her escape.

Well, she tried to, anyway. Carrie scooped up her stinky shoes and followed her, hobbling a bit, toward the bar.

"Do you even know what wearing a ring like that means?" Carrie whispered, behind her, as they hit the main hallway.

Summer stopped and glanced down at the enormous bloodstone on her finger. The gold setting glinted off the light from all the chandeliers, and the gem suddenly felt hot and heavy.

She was more annoyed now than creeped out, though. "No," she answered Carrie. "What?"

Carrie glanced up and down the empty hall. "Those superexpensive rings are given by Maxwell & Perkins to their best authors," she said. "After they sell their first million books, usually. You can't just buy one."

"There are plenty of cool rings like this out there," Summer informed her. "I know, because my mom happens to own a jewelry store." Well, Harmony did used to have that crystal place on the Santa Monica Pier. "She had this made, just for me."

"Oh. It's just a coincidence, then." Carrie looked doubtful.

"Yep." Summer strode into the bar without looking back and slid onto a red leather-backed stool next to Parker, who was well down Cosmo Road by now.

As she'd expected, Carrie joined them, but at least she wasn't talking about the ring anymore. She and Parker made up after their little spat, and Summer got to order another drink in peace.

Temporarily. "Hey, I was thinking, Summer," Parker said, slightly slurring her words. "Carrie has that TV interview tomorrow, and she really needs a makeover, if she's going to appear live next to Georgiana. You know, a little jazzing up. I mean, this is Milano, so she has to look supergreat. And it'll help build her confidence."

Summer reluctantly turned toward Carrie. Right now, after hearing her publicist diss her style, the girl seemed completely deflated. Obviously, Parker had hit a nerve.

"You always look awesome," Parker went on. "You have to know all the best places in town, right? I'm going to be so busy, between the TV prep and the beach party arrangements, so…what if you took on setting up the makeover for us?"

"Sorry, I really can't," Summer said. "I'm superbusy right now, with…stuff."

"Oh my gosh, I'm going to look like a total freak, then, right?" Carrie's head ping-ponged between Summer and Parker. "Maybe we should cancel the TV thing."

"You could make some major cashola," Parker murmured to Summer, half into her drink glass. "Stylist services are pricey in this town."

Beside her, Carrie sniffled in a disgusting, sniveling way. The girl was desperate. And Summer could use the dough. "Okay," she agreed. "I'll look into it, and give Carrie a call tomorrow so we can set things up."

"Oh, I can't thank you enough!" Carrie beamed instantly. "You're saving my life."

"No problem." Summer threw down a few bucks for the bartender and hauled it out of the Algonquin Club bar. She couldn't deal with either of those crazies for another second and it looked as if Professor Bell was nowhere in sight.

Luckily, Dash's car was parked outside the restaurant entrance, with him behind the wheel—and both his mom and Dorothy in the passenger seats, ready to go.

As she headed toward the Mercedes, Summer twisted Lorella's ring off her finger and tucked it carefully into the inside pocket of her bag. She was never wearing the stupid thing again.

EIGHTEEN

GEORGIANA HAD BEEN unusually quiet in the car on the way home from the Algonquin Club, Dorothy noticed. Since their conversation earlier in the ladies' lounge, in fact, she hadn't said a single word.

No one had said much on the drive, come to think of it. Dash seemed to be eager to make it back to Hibiscus Pointe as quickly as possible, and even Summer had seemed preoccupied.

She hadn't had a chance to tell her sleuthing partner yet what had transpired with Georgiana—and what she'd found out about Lorella.

"What would you think about spending the night at my place, dear?" Dorothy asked her, as soon as Dash had dropped them both off in front of Hibiscus Gardens. Georgiana hadn't even said goodbye. "We need to discuss a few things for the case. I had a very interesting conversation with Georgiana this evening."

"Sure," Summer said. "I'm feeling pretty beat. I think Carrie wore me out. I wouldn't mind having a glass of wine, though. So, what did you find out?"

"Something quite intriguing about Lorella," Dorothy said. "Let's get to the condo first so we can be more comfortable."

But as soon as Dorothy unlocked the door, she knew that would be impossible. Mr. Bitey had torn half the living room to shreds, in some sort of jealous rage.

"Whoa," Summer said as she stepped over a trail of torn Kleenex, "he really did a job on the place this time. Maybe you need to call those cat rescue people and have them come get Guinevere."

"No," Dorothy said as she spotted Lorella's small gray cat hanging on for dear life to a curtain valance. "I believe I'll have them cart Mr. Bitey away."

After a quick hunt, she located her skulking pet pawing at the throw cushions of the armchair in her bedroom. "Bad kitty," she said to him, and deposited the protesting tomcat in her own bathroom after tying back the shower curtain. "You're in time-out. Again."

Summer, bless her heart, was sweeping up dirt on the carpet from some overturned flowerpots that Dorothy usually kept on her balcony. If only she hadn't decided to bring them in out of the hot sun earlier that day.

"Thank you, Summer, but don't worry about cleaning up," she said. "I'm going to leave everything until tomorrow morning. We have something much more important to do."

"Like what?" her friend asked, leaning back on her heels in her good pink dress and brushing a smudge of dirt from her face.

Dorothy told Summer about her conversation with Georgiana in the Algonquin Club powder room, and Lorella's secret life as the famous romantic suspense author Angelina St. Rose.

"Ohh…" Summer stared down at the Maxwell & Perkins ring on her finger. The potting soil had made it a lot darker. "I guess Carrie was right, then. It all makes sense." She relayed to her friend what the young author had told her about the signature bloodstone.

"So it's not just that Georgiana and Lorella knew

each other," Dorothy said. "They actually had a good deal in common."

"But I still don't see why Georgiana was trying to keep Lorella's secret after she was gone." Summer frowned. "Unless…"

"Unless she had something to do with her death, perhaps," Dorothy finished.

Summer got to her feet, with a vain attempt at smoothing her dress, and shook her head. "There's no way Dash's mom would be involved in something like murder. I mean, okay, she writes about it, but that's a whole different thing."

"True, but I can't think of any other explanation," Dorothy said. "Can you?"

Summer sighed. "Not really, I guess."

"Lorella's secret identity must have had something to do with her untimely death," Dorothy said. "That's why we should go back over to her condo right now and take another look around. Maybe there's something both we and the cops missed earlier—and we certainly need to take a closer look at those files."

"Um, right now?" Summer eyed the mini wine rack on the breakfast bar. "Can't we just wait until morning? We can get up really early."

"No," Dorothy said. "We don't know when they'll start clearing Lorella's apartment, but it's sure to be soon. And if we need to bring any of those files back with us, it's better to go in the dark. I believe you left a pair of flip-flops here the other day. They're in the guest room."

A few minutes later, armed with the sturdy flashlights Dorothy kept for storm emergencies, she and

Summer let themselves in through the sliding glass doors from Lorella's ground floor concrete porch.

"Still open," Summer said cheerfully.

"Let's check those file cabinets first," Dorothy suggested. "I'm sure they'll be able to tell us something, now that we have a better idea of what to look for. Notes, royalty statements, correspondence…"

They headed through Lorella's dark condo, their flashlight beams occasionally crossing as they played into corners and over the walls. "Over there," Dorothy directed. "There's a cabinet in the alcove behind the desk, remember?"

"I feel like Nancy Drew." Summer switched her flashlight to her left hand and pulled on the top file drawer.

It was empty.

"TOTALLY GONE," SUMMER announced in frustration, after she'd yanked open the drawers of every last file cabinet in Lorella Caldwell's—aka Angelina St. Rose's—condo. "Every single folder."

"I was afraid of that." Dorothy sighed. "We should have taken them earlier. Or at least given them a closer look while we were here."

"The cops must have come back for them, I guess," Summer said.

"We can't be sure of that," Dorothy said. "I suppose, once we talk to Detective Donovan…"

"And let him know we were sneaking around in here before?" Summer said. "No way. That'll just make him really mad."

"Well, that's possible, but we do have to let him know about those files. Especially if Georgiana doesn't tell him about Lorella's—and her own—connection to Angelina St. Rose."

"He's probably figured all that out already anyway if he has the files," Summer said. "He's a very nosy person."

"That's his job, dear. I think you're missing the big picture here."

Summer frowned. Was that a clunking noise she'd heard out in the living room? Or…more of a sliding noise, from the porch? "Shh," she said. "Turn your flashlight off, quick."

"Maybe someone else left that door unlocked, too," Dorothy whispered. "So they could come back and forth, just like us."

Summer nodded in the darkness and moved toward the doorway, crouching as she tried to see around the door. There was definitely another flashlight out there in the living room, but she couldn't see the person behind it. Just a shape. Moving straight toward them.

She turned to warn Dorothy but knocked into something—a little table?—as she whirled around. There was a huge crash, and then the sound of shattering glass.

Uh-oh. They were nailed.

Summer jumped up and turned on her flashlight, aiming it into the living room. "Police!" she shouted. "Hold it right there."

Behind her, Dorothy gasped. But it was their only chance, Summer told herself. There was no other way out of the condo from the bedroom, except through the living room.

She flashed the light around the otherwise dark condo, but there was no sign of the other intruder. He or she had to be hiding somewhere now. But if she hit the overhead lights, the person would see her and Dorothy, too, and know they weren't the cops.

There was a rustling from the drapes and a sudden breeze as he or she threw open the sliding glass doors and ran out into the night.

Summer switched on her flashlight again and ran from the bedroom. She'd take her chances now that she wasn't trapped like that, and the person wouldn't know about Dorothy. "Freeze!" she called as she reached the porch.

She was about to take off after the perp, like she'd seen on *Citizen's Arrest*, when a firm hand fell on her arm.

"No, dear," Dorothy said. "Let them go."

"But he's getting away," Summer protested. "Or she."

"Better safe than sorry," Dorothy said. "That person might be armed. And it's likely they've already killed once. We can make an anonymous tip from one of those blue-light security stations. There's one just across the way."

Summer sighed. She was positive she could have caught up with the perp. If he'd run, he was scared, so he probably didn't have a gun.

On the other hand, he or she had thought Summer was a cop.

There was another thing, too, she realized, as Dorothy gave her a little push through Lorella's sliding doors. It would be a bad idea to return that bloodstone ring to Lorella's jewelry box, now that it definitely seemed important to the case.

Dorothy was already making that anonymous call to Hibiscus Pointe Security. Time to go.

NINETEEN

DOROTHY BIT INTO the scrumptious, pink-frosted donut
Summer had brought up from the early bird Sunday
morning continental buffet downstairs. Strawberry or
raspberry? Or possibly rhubarb.

Hard to tell, but deliciously sweet, at least.

After the long night they'd had, between the author
parties and the frightening ordeal in Lorella's condo, she
could definitely use the extra sugar boost. Ernie would
be here in less than half an hour to take her to church.

"So here's the big surprise I promised to tell you
about as soon as you had your donut," Summer said,
settling herself at the breakfast bar with her coffee.

Dorothy looked up from the table. "Oh, right, dear.
How nice. What is it?"

Summer smiled broadly. "You'll love it. I just found
out when I looked at my phone this morning. You have
a date tonight, at La Volpe!"

"What?" Dorothy fumbled her donut, which landed
frosting side down on the tablecloth.

"Remember when I took that cute picture of you at
the bistro with Esmé the other night? You know, with
the rose on the table?"

"No," Dorothy said. "I don't think I noticed."

"Well, I did, and I used it when I signed you up for
that Silver Sweetheart online dating site."

"Summer Smythe-Sloan! You did not." Dorothy was

so flabbergasted she was almost speechless. "I am not in the market for a romantic partner."

"I know," Summer said. "You have Ernie, sort of."

"That's outrageous, young lady." Dorothy rarely became annoyed with her friend, but this was too much. Ernie was very much married. And even though Grace was sadly afflicted by Alzheimer's, he remained entirely loyal and faithful to her, as he should. "Ernie and I are just good friends and you know it."

Summer looked sheepish. "Sorry, Dorothy. I didn't mean it like that. I meant you both really like spending time together, that's all."

Dorothy sighed. "So who is this date, and how can I get out of it? Immediately."

"Okay, I was kind of joking about the date thing," Summer said. "It's Charles Bell, and the setup is just for the case, I thought, since he goes on so many dates and all, that this would be a perfect way for you to find out more about him. And maybe whatever was going on between him and Lorella."

Dorothy rubbed her temples. This was no way to start a Sunday morning. Or any morning.

"I filled out the questions, you know, like do you enjoy books and reading, and a few other things," Summer rushed on. "He likes mature women, and I knew you two would be a match, but I was afraid you'd say no if I told you first. You matched up with some other guys, too, by the way."

"It's a terrible idea," Dorothy said. "The most ridiculous one I've ever heard, in fact."

"Don't worry," Summer assured her. "I didn't use your real name. I mean, Professor Bell knows who you are, but everyone else thinks you're Foxy Dot."

"Foxy Dot? *That's* what you came up with?" Dorothy was appalled. "Couldn't you think of anything better than that?"

Summer grinned. "Well, you *are* foxy. And hey, that's the kind of name that gets you lots of hits."

"I'm sure," Dorothy murmured. No wonder Charles had winked at her last night.

"But anyway, all you have to do is show up at the restaurant and get him to trust you. Then maybe you can ask him some questions for the case. And don't worry, I'll be right there at La Volpe, too, in disguise or something. And Esmé will call the cops if anything starts getting weird."

"It's already weird," Dorothy said. "We really don't know anything about this man."

"I did do a little more research on my phone this morning," Summer said. "I looked ol' Chuck up on ProfessorRater. He's not superpopular with his students. Really boring and a tough grader. But I also found out a few other things. He went to a fancy prep school outside Boston and stayed in the area for college and grad school. Oh, and his dad was a professor, too—at Wellsmount."

Dorothy sighed. "Of course. What on earth was going on behind those ivy walls? I'm sure the professor and I will have a scintillating conversation." She stood up from the table. "I'd better get dressed. Ernie will be here to get me any minute."

"Just another thing or two," Summer said, following her partway to the bedroom. "He does a little stand-up comedy on the side. Pretty funny, huh? For a murder suspect, anyway."

"I would never have guessed," Dorothy said, through

the door. On the other hand, she would never have believed Lorella Caldwell was Angelina St. Rose, either.

"And no criminal record," Summer called. "Not that I could find, anyway. See, everything will be fine."

As DOROTHY HAD EXPECTED, Ernie was less than pleased to hear about her "date" on the way to church. In fact, he was quite possibly even more upset than she had been.

But she had to tell him. What if he found out somehow she'd joined an online dating service, and hadn't been the one to tell him? Friends were supposed to share things like that.

"And with a name like Foxy Dot, no less." He was really fuming now, over the steering wheel. "Who knows what kind of scoundrels and screwballs will try to contact you? It's not safe, I tell you."

"I appreciate your concern, Ernie, but there's no need to worry. It's for the case, so it isn't a real date. And I'll be very careful. Summer will be there."

"Summer?" Ernie almost went through a red light. "That's it. I'm going with you. I'll be sitting at the next table."

Dorothy had a difficult time concentrating on the sermon. The upcoming evening with Professor Bell weighed on her mind, but she also couldn't stop thinking about Georgiana. She and Lorella had known each other at college. Later, they'd shared correspondence and the same publisher.

But here was the million-dollar question: Why would Georgiana want to eliminate Lorella? Had they been rivals or enemies in some way? So far, that didn't appear to be the case.

It was possible, though, she told herself. Look how

competitive—even threatened—Georgiana seemed by a new, ambitious young author like Carrie, who had a promising future. Or would, if she didn't manage to drive her own readers away.

Georgiana could have arrived from New York earlier—hadn't she caught Dash by surprise?—and disposed of Lorella with the bookend. Then she could have simply pretended she'd just come from the airport and an impromptu appearance at Murder by the Sea.

Of course, Georgiana's true itinerary would be easy enough for the police to check. But Dorothy knew she still needed some kind of hard evidence before she even breathed a word of anything like that to Detective Donovan. Dash was a good friend, and somehow it just seemed too unlikely that his mother was a murderer.

After the service, Dorothy took Ernie's arm and stepped out into the bright sunshine, feeling guilty for not having paid a whit of attention to prayerful reflection. She was about to suggest a nice, relaxing brunch when a silk-muumuued Gladys Rumway met her and Ernie at the bottom of the church steps.

"Morning, Dorothy! And Ernest." Gladys's enormous hat blocked the sun. "The girls are saving me a place in line for the Hibiscus Pointe shuttle, but I just had to share a quick something about Lorella with you."

Dorothy composed a smile. "What is it, Gladys?"

"Merle shared some info with me about Lorella's will." Gladys leaned in, fanning herself with a badly wrinkled church program. "She left practically everything to charity. No surprise there, who else would she give it to? But here's the kicker."

Gladys paused dramatically, and Dorothy braced herself.

"Word is, it's a whopping fortune! Who woulda thought?"

Well, that made sense. Lorella—aka Angelina St. Rose—had to have been financially blessed. "My," Dorothy said vaguely. There was no sense in encouraging Gladys.

"I also happened to hear some of that dough is earmarked for the Hibiscus Pointe Library. So there should be plenty left over to fund more of these big, fancy book club events, don't you think?"

No, Dorothy answered silently. That was the last thing they needed, in her view. She stepped aside to let a flood of churchgoers pass, but Gladys didn't budge.

"By the way, Dorothy, you know that odd-duck professor who's been showing up? Just so you know, he's my top suspect in Lorella's murder—and the Milano PD's, too. We'll need to keep a sharp eye on him."

Beside her, Dorothy could feel Ernie's glare. But Gladys wasn't finished. "Oh, and one more thing," the big woman went on. "I find this really hard to believe, Dorothy, but did you join Silver Sweethearts? There's a woman named Foxy Dot who just popped up, and she looks just like—"

"Whoa there, you're missing your bus, Gladys," Ernie broke in. "Look, away it goes. If you run, maybe you can catch it."

Gladys whirled to check the shuttle stop, and Dorothy found herself being hustled away in the opposite direction by a furious Ernie.

He looked like a thundercloud. But thank goodness she didn't have to endure any more gossip from Gladys Rumway.

TWENTY

AFTER DOROTHY LEFT for church, Summer helped herself to some cereal and hung around the condo for a while, psyched that her friend had finally agreed to the fake-date sting tonight. Then she headed to Jennifer's office in the main building and let herself in.

Resident Services was closed on Sundays, except for emergencies, so Jennifer had the day off. Summer knew she'd be okay with her taking a peek at those confidential resident notebooks—as long as she didn't have to officially give her permission.

Summer went straight to the large binders lined up behind Jennifer's desk, selected C for Caldwell, and took it straight to the photocopy machine outside Roger's office. No way was he going to show up on a weekend, so she was free and clear.

She could give the copy to Dorothy to read after she was done reading it. At the pool.

As she'd expected, someone had posted the copier's security code on the wall just above it. Good for her, bad for Hibiscus Pointe. Jeez. If they were that dumb, it served them right.

While she was at it, she took a peek at the *S* folders—there were three of them—and her own file.

Yikes. The word SUBLET was stamped across the top in red ink. And right under it was a long list of notes and complaints from the Residents Board. Illegal camping. Excessive noise. Community age requirement violations. Late payments.

Well, nothing new there. But there were some good things, too. Like her volunteer work as aquatics director—so far it hadn't been much actual work, since she just had a beginner class of two students and a couple of aqua aerobics classes per week.

She'd better get that water ballet team officially going. Helen Martin was very eager to compete in community intramurals. Probably because she wanted to parade around in a bathing suit in front of all the guy residents. The older and richer, the better.

Someone had to foot the bill for all that plastic surgery.

Summer's cell rang, and she answered it without looking, still reading her file.

"Hi, Summer, Carrie here. Just checking in on the plan for my spa appointments."

Oops. She'd totally forgotten about the makeover deal. "Oh, hey, Carrie. I'm still working things out—waiting for a few places to get back to me. I'll call you back, okay, as soon as everything's confirmed."

"Thanks soooo much," Carrie said. "I can't tell you how much I appreciate this. I really want to look my best on TV. Appearance counts a lot for authors. Do you think I have the right image? I want to look cool and smart, but approachable. Should I pick up some fake glasses? And a new outfit, too, maybe?"

Like that would make a difference. This girl was sadly deluded. "Sure, go for it," Summer said. "Never hurts to change things up sometimes, right?"

She hung up as fast as she could and racked her brain for a decent place that was open on Sundays. She'd have to pray someone would have a cancellation. Every spa and salon in town was closed on Mondays.

Summer was not looking forward to spending a long afternoon with Carrie Dunbar. But bucks were bucks. Maybe she'd see if Jennifer wanted to go with them, Carrie's treat. Jennifer would have fun, and maybe she could find out how things went with Detective Donovan last night.

There was also another big plus to that plan: She wouldn't be stuck alone with Carrie.

THERE WAS ONLY one place Summer could get Carrie, Jennifer, and herself into on such short notice. Sunday afternoons were especially slow at the All About You Spa located inside the dated Hotel Milano.

It wasn't that great, and way overpriced, but hopefully, Carrie wouldn't realize that. Didn't seem as if she was much of a spa regular. And, with luck, no one was likely to see them there.

"Oh, wow, this place is amaaaaazing," Carrie said as they walked into the All About You reception area. "Gosh, it sure is dark in here, but that's really cool. Very peaceful."

The whole place was done in tones of gray. Probably hid all the dirt and mold, Summer thought.

"Thanks so much for including me, guys." Jennifer seemed equally thrilled. "We should put a spa in at Hibiscus Pointe. I bet the residents would love it."

"I would," Summer said. "Maybe you should bring the idea up to Roger."

Jennifer sighed. "Don't think so."

The receptionist looked up from the movie she was

watching on her phone. "Hi," she said. "You must be that last-minute booking. Sloan, right?"

"That's me," Summer said quickly. Using her dad's name to book things was probably a waste here at All About Gray. "Jennifer and I are having the massages and seaweed scrubs and Carrie is getting the Milano Makeover package."

It was the best combo she could get for three hours. New hairstyle and highlights, restorative manicure for those badly bitten nails, and makeup application instruction. Summer figured Carrie could really use a little stress relief, but there wasn't time for the works.

As the three of them came out of the locker room in their gray robes and slippers, Carrie slipped her cell phone from her pocket.

"You're not supposed to have a phone in here," Jennifer whispered, looking around nervously as if the place was bugged or something.

"I have to text Parker," Carrie said. "I need her to get me booked to have my author photo retaken tomorrow morning, while my hair's all perfect."

As Summer waited for her massage, sipping warmish lemon water, she read Lorella's file behind a magazine. Jennifer had cucumbers over her eyes, but it never hurt to be extra careful.

The information was snooze city, nothing really new. Lorella was from Massachusetts, no kids, never married. Moved to Hibiscus Pointe a little over a month ago. Condo 1-B, Hibiscus Gardens. Milano resident, ten years. Recently retired as English Department secretary at Santa Teresa. Previously professor and also alumna at Wellsmount College. Hobbies: reading, poetry, and classic films.

Blah, blah, blah. "Tell me something I don't know," Summer muttered, under her breath.

Excellent health. Occasional arthritis. Personal physician: Dr. Lydia Bundtzen. Vehicle: 1999 Mazda Protégé, white. Possible volunteer interests: Newsletter, library, reading to the blind.

Lorella Caldwell might have been a famous author, but she sure was boring.

Jennifer peeled the cucumber slices from her eyes and Summer quickly stashed the residents form away under her gray spa towel. Carrie was still absorbed in her phone.

"Hey, Summer, can you recommend a nice, quiet place for dinner tonight?" Jennifer asked. "I actually have a date with a new guy tonight and he asked me to choose. I don't go out much, so…"

"Hey, that's great." Summer's stomach gave a tiny twist. "Who is it?"

So Jennifer and Detective Donovan were dating now. Well, Summer had expected that, right? And it was perfectly fine, she reminded herself.

Jennifer blushed and swiped at the stray cucumber seeds left on her face. "I'd sort of rather not say yet, if you don't mind. I'm afraid I might jinx things, you know? But I want us to go somewhere that isn't too crowded so we can at least talk."

"Well, it might be hard to get last-minute reservations at most of those kinds of places," Summer said. "But Dorothy and I are going to La Volpe around seven. It's totally quiet, trust me."

Oh no. Had she actually just said that? What was the matter with her? She'd blown her cover for tonight, and her partner's. The last thing they needed was Detective Donovan and Jennifer showing up there on a romantic date.

Jennifer brightened in the creepy, grayish light. "That's a great suggestion! I went to La Volpe once, ages ago, and I'd forgotten all about it. Perfect."

Yep. Unbelievably fabulous. Summer mentally kicked herself. At least there was one good thing about Detective Donovan and Jennifer joining the party on their superromantic date. Dorothy could feel even safer during her dinner with a possible murderer.

TWENTY-ONE

DOROTHY COULDN'T HELP feeling a twinge of regret after she finally brought herself to leave that message on Gladys's cell about Guinevere.

Lorella's kitty desperately needed a new home and Dorothy knew it would be the best way to get the word out community-wide. And no doubt beyond. But still… Dorothy wished she could keep her.

While Mr. Bitey took a nap in a sun patch on the bedroom carpet, she took the little gray cat on her lap and began to flip through the Moleskine notebook she'd taken from Lorella's condo on her and Summer's first trip.

Why hadn't she done this earlier? They'd been so busy…and now that those folders were missing from Lorella's file cabinets, it was the only thing they had to go on.

It wasn't a personal journal, as Dorothy had hoped. Just snippets and a few longer passages of lovely writing—probably for Lorella's next book. There were character sketches, too, and notes for clothes and setting.

Finally, there it was: a calendar at the back. With renewed hope, Dorothy perused the monthly pages, in which Lorella had made sporadic entries. Book deadlines, occasional reminders to order various items for the Hibiscus Pointe Library—and a few fairly recent references to "C." Underlined.

Were those the assignations Lorella had had with Charles Bell? The very man Dorothy was committed to meet, in just a few short hours?

She shivered, remembering the bloody bookend that had killed the earnest librarian and author. Maybe Summer should tuck the professor's matching piece back into her bag tonight, just in case they needed it to defend themselves.

No, that was absurd. The two of them—plus Ernie and Esmé, of course—would be perfectly safe in a public place like La Volpe.

A heavy, furious shape launched itself at Dorothy, startling her from her thoughts. Mr. Bitey had woken from his nap and detected that his unsuspecting rival was curled, peacefully purring, in his owner's lap.

As Guinevere beat a hasty retreat to the drapes again, clawing them half-threadless with flailing paws as she tried to ascend them in a panic, Dorothy grabbed the hissing tomcat firmly by the collar and deposited him in his new powder room jail.

Perhaps she should tuck her attack cat into *her* purse tonight, for extra protection.

"So you're all set?" Summer asked as Dorothy settled herself at the small, marble-topped bistro table. "Are you sure you don't want me to run over to Fleurs de Paris and get you a red rose?"

"No, thank you," Dorothy said. It was almost mortifying, to be in this position, even if it was for a case.

"I put in your reply to Professor Bell that you'd have one sticking out of a book, so he'd know it was you. It's a Silver Sweethearts thing. I saw it in a movie once, too. And Esmé said…"

"He knows who I am," Dorothy broke in. "And there's a rose right here on the table, see?"

"But it's white," Summer pointed out.

"White rose, red rose, who cares?" Ernie was looking stormy again. "This jerk won't even notice the difference. All he wants to do is try and seduce Dorothy."

Dorothy closed her eyes. "No one is going to do anything of the sort. Really, Ernie. I believe I can handle things. Now both of you go sit down and order your dinners. I will be just fine."

"Well, okay, if you're sure." Ernie still sounded reluctant. He and Summer chose a table a ways back against the brick wall, but it still seemed oddly close in the nearly empty restaurant.

Summer's choice of outfit was somewhat inappropriate as well, Dorothy noted. For one thing, her friend was wearing a big, floppy hat and tinted sunglasses—indoors *and* during the evening. She'd also draped herself in an unusually baggy dress that failed to flatter her trim, toned figure.

Surely the girl didn't think such extremes were necessary to disguise herself from Charles Bell. He might remember her from their chance meeting in his office or the book club events, of course, but that look was definitely overkill.

It was so obvious it might even scare their suspect off.

"Hey, Dorothy, what can I get for you?" Esmé materialized at the table in wide-leg black pants and a wrap-style white leotard. "A glass of wine, maybe? Summer says she's buying, but it's on the house."

"No, thank you," Dorothy said, smoothing her plain

navy dress. She'd worn as dull an outfit as possible. "I'll wait. How about some nice peppermint tea?"

"Coming up," Esmé said. "By the way, good luck with that creep tonight."

Lovely, Dorothy told herself, trying not to cringe with humiliation. There was probably a reason the man chose a restaurant named after a wolf to meet his dates.

She opened the book she'd brought with her—she was rereading *Mansfield Park*—and tried not to notice that Professor Bell was late. A gentleman should never keep a lady waiting. No wonder his dates didn't go well.

The minutes ticked slowly by, and melted into half an hour. Then forty minutes. This was ridiculous. Dorothy put her book aside and took out her little pen and pad set from her pocketbook. Maybe she'd make a few notes for the next book club meeting, since she had so much time to kill.

At eight o'clock sharp, Dorothy clicked off her pen. Obviously, her "date" was not going to show up, the cad.

Had he spotted Summer through the window? She'd been craning her neck and looking around every two minutes. Perhaps her sleuthing partner had scared him off.

Dorothy felt a sharp stab of annoyance, and not just because she wouldn't have the chance to prod Charles into spilling information about him and Lorella.

She'd been stood up, for the first time in her life. How embarrassing, as well as infuriating. What would Ernie think?

"Hey, Dot," he said, looking considerably more cheerful as he put his napkin down and came over to Dorothy's table. "Looks like you haven't had much to eat yet."

She glanced down at the telltale crumbs of the bread sticks she'd nibbled with her tea. Maybe she shouldn't have waited to order dinner. "No, I guess not."

"Well, come on over and join us," Ernie said. "We'll order another plate of clams marinara and Summer and I will save you some cannoli. The chef has nothing to do back there, so it'll make him real happy."

Dorothy grabbed her pocketbook. "Thank you. I believe I will."

"Oh well, we tried," Summer said, removing her sunglasses as Dorothy sat down. She looked as dejected as Ernie was full of new energy. "I knew Professor Bell was a loser. Let's get some spumoni, too, okay, Ernie?"

Esmé brought a decanter of red wine and two more glasses, and pulled up another uncomfortable bistro chair. "Mind if I join you?" she said. "And if your date shows up, Dorothy, you can use some of this to throw at him."

"Thank you," Dorothy said. "I just might."

SUMMER WAS STILL feeling out of sorts the next morning, even after a quick mile or so of laps in the pool. Now she was reading Georgiana's book, which was actually pretty good—better than *Citizen's Arrest*—in an attempt to distract herself.

Charles Bell hadn't shown last night, and neither had Jennifer and her "date," aka Detective Donovan. Where had the two of them gone? Plus, her sister Joy in New Jersey woke her up at 8:00 a.m. to rant about having to kick in their joint rent payment to Syd again this month—even after Summer had sworn she'd take care of the next two in a row for sure.

Also, the home theater guys had come yesterday afternoon, while she was out at the spa with Carrie and Jennifer, so they hadn't installed anything. Again. And to top things off, she had a freaking killer headache from all that cheap wine last night.

Her cell rang, and Summer answered it without rolling over in the pool lounge chair. If it was Carrie, she would tell her her phone was running out of juice and hang up.

"Hey, it's Dash." He sounded totally panicked, and he hadn't even called her Cali Girl the way he usually did when he called.

"What's the matter?" Summer quickly sat up.

"It's that blasted turtle you got Juliette-Margot. Skipperdunk, or whatever she calls him."

"Skipperdee," Summer corrected.

"Right. He's not doing so well. The thing looks kind of floppy, he's not eating, his shell is all mushy, and he's moping around the soap dish with these little bubbles coming out of his nose."

"Uh-oh," Summer said. That did not sound good.

"Juliette-Margot won't eat, either. Not even the pancakes à l'orange I made her this morning. She's posted watch beside the tub—and I really think this turtle will need Last Rites soon."

"I'm sure it's not that bad." Summer's head started to pound again. "Maybe he's just getting used to living at your house."

"Don't think so," Dash said. "And the vet at Purr-fect Angels Pet Hospital and Resort refuses to call me back. I've left a thousand and one voice mails. Anyway, can you run over to wherever in Hades you got this bloody reptile and pick up another one, just in case?"

"In case what?" When Dash didn't answer, Summer

finally swam out of her hangover fog and filled in the blanks. "Oh, right. Got it. Sorry."

"I'd go myself, but to add to the high-drama chez Hamel-LeBlanc, Mother has misplaced her precious writing notebook and she's beyond hysterical."

"I'm on my way to the pet store," Summer said, sliding into her flip-flops. "I'll be at your place as soon as I can."

The trip to Camo's Exotic Pets was a good thing, she told herself as she pulled into the empty parking lot. Hopefully, she'd run into Ray, or at least get some intel on his whereabouts, while she was doing a good deed for Juliette-Margot and Dash.

With everything else that had been going on, she and Dorothy hadn't been focused enough on cornering Ray and Trixie and their vanishing RV. So many suspects, so little time.

The same teenage kid with the ball cap was manning Ray's store. This time Summer headed straight to the counter, without looking at any of the cages and glowing tanks or snakes and lizards and furry spiders.

"Is Ray here?" she asked the kid.

"Nah, he ain't been around much, but that's the way he is. If he don't give me a paycheck soon, though, he'll be here a lot, because I'm quitting."

"I know what that's like," Summer said. "I've had some pretty bad bosses myself. By the way," she added, glancing nervously around at the filthy floor, "did Ray ever find Camo the snake?"

"Nah," the kid said. "But that cop came in here again yesterday and asked more questions about Ray. He didn't seem that interested in Camo."

Detective Donovan, Summer thought. No wonder

he'd been over at the golf course. But ugh. She'd better wrap this turtle mission up quick, in case that slimy giant python showed its ugly snake face around here again.

"Hey, where are all the little green turtles?" she asked, peering at the empty tank near the counter. It was completely dark today and the bubbles were gone.

"Uh, we had a filtering malfunction." The kid shrugged. "Happens a lot."

"That's terrible," Summer said, horrified. "So...you don't have any more turtles? Not even one?"

"Nope. Don't know when we'll get a new delivery, either. Our suppliers ain't real reliable."

Well, that wasn't good. Summer explained the mopey turtle problem to the kid. "What can I do?" she asked. "Can I get another one somewhere?"

"Dunno," the kid said. "But if the turtle ain't dead already, you can take it to Safari Sue's Wildlife Park and Zoo over on the Trail. Maybe they can help you out."

Fabulous. Summer wasted no time in beating it out of the creepy-crawly pet store.

TWENTY-TWO

DOROTHY STRUGGLED TO jam one more slim volume onto a dusty, overcrowded shelf in the Hibiscus Pointe Library. At this rate, she had only managed to shelve two boxes worth of donated titles—and there were a good two dozen more to go.

Perhaps the book club might sponsor a book sale to help create a literacy program for migrant children. She'd overheard Summer talking about something like that to her date at the author signing party. What a marvelous idea.

The two of them could bring the subject up at their first actual book discussion meeting, if they ever managed to have one.

Someone knocked softly on the closed library door.

Startled, Dorothy nearly tripped over Guinevere, who'd been winding around her ankles. She'd brought Lorella's cat with her this morning, for company. And to give Mr. Bitey a breather from the powder room.

"Come in," she called. "And close the door behind you, please."

Instantly, she regretted those words. Standing just inside the library now was Charles Bell, smiling with unsuccessful charm. She was trapped.

"What can I do for you, Professor Bell?" she said stiffly. She certainly wasn't going to bring up his failure to appear for their appointment at La Volpe last night. *And what are you doing here?* she wanted to ask.

"The staff at the desk told me I might find you in here," he said, still smiling. "I wanted to apologize for standing you up last night."

Dorothy crossed the room and busied herself arranging papers on Lorella's old desk. She was hardly about to stay back there in the stacks, where her predecessor had been murdered.

Possibly by this very man.

"I was unavoidably detained," he said.

Dorothy briefly glanced up. The professor was blocking the door now. Had he really told people he was looking for her, and they'd directed him to the library? If so, then if anything happened to her, they'd know who to look for. But if he'd been lying...

"I'm so terribly sorry. Please allow me to make it up to you. I know a lovely little sandwich shop that's just opened over on Periwinkle. Would you be willing to go to lunch with me?"

Absolutely not, Dorothy thought. She had a policy of not riding in cars with suspects, if at all possible. No one would even know where they had gone. She needed to make a graceful—or less than graceful, if need be—exit from the library.

On the other hand...how could she pass up the opportunity to interview Professor Bell for the case? She and Summer badly needed that information. "I'm extremely busy today, so I'd prefer to stay on the premises," she said finally. "But there's a buffet lunch set up at the pool. We could talk there, perhaps."

At her feet, Guinevere gave what sounded like a

warning meow. Oh, heavens. She'd forgotten about the cat.

The professor seemed delighted. "I assure you, you won't regret it."

Dorothy barely suppressed a shudder of disgust. The man certainly had an overly high opinion of himself. She reached down to scoop up Guinevere and grab her cat carrier from under the desk, just as the professor stepped closer.

"What are you doing?" she demanded, quickly putting the carrier between them.

He stepped away, looking a bit taken back. "Sorry," he said. "I was just going to help you with that heavy-looking crate."

"No need, thank you." Dorothy sidestepped the professor and headed straight for the door.

He followed at her heels, like an admiring puppy. "You're something else, Foxy Dot. I must admit, I love a woman who's a challenge."

SUMMER DROVE AS fast as she dared to Safari Sue's, after a brief stop back at Hibiscus Pointe to pick up Juliette-Margot and Skipperdee.

"You know what, JM?" she said as they stopped at about the eighty-fourth red light. "I think Skipperdee is looking pretty good there. He's probably just sleeping inside his shell."

Juliette-Margot stared sadly down at the see-through container on her lap with the little plastic palm tree. "It is *très* grave," she said.

When they got to the animal park, which the entrance sign said had been established in the 1940s, Summer rushed Juliette-Margot past the line to get Skipperdee out of the brutal heat. They couldn't have him baking in that Tupperware-looking thing.

"Hi," she said to the girl at the customer service desk. "We have a turtle emergency."

"Huh?" The girl, whose name tag read Mandy, snapped her grape gum.

Summer explained the situation, and asked for Safari Sue.

"Sorry, Safari Sue is in Africa getting more animals right now," Mandy said. "But I'll page Dr. Josie for you. She's our head veterinarian. You need tickets, too?"

Summer glanced over her shoulder. The perspiring people behind them were looking pretty ticked off that she and Juliette-Margot had skipped the line. "Sure. One adult, one kid," she said quickly. If things went south with Skipperdee, maybe a quick trip through the zoo would help make Juliette-Margot feel better.

Summer carefully pried the turtle box from the kid's hands. Today Dash's daughter was dressed like a turtle herself, in a green sundress with a little green smock thing over it and matching sunhat. "Come on," she said. "We have to go wait in the animal hospital for Dr. Josie."

The vet, a pretty young woman wearing all khaki and a Safari Sue scarf around her neck, introduced herself and gazed down at Skipperdee flopped out on his little plastic island. "Hey, a baby red slider," she said, smiling at Juliette-Margot. "Where did you get him, sweetie?"

Juliette-Margot pointed to Summer. "My friend."

Dr. Josie raised one eyebrow. "Oh. I see. Well, let's go into one of the examining rooms and I'll take a look at him."

Summer held her breath as the vet put Skipperdee through his paces. Or tried to, anyway. The little creature was pretty lethargic, but on the other hand, turtles were always slow, right?

"Okay, guys," Dr. Josie said when she was done. "Why don't we sit down over there and we'll talk."

That did not sound good, Summer told herself with a gulp. Skipperdee was doomed, Juliette-Margot was going to be totally devastated, and it was all her fault.

"So here's the thing." Dr. Josie pulled up a stool as Summer sat down on a plastic chair and took Juliette-Margot on her lap. "I really think Skipperdee is going to be okay."

Summer almost dropped Juliette-Margot in relief.

"But he needs a proper environment and the right food, not a bathtub of chlorinated water and lettuce."

For a second, Summer wondered what Dash would think of Skipperdee not having a good enough home. Jeez, he had to be the most pampered reptile on earth.

"You see, this tiny turtle will grow into a very large turtle. And red sliders are endangered. I'm really sorry, but they're not allowed as children's—or anyone's— pets. And they sometimes carry salmonella, so kids shouldn't handle them." The vet looked at Summer. "Where did you get this one?"

"At a place called Camo's Exotic Pets," Summer said. "It's owned by a guy named Ray."

"Well, I'll have to report him, I'm afraid." Dr. Josie leaned forward until she was almost eye level with Juliette-Margot. "Sweetie, if you leave Skipperdee here with me and Safari Sue, he'll get the best of care. And he'll get to be with all his friends. What do you say?"

Summer felt Juliette-Margot freeze up in her arms. "But Eloise has a turtle like Skipperdee," she said, sniffling. "He lives in her bathtub at the Plaza Hotel on the tippity-top floor."

The vet looked at Summer again. "It's a book," Summer told her. "But hey," she added to Juliette-Margot, "guess what? I got us tickets to the zoo. You and I are going to see all the animals while Skipperdee hangs out with Dr. Josie. She's going to make him well. Is that awesome, or what?"

"Juliette-Margot does not want to see the zoo." The kid gave a weird little hiccup.

"Tell you what," Dr. Josie said. "How about if I show you where Skipperdee is going to live with his new turtle family after he gets better? And then I'll give you and your friend a special pass to Safari Sue's, so you can visit him whenever you want."

Juliette-Margot thought about that one. "Okay," she said finally.

The turtle habitat tour was short and sweet, for which Summer was grateful. It cheered Juliet-Margot up at first, but after they'd thanked Dr. Josie and headed to the car, she looked a little down again.

"How about we stop at Lime Rickey's for an orange crème shake?" Summer said. She had to talk the kid into it, but by the time they were halfway to the fifties-style ice cream drive in, Juliette-Margot had warmed to the idea.

After the two of them walked back to the MINI with their ice creams—Juliette-Margot with the orange crème and her with a Blue Hawaiian Freeze, Summer reached for the driver's-side door—and screamed.

Something dark, hairy, and almost the size of her fist was emerging from under the handle. The gnarliest freaking spider she'd ever seen.

TWENTY-THREE

DOROTHY TRIED NOT to notice that Gladys Rumway and half a dozen other ladies at the poolside buffet were eagerly watching as she and Professor Bell carried their plates to a table in a far corner of the pool deck.

She spread a towel beneath Guinevere's carrier in the comfortable shade of a nearby cabana and gave the kitty fresh water from a drink cup lid.

It would be better to drop her off back at the condo, but Dorothy didn't want Charles to know where she lived—not that it would be difficult for him to find out—or try to accompany her.

"So, why don't you tell me about yourself, Professor?" Dorothy said, trying to spear a tough piece of pineapple.

"Please call me Charles," he said. "What would you like to hear?"

The truth, Dorothy thought.

"Well, let's see," he continued, before she could answer. "I'm not sure where to start, there's so much to know about me. I was born in New England—Marblehead, Massachusetts, to be precise. I was exposed to the world of literature exceptionally early, by virtue of the fact that my father was a distinguished professor of English with a specialty in the Romantic poets..."

Oh my. Professor Bell continued to drone on, and Dorothy nearly fell asleep in her fruit salad. He was quite possibly the most boring man she'd ever met. And the worst part was, so far he'd told her nothing she didn't already know.

As he went on at length about his academic research and publications, Dorothy tried her best to force her facial muscles into what she hoped was an expression of mild interest.

"I'm sorry, I fear I must be boring you," the professor said suddenly. He hadn't touched a bite of his sandwich, with the all the talking he'd been doing. Before Dorothy could politely protest, however, he started up again.

"Rather surprisingly, I have never had a wife." Professor Bell finally took a few forkfuls of pasta salad, and Dorothy averted her eyes so she wouldn't have to see him talk with his mouth full. "I suppose you could say I am married to my work."

"Of course," Dorothy murmured.

"In fact, in addition to my extensive research and teaching duties, I am writing a romantic novel," the professor said. "Currently, the manuscript runs a shade under one thousand pages. Quite a literary undertaking, you understand. Each time I think I'm about to reach the conclusion, those words just keep writing themselves."

Good heavens. If she ever needed a book to cure her occasional insomnia, Professor Bell's lengthy opus would surely fit the bill. "Have you considered dividing the story up, perhaps—say, into a three-book set?" Dorothy asked.

The professor put down his fork. "Funny you should suggest that. I've been told that before, by my editor. But really, I anticipate this entire manuscript will be Book One. Would you like to hear the plot?"

"No," Dorothy said quickly. "I mean, I'm very impressed that you have an editor. When will your book be published?"

"Oh, it's not under contract," Professor Bell said. "Not yet. My editor was more of a prepublication consultant, really. I was lucky to have her, as she had an academic specialty similar to mine, but sadly we are no longer working together. However, when I…"

The editor had to have been Lorella, Dorothy thought. Why had he failed to mention her by name—or the fact that she had passed away? He had been her employer, for heaven's sake, and who knew what else? "Yes, wasn't it very sad about Lorella Caldwell?" she said.

The professor stopped talking. "You knew her?"

Dorothy nodded. "Not extremely well, but she was our librarian here at Hibiscus Pointe. You two must have been much better acquainted." She paused, expectantly.

Professor Bell cleared his throat. "Yes, I knew Lorella. She was a nice lady. And she had excellent grammar."

Grammar? What was the matter with this man, and how could he be so selfish? "I'd love to hear more about her. Since I've assumed Lorella's duties in the library, and the book club was a project close to her heart, I'd love to make sure I'm carrying out her wishes to the fullest extent possible."

The professor shrugged. "I'm not sure there's much to tell. She was actually my administrative assistant at Santa Teresa, did I mention that? She didn't list it on her résumé, but I learned not long after I'd hired her that she'd once been a professor at Wellsmount College. It just so happened, my father was also on the faculty there. As a student, Lorella had even been his teaching assistant. Quite a coincidence."

"Yes, quite." Dorothy decided it might not be the right time to bring up the possibility of an affair between Lorella and his esteemed father. "You attended Wellsmount's brother school across town, didn't you, Charles? You never met Lorella, then?"

He frowned. "No. I was just a kid. And I never took any classes on the Wellsmount campus, so our paths never crossed."

"I see," Dorothy said. "Well, how nice for you that Lorella agreed to edit your manuscript later."

"When she had a little downtime on the job." The professor went back to his pasta salad. "She thought I was very talented."

"She didn't do any extra work on her own time?" Dorothy pressed. "With you, by chance? You must have visited her lovely Tudor home."

The professor wiped his mouth with his napkin. "Once or twice, maybe, before she suddenly quit working for me and moved without a forwarding address. And I did stop by there recently to see if she'd perhaps left behind any further editorial notes. Not that I really needed them that badly, of course. Sadly, she never finished reading my manuscript, and now she's gone."

How heartless. And his whole story sounded fishy, in Dorothy's view. But she couldn't blame Lorella for leaving her job and moving to a gated community like Hibiscus Pointe to avoid this man and his terrible novel, if that was the case.

"So it sounds as if Lorella was an excellent editor," Dorothy said. "Did she write, as well?"

"No," Professor Bell said. "Some people are born to write, like I was, but Lorella didn't have that gift."

Obviously, this pompous man had no idea that Lorella was a bestselling author. Or else he was lying. "What a shame. I could have sworn I heard something about her working on a book or two. You would have known that, though, wouldn't you?"

"I'm not sure what you're getting at." Professor Bell leaned across the table and placed a large hand over Dorothy's much smaller one. "Why don't we talk about you now, Foxy Dot?"

Dorothy snatched her hand away, glancing nervously across the pool. Sure enough, Gladys and her cronies were staring and whispering. But she needed to ask the professor whether he'd been acquainted with Georgiana back in their small college town.

Maybe he hadn't known quiet Lorella, but the future GH Hamel might have been harder to miss.

"So, how about it?" the professor was saying. "Dinner tonight? I can tell you more about my novel."

Dorothy jolted back to attention. "What? Oh my, no. I'd love to, of course, but I already have plans."

"So, you two are looking very cozy over here." Gladys Rumway planted herself beside their table, grinning widely under her enormous zebra-print sunglasses.

For once, Dorothy was happy to see her. "Oh my, what *is* the time? I need to get my cat inside before she overheats." She rose quickly, nearly toppling her light plastic chair. "It's been lovely, Professor Bell, but I really must go."

Gladys put a heavy, sweaty hand on her arm to stop her. "Hey, Dorothy, where's the fire? Your cat's fine.

Helen just took that cute little Yorkie-wow-wow over to play with her."

Oh dear. Now Dorothy could hear sharp, excited yipping sounds from the nearby cabana. And a tiny, terrified meow.

"You are going down to the TV station tonight for GH Hamel's interview tonight, right? Oh, and that other one, too. The Carrie girl. They're looking for bodies to fill the studio audience, so since you're book club prez I let them know you'd be there."

Dorothy sighed. She'd secretly hoped to skip the live show, actually, but it was probably a good idea to attend, and keep an eye on Georgiana. "I'll be there."

"Wait, GH Hamel's going to be on TV live?" the professor said. "Where? What time?"

"WMLO. Doors open at five," Gladys said as Dorothy gracefully removed herself from the big woman's grasp. "Use the bathroom first, though. They don't let anyone out of the room once the cameras start rolling."

"On that note," Dorothy said, "I'm sure I will see you both later."

She hurried away to rescue Guinevere, before anyone could try to stop her this time. She would broach the subject of Lorella again—and Georgiana—with Professor Bell later, and listen to what he had to say.

But she had definitely heard enough from him for now.

"ARE YOU TWO OKAY?" Dash asked Summer, the second she and Juliette-Margot stepped into the foyer. "I got your message, but it was all garbled."

"We're fine. Well, we are now, anyway." Summer headed straight for the living room and flopped onto the nearest white couch.

Dash scooped Juliette-Margot, whose eyes were still a little red and puffy, into his arms. "What happened? You both look like you've been through the spin cycle."

Summer stuck a throw pillow over her face. "Don't ask."

"I take it things didn't go well at Safari Sue's," Dash said. When Summer peeked out at him from under the cushion, he nodded toward the empty plastic turtle carrier on the Berber rug.

"We saw a big, *très* poisonous spider," Juliette-Margot said. "But Summer grabbed Juliette-Margot and we ran back into Lime Rickey's."

Dash seemed speechless.

"Don't worry, everything turned out okay," Summer assured him. "There was a cute, off-duty fireman there and he captured the tarantula thing with his helmet. Scooped it right off the car door." It was a good thing, too. She drew the line at gross bugs and all snakes.

"A *tarantula*? On your car? You're joking, right?"

"Nope. I called that nice vet who's taking care of Skipperdee, Dr. Josie, because I thought maybe the thing came from Safari Sue's, but it didn't."

"It came from the store where the big snake lives," Juliette-Margot put in helpfully. "His name is Camo."

"Camo from the sign for that sleazy exotic pets store over on Immokalee? With the bars on the windows? You took my daughter *there*?" Dash's face turned an unflattering shade of violet. "If Julian finds that out, we're both dead."

"No, no, no," Summer said quickly. "That was before I picked Juliette-Margot up. Besides, the tarantula might have just been a random deal. You know, it might have dropped off a piece of fruit from someone's grocery bag in a parking lot or something."

"Right." Dash did not sound convinced.

Summer wasn't, either. Could Ray have been lurking somewhere while she was talking to his employee about Skipperdee, and dropped the nasty spider into her car?

"Skipperdee is going to live with Dr. Josie and Safari Sue and all the other turtles," Juliette-Margot told her dad. "Because he can't live in our bathtub anymore."

He sighed. "Well, that's nice, honey."

Georgiana suddenly swept into the living room from the lanai, dressed in a black-and-gold caftan. "I couldn't help overhearing," she said, taking her granddaughter from Dash and sitting down in the armchair across from Summer. "Don't worry, darling, *Grandmère* will get you a much more interesting pet. How about a pony?"

"Mother," Dash warned. "Don't start."

Georgiana turned to Summer. "You are a most intriguing young woman, my dear. Tell me, does trouble always follow you like this? I must create a character..." Her face clouded over. "But I still don't have my writing notebook."

"I'm sure it will turn up," Dash said. "I saw it in your bag at the Algonquin dinner."

"Yes." Georgiana frowned. "I always carry it with me in case I need to jot ideas. And I am quite sure someone stole it."

"Maybe it just fell out somewhere," Dash tried. "I've already checked with the club. Twice."

Georgiana sniffed. "Well, I really don't think I'll be able to attend that TV interview tonight unless I find it. Why should I have to share the stage with that journeyman hack Carrie Lumbar, anyway?"

"Dunbar," Summer corrected. It almost sounded as if the newbie author was more of a problem for the great GH Hamel than any missing notebook.

"They can just do the show without me," Georgiana said, with a dismissive wave. "I'll stay home here and cheer up my precious granddaughter who's mourning the loss of her beloved pet."

Juliette-Margot started to droop with gloom again.

"He's not dead," Summer said quickly.

"Here's an idea," Dash said. "Julian and I will take care of our daughter tonight, Mother, and Summer will take you to the interview. Maybe you can stop for a cocktail or two on the way."

"Sure," Summer said, eager to make up the turtle and tarantula fiascos to her friend. "You can't let all your fans down, Georgiana. They'll be dying to see you on TV. I'll be back to pick you up at three-thirty."

TWENTY-FOUR

DOROTHY TRIED TO give herself a silent pep talk as she, Summer, and Georgiana pulled up to the WMLO studios at almost exactly five o'clock.

Accompanying GH Hamel to this interview was definitely the right thing to do. As she'd reminded herself several times, she needed to support Georgiana and Carrie. It was her unwritten duty as the chief organizer of the Hibiscus Pointe Book Club.

Besides, other than her son, Georgiana didn't have a dedicated assistant, as Carrie did, to take care of any issues that might pop up. And having gotten to know GH Hamel, there were sure to be at least a few of those.

Plus, once everyone was occupied, she and Summer would have a chance to compare notes on the case so far for the day. They hadn't been able to talk freely over those cocktails, with Georgiana there.

The author had insisted on Larry's Lizard Lounge, a somewhat questionable establishment attached to a motor inn just off the highway. Dorothy suspected Georgiana might have had a drink or two before they'd picked her up at the house.

A breathless young woman in a bright blue WMLO blazer, most likely a college student, greeted them at the door. "Hi there," she said. "My name is Monesha, and I'm one of the interns here at the station. I'll be taking care of you, Ms. Hamel—it's an honor to meet you—so just let me know if there's anything you need."

"How about a drink?" Georgiana said.

Oh dear. That would be a very bad idea, Dorothy told herself. The woman was already tipsy. "Perhaps when you're all settled," she suggested.

"There's a bar set up in the greenroom," Monesha said. "The other author, Carrie—she said she's a friend of yours—is already there. Her publicist is helping set things up with our assistant producer—you know, sound check, teleprompter, that sort of stuff. For both of you, Ms. Hamel."

"Fine. I can't be bothered with minor details," Georgiana said. "And I always do my own makeup, just so you know."

The intern led them all into the greenroom.

"Hi!" Carrie said, from the makeup chair, where a stylist was struggling to curl her limp hair. "I've been waiting forever for you guys to get here."

Any changes resulting from the young woman's spa makeover yesterday were not immediately apparent to Dorothy, but she would never say so, of course. "Don't you look nice?" she said.

"Thanks," Carrie said. "Isn't this exciting?"

"So we're going to be featuring a very short excerpt from each of your books," Monesha told her and Georgiana. "But don't worry, you'll be reading straight from the teleprompter."

"I don't need a teleprompter," Georgiana called as the intern left. She pointedly ignored Carrie and accepted the gin and tonic Summer had mixed for her at the wet bar in the corner.

About two minutes later, the greenroom door opened

and Charles Bell stuck his head inside. Dorothy could see the top of Gladys's curly gray head just behind him.

Good heavens. What if someone had been in the middle of dressing?

"Just stopping by to say hello," the professor said. "Turns out I've been asked to join the literary conversation with you lovely author ladies."

"How...*nice*," Georgiana said. "We will see you onstage, then. Please let yourself out so I can"—she swirled her drink—"collect my thoughts for the interview."

"Of course," he said. "Maybe I can catch up with you after the segment, Ms. Hamel. It just so happens I have in my car that highly commercial manuscript I mentioned to you earlier. I've already had it edited by a literary expert, and I think—with your recommendation—it will be of great interest to your fine publisher, Maxwell & Perkins."

"We'll see." Georgiana took a large sip of her G&T. "Now get lost."

My, Dorothy thought as Charles scurried away, with Gladys right behind him. GH Hamel certainly didn't mince words.

"Sometimes you just have to get rid of wannabe vermin," the author said, with a side glance at Carrie.

Gladys poked her head back in. "Hey, Foxy Dot, not to worry," she said. "I have no lovey-dovey interest in Charles at all. I'm only tailing him for the case—which, by the way, I'm about to crack wide-open." Then she disappeared, to Dorothy's great relief.

Georgiana turned to Dorothy. "Who *was* that horrible woman and what was she talking about?"

"Nothing, really." Dorothy sighed. "Don't worry, Gladys is quite harmless."

"Just another wannabe rat," Summer added, from the back of the room. Dorothy frowned in her friend's direction, but if truth be told, she heartily agreed.

SUMMER AND DOROTHY slipped into the last seats left for the live interview—right in front of Gladys—just before a guy intern closed the studio doors.

"Oh dear," Dorothy said. "Parker must not have made it in time."

"She's in the wings," Summer said, pointing. "See, over there, pouring Georgiana's drink into a mug. Dash's mom can really hold her liquor."

"I'm not so sure of that," Dorothy said. "She should be more careful, don't you think? Especially speaking in public like this."

"Maybe she's nervous," Summer said. It was hard to imagine a famous author like GH Hamel freaking out, though.

"It's that Carrie kid." Gladys leaned over the backs of their seats. "She could make butter crazy."

Jeez. Summer guessed she and Dorothy wouldn't be having any private conversations. But they probably couldn't anyway, because another intern had just announced during the commercial break that the audience had to stay quiet. Except for lots of clapping after the interview, when the little Applause sign above their heads lit up.

It was just like being on a regular TV or movie set. She and Joy used to get to visit them when they were kids. Sometimes Syd had even let her sit in his folding producer chair. There was no food on this set, though. And all the walls were plain so they could use digital stuff like laser designs and weather maps and cheesy graphics to change things up.

Right now the background on the left side of the set said Book Corner. A hundred percent fake, and zero glam.

Another intern ran up and whispered something to the first one. How many interns did they have here at the TV station, anyway? Maybe she should send in a résumé. They probably didn't get paid, though.

"Okay, everybody," the first intern said to the audience. "Slight change of plans here. We need to do a quick, special news segment, so please keep the rustling to a minimum and no more talking, please."

The two news anchors, a square-jawed guy who looked like a blond Frankenstein and a bony woman in a supertight knit dress and tons of makeup, showed up a second later. They sat down behind their cheap news desk on the other side from the one where Georgiana, Carrie, and the professor waited in fake-leather chairs.

Felicia Hernandez seemed a little annoyed that she was stuck on the Book Corner fireside and wasn't going to deliver the breaking news, whatever it was.

The anchors tested the microphones and shuffled a bunch of papers. A stylist ran up and applied more powder to both of their faces. And then they were live.

"Milano police and wildlife officials are investigating reports of yet another spotting of a twelve-foot Burmese python that allegedly escaped Wednesday from an exotic pet store on Immokalee Boulevard in North Milano," the woman anchor read from the teleprompter. "The giant snake's owner, Ray Bob Slater, was unavailable for comment."

A photo of a huge, gross, evil-looking snake filled

the screen behind the news desk. "Oh my gosh," Summer whispered to Dorothy. "It's Camo! And if that snake's down there by the beach, Ray must be, too."

"Quiet!" Gladys said behind them, superloudly.

The background switched to the young woman reporter, Melanie Knight, who was filling in for Felicia Hernandez. She kept looking behind her as she tried to interview a cop about whether they knew where the snake was now, and a bunch of people in the crowd who all wanted to see it.

"Residents have been warned to keep their pets and small children inside, and avoid swamps, woods, and other areas of vegetation," Melanie told the cameras.

After viewers were treated to dark, fuzzy cell phone video footage of something long and slithery, the cameras cut back to the studio news anchors. They warned about the growing problem of invasive species in Florida, even right here in a highly populated area like Milano. Some were illegally imported into the country and escaped. Others were released into the swamps by illegal pet owners when they got too big to handle. And as the swampy habitats disappeared, from pollution and development, the creatures headed for the burbs for food.

Now the background showed a pic of some dinosaur-looking thing called a crocodile monitor lizard.

That did it. She was never going outside again.

She was almost relieved when the breaking news report ended, the lights went dim on the anchor desk side, and Felicia Hernandez launched right into the Book Corner segment.

She'd put on glasses so she'd look smarter, Summer noticed. "Hello, everyone, and welcome to Book Corner!" Felicia was all smiles again. "Today we're honored to have bestselling mystery author GH Hamel here in the studios—along with debut author Carrie Dunbar."

"Not really debut," Carrie piped in. "*Debut for Death* was my first book, and that one came out last year. But my new one is *A Killing Fog.*"

The interruption threw Felicia off her game, and Georgiana actually rolled her eyes as she took a long sip from her mug. "Oh. Of course. My apologies, Carrie," Felicia said. "And to my left, I'd like to introduce our local literary expert Professor Charles Bell, chair of the English Department right here at Santa Teresa College."

The Applause sign lit, and everyone clapped. Carrie looked as if she were about to pop with happiness. Georgiana seemed really moody, Summer thought, not exactly playing the charming author for her fans. And the professor was his usual smug self.

"So, Professor Bell, perhaps you could remark on GH Hamel's place in modern popular literature," Felicia began. "She's an established mystery novelist—a member of the Old Guard, some might say—but what do you see for the future of the genre?"

Carrie sat up superstraight. Beside Summer, Dorothy frowned in the dark. "Georgiana is hardly *old*," she said. "How ridiculous."

"Shh!" Gladys said. "I can't hear the professor."

Dorothy twisted in her seat. "He's not even talking, Gladys. Yet."

Ooo. Summer hardly ever saw Dorothy that annoyed.

"Well, if we look back through the entire history of the novel, and beyond the realm of the mystery genre..." the professor began. Summer tuned out as he began to drone on and on about books she'd never heard of. *Beowulf? Jude the Obscure?*

"Wake me up when it's over," she muttered to Dorothy, but her friend gave her a little nudge after what seemed like just a few seconds.

"But since we're considering literature of the future," the professor was saying—Carrie smiled at the audience—"I should mention, in full disclosure, that I have just completed a novel of my own. It's a story of high romantic intrigue, with elements of—"

"Thank you, Professor Bell." Felicia tried to cut him off. "I'm afraid we need to go to a commercial break right now." She urgently motioned to the guys in the control room booth. "And when we come back, our guest authors will share excerpts from their books."

All too soon, they were back to Book Corner. Summer was pretty sure Carrie read a different part of her book this time than she had at the signing party.

"That was lovely, don't you think?" Dorothy said. Everyone clapped as Carrie bounced back to her seat.

"I guess," Summer said. Carrie had finished reading just as she was starting to get half interested.

Georgiana strolled slowly to the microphone, carrying her mug. Then she waited, until the audience quieted down again.

When she started to speak, in that superlow, dramatic voice of hers, everyone was mesmerized. Even though she'd told the intern she didn't need the teleprompter, she was definitely reading from it, Summer noticed.

GH Hamel's story was just as good as Carrie's. Better, actually, because GH Hamel had already written tons of book. Even though she was obviously on autopilot, the scene she was reading was a lot more exciting.

The mystery writer character was confronting the guy who'd killed that old lady with all the money.

Summer sat up and paid more attention. Wow, this story was scary-amazing. But Georgiana was starting to slow down. She looked confused. And then really, really mad.

"This is outrageous!" the author suddenly thundered, whirling toward Felicia. "How *dare* you? What kind of ill-advised, unpardonable joke are you trying to pull here?"

"Oh no." Dorothy sounded really upset. "I knew she shouldn't have had those drinks."

Summer frowned. "I'm not sure that's it."

"Ms. Hamel, I don't know what you mean." Felicia sounded all fluttery, not like a reporter at all.

"You'll be hearing from my attorneys." Georgiana knocked over the microphone, which made a loud, muffled noise as she threw her empty mug at the dark news anchor desk. "Regarding blatant theft of intellectual property." Then she tossed her scarf over her shoulder and stomped off the set.

TWENTY-FIVE

THE MOMENT THE Book Corner host went to another emergency commercial break, Dorothy rushed for the studio door, with Summer right behind her.

Why had Georgiana stormed off the stage like that? Dorothy had heard of temperamental authors, of course, but no one could have expected that kind of diva behavior.

Georgiana was already on her way out of the green room. "Parker here has called me a town car," she said. "Clear the door, please."

"Georgiana, wait." Dorothy didn't budge. Neither did Summer. "Please tell us what on earth happened out there. Are you feeling ill? Is there anything we can do?"

"Hardly." The famous author sniffed. "I have my attorneys on speed dial, and they will take care of this matter quite expediently, I'm sure."

"Ms. Hamel, I can't tell you how sorry I am." Parker sounded extraordinarily anxious. "That wasn't even the section I chose for you, I swear. I don't know where that other one came from." She held out an open hardcover copy of *Murder in the Mist*, marked with sticky notes. "This is what I picked out."

Georgiana threw up her hands. "You ignorant girl."

Parker looked stricken.

"That's enough, Georgiana," Dorothy intervened quickly. "There is no need for any unkindness right now. Parker was doing you a favor, and I'm sure she had no intention of providing the wrong material."

The author turned toward Dorothy. "Obviously, none of you understand. The scene I read from the teleprompter was the climax of my next book. Not *Murder in the Mist*. The one that *no one* has read yet. That would be impossible, because it can only be found in my writing notebook."

"You mean, the one that's missing?" Summer asked.

Dorothy wished her sleuthing partner hadn't brought that up. She braced herself for Georgiana's reaction.

To her surprise, the author's broad shoulders slumped. "Yes."

"Georgiana, please let Summer and me take you back to Hibiscus Pointe," Dorothy said. "It would be so much better for you to be with friends right now. Parker can cancel the town car and make up some kind of explanation for your unexpected departure"—Carrie's publicist nodded—"and we'll have you home in no time."

The author agreed more readily than Dorothy had expected, and she and Summer bundled her into the MINI before she could change her mind.

"I simply cannot believe this," Georgiana said, from the tiny backseat. She definitely appeared to be in shock. "Who could have stolen my notebook? And picked out the spoiler scene for me to read in public, before the book was even published? I hadn't even typed it onto my computer yet. My story is ruined."

"No, it isn't," Summer said. "I really liked it. And you're such a great writer, I bet you can come up with an even more exciting scene on top of that one. You know—a double twist."

Georgiana fell silent for a moment. "Perhaps."

Dorothy was shocked by the turn of events—but then, maybe she shouldn't be. What had happened to Georgiana had something to do with Lorella's death, she was sure of it. There were just too many shared connections between the two authors for the teleprompter incident and the missing notebook to be pure coincidence. Their personal and academic backgrounds, their publisher, their parallel success, even Hibiscus Pointe...

A missing notebook, no matter what its contents, hardly compared with murder. But locating it might very well lead them to the other author's killer.

Could that same person be targeting Georgiana for something much more sinister than a crucial plot reveal from her next, not yet published, best seller?

And, Dorothy wondered, did today's fiasco at the TV station let Georgina off the hook for Lorella's death?

No. Not necessarily, anyway. She was a mystery author, after all. She could very well have engineered a plot twist of her own for the case, to divert suspicion. Georgiana had to know that Dorothy and Summer were considering her possible involvement.

But who could have gotten their hands on that notebook? Charles Bell. Parker. Carrie. Anyone who had attended the Algonquin dinner, in fact, if that was indeed where it had disappeared.

From what Summer had told her on the way to pick Georgiana up this afternoon, the author had seemed quite certain about that.

Even Felicia Hernandez could have snatched the notebook from Georgiana's bag Saturday night, before she was called away on the sudden assignment.

But the news story—a fire, if she remembered correctly, was legit. Ernie had mentioned seeing the live report on TV. And Felicia didn't seem to have any motive to harm Georgiana's career—or murder Lorella Caldwell.

It was the reporter's job to scout out news. Would a scoop on Georgiana's unpublished book or Lorella's secret identity as Angelina St. Rose warrant theft and murder?

Possible. But highly unlikely.

Two suspects in Lorella's murder did seem to be in the clear for stealing Georgiana's notebook, however: Trixie and Ray. Certainly neither of them had shown up to the Algonquin dinner.

From the backseat, Georgiana blew her nose loudly on a handkerchief with a little skull and crossbones on the corner. In today's interview, she had been painted as a fading literary star.

Was the great author shedding tears over that precious notebook, or her relegation to the so-called mystery-writing Old Guard?

And why wasn't anyone shedding tears for her pseudonymous colleague, Lorella Caldwell?

SUMMER DROPPED OFF a still-fuming and sniffling Georgiana at Dash's, then walked Dorothy to her door at Hibiscus Gardens.

"If you don't mind, dear, I'm going to retire early tonight," Dorothy said. "I have a few leftovers, and may even just crawl into bed right now, with a book."

"Okay," Summer said. Fine with her. She needed a break, too, to clear her head and blow off some steam. It had been a crazy day.

But first, a quick nap. She and Dorothy were missing something, Summer told herself as she flopped out on Grandma Sloan's ugly couch, feeling like Skipperdee on his plastic island.

They had a whole bunch of pieces right in front of them, and none of them fit. If this were a *Citizen's Arrest* episode, they'd be in the last ten minutes already. That was usually when she had the crime solved herself and headed to the freezer for ice cream.

Three hours later, Summer woke up, ready to go. It was almost eleven, but she didn't feel like going downtown.

Not to a bar or club, anyway. It was the perfect time to go for a swim—and maybe even a little surfing.

She'd go to a really quiet beach. Nowhere near where all those news crews and crowds were. That snake sighting was probably a bogus report someone put up on Twitter as a joke, anyway.

She threw on a bathing suit and grabbed a striped Hibiscus Pointe pool towel—she'd have to return it sometime—from the floor of her bathroom. Then she headed to the lobby, making a quick stop at the storage closet around the corner from the elevator.

That was where she kept her surfboard. It wasn't like any Hibiscus Pointe residents were going to use it or anything.

The clock in the MINI, which was usually wrong, said eleven-twenty when she parked at the little sandy spot off the parking lot that security patrols usually missed. Milano beaches were officially closed an hour after sunset—they posted the exact time, down to the minute—but no one really cared about that, except the cops.

Plenty of people showed up at the beach at night: couples making out, homeless people looking for left-behind food and a comfy place to sleep, even guys with flashlights using those crazy metal detectors to find treasure—watches, rings, spare change.

Tonight, though, the place was deserted. She had the whole beach to herself.

Summer stepped off the boardwalk and kicked off her flip-flops, feeling the welcoming, still-warm sand between her toes. There was a full moon and the lamp-posts along the pier also gave extra light, so she shut off her cell flashlight app and carefully left the phone at the base of the boardwalk steps.

The waves weren't killer, but that was okay. Night surfing could be a little dangerous and you really had to know what you were doing. She was always super-careful. She'd even worn an all-black bathing suit so any sharks lurking out there—they liked to feed at night—wouldn't think she was food.

Paddling out smoothly, Summer took a few gentle waves. She felt better already. After a while, she just floated around on her board, staring at the moon. It was so peaceful she almost could have fallen asleep again.

Finally, she decided to pack it in. Trudging out of the water with her board, she headed to rinse off her feet at the sprinkler near end of the boardwalk. The night sky was starting to cloud now and it was getting kind of misty. The disgusting smell through the mangroves and banyans in the swamp surrounding the boardwalk was really kicking up now, too. Yuck. The wooden boards, rotting in parts, creaked as she quickly walked along.

"Ouch!" She'd stepped out of one of her flip-flops and onto a nail or something. Wincing, she turned on her cell flashlight again. Yep, she was bleeding. Not too much, but enough to gross her out.

Yikes. Another light, a bigger one, was moving out there in the swamp. Straight toward her.

Who—or what—was that? Summer shut off her light

and stifled a gasp as the moon suddenly emerged from be-hind the clouds. An RV—mostly hidden by vegetation—was parked out in the swamp on a broken section of old boardwalk, which was half-sunken into the gunk. She could just make out the words "Happy Trailways."

Trixie and Ray! Summer had to call Detective Don-ovan, immediatamente.

She was so excited and nervous she dropped her cell phone. It fell through the railing of the boardwalk, straight into the freaking swamp.

Summer muttered under her breath, even though no one could hear her. Well…maybe Ray and Trixie. With-out her phone, she was dead meat. Plus, the moon had disappeared again and she was too far from the lamp-posts to see much.

Her phone was gone. Unless it got caught on a root or something. Maybe, if she leaned over the railing, she could try to scoop it up with her surfboard…

Summer laid herself flat on her stomach and reached out the board. It was way too short. But when the moon popped out again, she found herself staring into a large, gleaming eye.

Hoooly spumoni… She couldn't make out the whole thing in the darkness—but judging by the size of the head, she didn't need to.

Camo. And she was definitely out of here, suspects or no suspects.

Summer charged down the long, twisting boardwalk in her bare feet toward the deserted parking lot. She kept a good grasp on her long board in case she needed to fend off a ginormous reptile.

Which one would be worse, Camo or Ray? Or flying bullets from Trixie's buddy General Luger?

TWENTY-SIX

DOROTHY WENT TO bed almost as soon as she'd arrived home from the TV station, but even after reading for hours, she couldn't sleep.

Now it was just past midnight.

A ball of warm gray fur snuggled up against her, purring loudly. She'd been letting the cats take turns sleeping on the bed. Right now it was Guinevere's turn, while Mr. Bitey sulked in the kitchen.

"Sweet kitty," Dorothy said, scratching her under the chin. Still no messages on her machine from any potential adopters. That alone was enough to keep her up at night, but figure in her and Summer's murder investigation, and the bouts of insomnia had increased threefold.

Perhaps some warm milk would help.

Leaving Guinevere stretched out on her good comforter, Dorothy padded to the kitchen in her chenille slippers and set out a saucepan. Microwaved milk never tasted the same.

"Here you go, Mr. Bitey," she said to her other cat, placing a small saucer down on the linoleum floor. Maybe that would cheer him up.

Returning to the bedroom with her steaming mug, she flipped on the TV. Nothing was on other than infomercials and a repeat of the news—Georgiana's reading and her storming out of today's interview had thankfully been edited out, turning the spotlight on Carrie and her book.

Dorothy also found a Heartflower Channel remake movie based on, of all things, an Angelina St. Rose novel she'd read years ago. During one of the racier parts—now rather boring after being toned down for TV—she flipped through Lorella's Moleskine notebook again. Maybe she had missed something.

A burst of overly foreboding music sounded from the TV, and Dorothy's attention returned to the screen. Before she knew it, she became absorbed in the story, unable to stop herself from making comparisons between the original and the remake.

The new actors weren't quite as good, in her view, but the female lead was appealing enough and the hero indisputably handsome.

Almost before she knew it, the movie ended and the credits began to roll. When the book credit came onto the screen, Dorothy nearly flattened Guinevere as she jackknifed up in bed.

The "based on the novel by" credit didn't go to Angelina St. Rose. The name listed on the screen was Carrie Dunbar.

How was that possible? It had to be some mistake.

Then Dorothy looked down at the notebook that had fallen from her lap, open to the calendar section.

Were all those references to *C* for Charles? Or... Carrie?

FREAKED-OUT AND PHONELESS, Summer tried not to panic as she strapped her long board to the top of the MINI in record time. She wasn't leaving her board here, no matter what. Then she sped to the Milano PD Headquarters downtown.

When she arrived, she pulled on her shorts and a

T-shirt from the backseat over her still-wet bathing suit and ran into the station.

"I need to talk to Detective Donovan," she said breathlessly. "It's really important. Is he here?"

"He's done with his shift, but I think so." The young guy behind the enclosed booth just inside the door looked through the small, round window. "Can I ask what you need to see him for?"

"Information about the Caldwell case. Tell him it's Summer."

The guy nodded and made a quick inside call. "Detective Donovan will be out in a minute."

So he was going to escort her inside. Well, that was nice of him. But the tail of her oversize tee was dripping on the station house floor. Casually, she tried to wring it out behind her back and step away without the reception guy noticing.

That looked even worse.

The detective took longer than a minute. It was more like ten minutes. When he finally came out, he looked beat. And he had his laptop with him.

"Wow, you look tired," Summer said.

He smiled, sort of. "I am. Rough day. So, what did you want to tell me?"

"Well, guess what? I know where Trixie and Ray and the van are. And that crazy-big snake." Talking fast, she gave him the location of the van and exactly where she'd had the close encounter with Camo. Then she started to shiver. A lot.

"S-s-sorry," she said, sounding like a snake herself. But she was freezing, and she couldn't stop her teeth from chattering.

"Hey, are you okay there? You're in shock, or you

might be having a panic attack. And your foot looks a little bloody. Do you want to go into the squad room and sit down? Here, take this." He pulled a navy sweatshirt tied to the strap of his laptop bag and held it out.

"Th-th-thanks." Summer pulled the shirt over her head. Milano PD. Pretty cool. But she still couldn't stop shaking.

Detective Donovan rapped on the window of the little booth. "Hey, Mike, can you get us some Band-Aids and a cup of hot chocolate?" He looked back at Summer. "Unless you'd rather have tea or coffee? I thought maybe the extra sugar might help."

"Hot chocolate's f-fine," Summer said. She hadn't had much of it since she moved to Florida, but right now it sounded great.

The detective nodded and gestured toward the chair she'd used while waiting for him to come out. Then he made a couple of quick calls, but he stepped away toward the squad room door and she couldn't hear what he said.

"So, do you want to go downtown with me?" he asked her after he'd hung up.

"Sure." Oh, good. She was going to be in on the action when the detective brought in Ray and Trixie. And maybe Camo. Ugh. That wasn't quite as good. She'd stay in the squad car for that.

To Summer's surprise, Detective Donovan pulled the unmarked car into the parking lot of the Tick-Tock Diner, not far from the beach. The sign in the window said, "Open Round the Clock."

"What are we doing here?" Summer asked.

He smiled. "Waiting. I come here a lot."

"But what about Trixie and Ray and that freaking

snake? I don't know whether they saw me—well, Camo did, I guess. They might get away."

The detective got of the car and came around to open her door. Wow. The only other guy she knew who did that was Dash. "No, they won't," he said. "I made a couple of calls before we left the station. My team and Animal Control can handle things for now—and this way, I can be sure you're not going to be in any danger."

Summer frowned. "But I found the RV and your suspects for you. And the stupid snake. Can't I at least be there when Ray and Trixie get arrested?"

"I can see you're already feeling much better." This time Detective Donovan opened the diner door. "But I didn't have dinner, and maybe something to eat will help calm you down. We'll be notified as soon as anything happens, okay? And I'm buying."

The Tick-Tock Diner smelled like bacon. And sausage and eggs and pancakes. "Okay," she said.

It was hard to decide what to order off the huge, multifold menu. Everything sounded delicious. "I'll have the Milano Medley," Summer said. "With extra whipped cream on the waffles. Oh, and a side order of bacon, please. It comes with sausage and biscuits already, right?"

The waitress just nodded and scribbled on her notepad. She looked a little like Carrie, but she definitely wasn't as talkative.

Detective Donovan ordered two eggs over easy with toast, coffee—black—and a side of fruit. When the silent waitress brought their plates, he seemed amused by her towering breakfast. "Are you sure you can handle all that?" he asked.

"Yep," Summer said. "Can you pass the syrup, please?"

They didn't talk much, since they were both busy eating, but it wasn't one of those awkward silences or anything. Just kind of comfortable. Summer was digging into her home fries when the detective's cell buzzed on the table.

"Donovan." She strained to hear the caller on the other end, but the detective turned away from the table slightly, and frowned. Uh-oh. Had Ray and Trixie gotten away?

They could have gotten out of that swamp fast, on the broken, sinking boardwalk.

"So what happened?" Summer asked the second he hung up. "Did they get them?"

"The RV has been located and secured," the detective said. "And Ray was taken into custody without incident. We can only question him for the Caldwell case, I'm afraid, but we can hold him for a while on possible RV theft. And maybe a few other things."

Summer's stomach tightened, and not from the waffles and breakfast meat. "What about Trixie? She's pretty slippery."

He sighed, and took another sip of his coffee. "She didn't seem to be around, and the team is very thorough. They've got canines in the area now. Ray isn't talking. Says he has no idea where Trixie is now."

"And what about"—Summer shivered again—"my buddy Camo?"

"No sign of the snake, either."

Summer looked down at her plate. The syrup-logged waffles didn't look very appetizing anymore. How could Trixie have given everyone the slip?

If she was even down by the beach in the first place.

Summer hadn't actually seen her tonight. That woman could be anywhere.

Plus, no one was going to believe her about Camo. This was the second time she'd seen the python. How could people not find something that big?

Summer and the detective finished eating in silence—not so much the good kind anymore, either. He seemed preoccupied now, and she was bummed about Trixie.

And this diner date didn't really count as a date. It was more like a work thing. Or worse, maybe he'd just felt sorry for her, because she'd been a hot stuttering mess tonight. His hand had brushed hers when they both reached for the ketchup. That was it.

She hated to admit it, but his grandma was right. He needed a nice, careful, put-together girl like Jennifer.

"I know someone you could call about the snake," Summer said, suddenly remembering as Detective Donovan signaled for the check. "Dr. Josie over at Safari Sue's." She handed him the vet's crumpled card from her bag.

"Fish and Wildlife is working on it," he said. "As well as Milano PD. But I guess it wouldn't hurt to see if she might be willing to consult. Thanks. So far, no one's managed to bring that reptile in."

Just like Trixie, Summer thought.

The ride back to the station house was supershort. Detective Donovan drove like a guy in a hurry, which was a good thing. They needed to be there when Ray arrived in handcuffs.

The detective pulled into a space and opened the car door again. "So, will Ray be here soon?" Summer asked him as she got out.

"Should be," he answered. "But *you* won't be here then."

Was he kidding? "Why not?"

"I'm sorry, but this is police business," the detective said. "Besides, you were one of the people who found Lorella Caldwell's body. That makes you a witness. So it's better if you're not around when Ray is brought in."

"Why is that a problem?" Summer said. "I can identify Ray in a lineup or something."

"We really don't need you to do that," Detective Donovan said. "You shouldn't even be here right now, in fact. How would it look in court if a detective was personally involved with a witness?"

Wait. What? They were "personally involved" now? "Okay," she said reluctantly, leaning back a little against the car. "I get it."

"But hey, thank you," he said. "You've been a big help in the case. And now it's time for you to step out, okay? You could have been in real danger tonight."

She was about to answer when he suddenly leaned in and kissed her, quickly and very gently. Almost without thinking, she put her arms around his neck and kissed him back, longer, feeling his broad, windbreakered chest against her damp sweatshirt.

But oh noooo. *Jennifer.*

She still didn't know for sure what the deal was between them, but this didn't seem like the right time to ask. And now she was weirdly shaking again.

"I h-have to go," she said, moving away. "Before, uh, Ray gets here."

He looked confused, then embarrassed. "Right." He sounded all business again. "Sorry, I don't know why I did that. It was a mistake."

"That's okay," Summer said. "Well, bye. Thanks for dinner. I mean, breakfast." Jeez. This was awkward. And it was killing her. Before he could say anything else, she jumped in her car and pushed the ignition.

He leaned in the open window. "Straight home, right?" he said. "Please?"

She gave him what she hoped was a reassuring smile in the glow from the round lamps outside the PD. "Right."

For once, she wasn't going to argue.

TWENTY-SEVEN

By now it was nearly 2:00 a.m., but Dorothy was up and dressed. She was determined to find some answers—in the Hibiscus Pointe Library.

She was fairly sure she'd seen a particular title she needed in Summer's grandma's estate collection. She'd just shelved it the other day. And she definitely couldn't sleep now, after seeing Carrie's name in the book credit for the remake of Lorella's movie. If she headed over to the library at this hour, no one would see or bother her.

Dorothy felt very alone as she made her way through the Hibiscus Pointe complex to the main building. It was dark and still, although there were a few points of light here and there in the condo windows. Other insomniacs, no doubt.

Maybe she should have called Summer, in case she was still up. But her friend had said she was going down to the beach earlier. Hopefully, she was being careful.

Dorothy slipped past a dozing Bill Beusel and let herself into the library. Maybe she should leave the door ajar, in case anyone was lurking inside.

Ridiculous, she told herself. That movie must have spooked her.

It looked as if someone had undone a bit of the organizational work she'd done the other day. Just a few little things here and there, but still. Fortunately, it didn't seem to be the work of the library vandal who might have also murdered Lorella.

Probably one of the library patrons who'd been in a hurry. Or confused. But who had been the vandal on the day Lorella died? Was that person also the murderer? And what had they been looking for?

Dorothy went straight to the extensive romance section and discovered that the Angelina St. Rose title she'd wanted, and had just shelved, was no longer there.

Very disappointing. She'd have to try the Milano Library, then. Was it more than a coincidence, though, that the book had disappeared so quickly?

Click.

Oh dear. Was that someone coming into the library? No. She'd left the door open.

Very slowly, Dorothy turned.

"Hold it right there, hon." Trixie was standing in the middle of the library—with General Luger pointed straight at her.

Dorothy cleared her throat and tried to speak, but the words wouldn't quite come out. "What are you doing here, Trixie? And what do you want?"

"It's real simple," Trixie said. "I'm lookin' for that book on the Berkeley Pit copper mine. You know, in Montana."

Dorothy tried not to look at the pistol. What on earth? She'd read an article once on that mine, in fact. It had closed years ago, and now it was a major Superfund cleanup site. "There's no need for the gun, Trixie," she said. "For heaven's sake. I took that title out of circulation to repair it. All it needed was a touch of glue."

"So where is it?" Trixie was growing impatient.

Dorothy glanced toward Lorella's desk, where she'd set the book to dry. "Over there."

"Let's go find it, then." The blond woman, her heavy jewelry clanking, marched Dorothy toward the desk. Her eyes lit with glee when she spotted the thick volume, opened out on the ink-stained blotter. "That's it!"

Eagerly, she began to flip through the pages, still keeping the pistol trained on Dorothy. When she reached the end, she frowned. "There's supposed to be a map in here. It shows all the places you can find copper."

And noxious chemicals, no doubt, Dorothy thought. "I'm sorry, Trixie. It looks as if that page may have been torn out. See, the jagged edge there, where it should have been?"

Trixie stamped her black-and-red cowboy boot. "That is not fair! The book is out of print, and I can't find another copy anywhere. I need it for my trip. Find that page right now, or you're Texas toast."

SUMMER ARRIVED BACK at Hibiscus Pointe feeling totally wired. The last few hours had been too crazy for her to deal with. No, the whole day had been a disaster, too.

But she'd found the RV and Ray, she reminded herself. And the snake. And she'd helped keep Georgiana from self-destructing. Oh, and she'd survived a gnarly, hairy tarantula.

Was she forgetting something? Probably. She wasn't even going to count the whole thing with Detective Donovan. Or think about it. If she went to bed right now, she'd probably have nightmares.

Which reminded her of something else. When she'd dropped Dorothy home earlier, after all the crazy stuff went down with Georgiana, she promised she would help her in the library. First thing in the morning so they could talk about the case.

No way was she going to make it before noon. She'd probably crash when the sun came up. What if she went to the library now and got rid of some book boxes and stuff? She could leave Dorothy a note telling her she didn't feel so great and knew she'd have to sleep in, so she came in a little early?

That would work. She couldn't wake up Dorothy now to explain. Besides, it was true, right?

Summer passed Mr. Bill the security guy on her way in to the main lobby. He didn't even hear her, because he was watching a breaking news report on a tiny TV about the snake hunt down by the beach. She was tempted to stop, but if she did she might never make it to the library.

She didn't want to see Camo again, anyway. Ever.

When she reached the hallway outside the library, the door was open. *Oh my gosh*, was that Dorothy working at two in the morning? Her friend sure was dedicated.

Oh. No. Trixie was there, too. And she had a gun.

There was no time to think. Her stupid cell was gone. And she wasn't going back to tell Bill. He was useless. And what if Trixie killed Dorothy while she was gone?

Summer removed her tennis shoes. She knew, from years of sneaking into her dad's house from the clubs as a kid, that bare feet were always quieter.

Very, very slowly, she moved toward the door. Neither Dorothy nor Trixie had seen her yet. If she could get the gun away from the rodeo queen's sister, everything might be okay.

The two of them were looking at a book, but they

faced the door. If Trixie glanced up, she was dead. Well, hopefully not.

She'd have to go for it. Luckily, Hibiscus Pointe's carpets were pretty thick. It was those wooden floors she had to worry about. Much worse than the marble.

"Trixie, I just don't think that page with the map is still around here," Dorothy said. Her friend sounded supercalm, even with a pistol pointed at her. "If it was damaged, I may have discarded it. I'm sorry. Why don't we—"

"No, we have to find it." Trixie waved General Luger around over Dorothy's head. "Keep looking."

Dorothy glanced toward the door and saw her. Summer put her fingers to her lips, and Dorothy frowned and shook her head very slightly as Trixie grabbed a folder from the desk and started frantically throwing all the papers around.

Summer's partner didn't want her to risk her safety.

"Wait, let's check this page, Trixie." Dorothy flipped a few pages in the big, open book on the desk. "We missed this one, I think. Is this the map you need?"

Trixie peered down at the book, and Dorothy gave Summer a quick nod toward the lobby. She wanted her to leave.

Sorry, Dorothy. Summer lunged through the library doorway and knocked the pistol from Trixie's hand before she knew what hit her. Then Summer tackled the blond woman to the floor and sat on her.

"Oof," Trixie said. She looked a little dazed. Well, that was easy, Summer thought. Maybe she should take up rodeo.

Dorothy kicked the gun away. "Grab it," Summer said.

"No need," her friend said. She took the big book

from Lorella's old desk, rushed to the wall, and slammed the book through the glass on the fire alarm.

The alarm actually worked. They'd have the fire department and cops here in no time. And maybe even ol' Bill.

Too bad it couldn't have saved Lorella. "You're going down," Summer told Trixie, "for the murder of Lorella Caldwell. And the attempted murder of Dorothy Westin."

"What? That gun isn't even loaded. Get off me, you understuffed scarecrow." Trixie tried to give her a push. Pieces of light brown hair were sticking out from her wig now. "And y'all are crazy. I didn't kill Miss Lorella, no, sirree, Bob. And neither did Ray. She was one nice lady."

TWENTY-EIGHT

"WE DON'T BELIEVE YOU," Summer said to Trixie as the fire alarm continued to blare. Dorothy's partner was still sitting on their slightly deflated suspect.

"You and Ray bumped off Lorella together, didn't you?" Summer went on. "Well, just so you know, your skeezy boyfriend is in Milano PD custody right now."

Dorothy raised an eyebrow. She hadn't heard *that* news yet. But she hadn't had a chance to tell Summer her new theory about Carrie, either. "Trixie may be right," she said to her partner.

"Dang straight I'm right." Trixie looked furious. "Ray and I were gonna strike it rich in Montana. At a closed up mine that's chock-full of copper."

"Not the Berkley Pit Mine, I hope." Dorothy shuddered. She'd learned a few things about the current Superfund site when she was mending that book, and they didn't sound pretty. Quite toxic, in fact.

"Nope, another one," Trixie said. "But it's close by, in a very secret location. That's why I need that map. Now let me go so I can make me a fortune. I'll do it for Ray while he's in the slammer."

"I'm sorry, Trixie," Dorothy said. "That isn't going to happen."

"No, it isn't." Detective Donovan, looking a little less crisp than usual, strode into the library.

My, that was fast. He'd beaten the fire department here.

Summer almost tumbled off Trixie, she looked so surprised. How had her friend gotten her hands on an extra-large Milano PD sweatshirt? "Where's the team?" she said. "I can't believe it's you again."

"Likewise." The detective's voice was clipped, but Dorothy was almost sure she'd seen an amused quirk to his lips.

He turned to Trixie. "Your buddy Ray sang," he told her as Summer got out of the way so he could place the still-struggling woman in handcuffs. "Guess he wanted to lessen those possible charges of illegal, exotic animal possession and trade, fraud, check bouncing, unarmed robbery, and vehicle theft." He nodded toward the pistol on the carpet, a few feet away. "You might want to consider the same."

"I'm not talkin'," Trixie said. "And I need me a lawyer."

Detective Donovan turned back to Dorothy and Summer. "I'll speak with you ladies tomorrow. Get some rest."

Standing beside her friend as the detective led a babbling Trixie away, Dorothy felt an overwhelming sense of dizziness and fatigue at the mention of rest. "I think I should get home," she said to her friend. "Quickly."

"I've got the car right outside," Summer said. "Do you think you can make it to the lobby with me?"

"Of course, dear." Dorothy's voice sounded faint even to her own ears. "I have a new theory for the case I want to share with you, about our friend Carrie, but… it may have to wait until morning, I'm afraid."

"Don't worry, Dorothy." Summer took her arm as the two of them slowly left the library together. "I've got your back here."

"I know," Dorothy said.

WHEN SUMMER WOKE up in Dorothy's guest room, sunshine was streaming through the condo. She had no idea what time it was, and she didn't care.

The phone was ringing out in the kitchen. Summer was tempted to let it go, but she didn't want it to wake Dorothy. Her friend needed her sleep more than she did. She stumbled out to the kitchen, but the message machine had already picked up.

"Hi, Dorothy," the male voice said. "It's—"

"Hey, Dash," Summer said. "You're on speaker. What's up?"

Dorothy came up behind her, tying her fuzzy robe. "Ask him whether Georgiana's writing notebook has been found yet," she whispered.

Huh? That had to be the least of their problems right now.

"No." Dash sighed. "But I have other news. You're going to love this. Your pal Gladys has taken it upon herself to organize a book club boat trip—for this afternoon."

Ugh, Summer thought. She was definitely not up for that today.

"I'm going to take Mother, in an effort to distract her—she's still agitated about the notebook, so I can't be responsible for anything she says—and Juliette-Margot."

"Sounds, uh, fun," Summer said.

"My beloved has begged off, pleading nausea that sea sickness will apparently not improve," Dash went on. "But there will be box lunches and champagne. You and Dorothy are going, right?"

"Yes," Dorothy said, behind her.

"Do we have to?" Summer asked after Dash had re-layed the details and signed off.

"I don't care to go, either." Dorothy sighed. "And I never budgeted for champagne and a party boat, no matter how much money Lorella left the book club. But we need to be there to watch Georgiana. And Carrie."

Summer listened as her friend told her about the Heartflower movie she'd seen last night, and the idea of Carrie possibly plagiarizing Angelina St. James's work.

"Lorella must have found out, and threatened to expose her," Dorothy said. "But if she did so, you see, Lorella's identity as Angelina would also come out."

Summer hopped on a stool at the breakfast counter. "Well, if Angelina's books are so famous, how come no one's noticed yet that Carrie is ripping her off?"

"I'm not sure," Dorothy said, "but that Heartflower movie was based on one of Angelina's earliest works, so it's lesser known. And Carrie writes to a younger generation."

"True." Summer leaned her elbows on the counter. "No one's really noticed Carrie's books yet, either. Even after she hired her own publicist."

"Exactly." Dorothy dodged Mr. Bitey as she rummaged through the cupboards for any remnants of instant coffee. "Your breakfast is coming," she told him. "Be patient like Guinevere."

So she and Dorothy definitely had to go on the boat lunch. If it was true Carrie stole Angelina St. Rose's ideas, then the wannabe probably wouldn't turn down a chance to pick up any tidbits from other famous authors, now that Lorella was dead.

Like GH Hamel, for instance.

"I just don't get it, though," Summer said to Dorothy.

"Why would Carrie release spoilers from Georgiana's brand-new, unpublished book on that teleprompter during a live TV interview, then? I mean, it would spoil things for her own book, too, if she stole the story and published it before GH Hamel."

"True..." Dorothy tapped her chin.

"Wait, how about this?" Summer said excitedly. "Parker hates Carrie. What if she knows her client's been stealing other writers' stuff, and she's setting her up to fall?"

"A bit far-fetched, I think," Dorothy said. "Don't worry, I have a plan to help us prove who stole GH Hamel's notebook. But we'll need Georgiana's help."

"I thought you were really tired," Summer said as Dorothy poured them each a glass of expired orange juice.

Dorothy smiled. "Not anymore, dear."

TWENTY-NINE

SUMMER AND DOROTHY arrived at the Milano Marina Dock just in time to make it onto the book club party boat.

"Am I glad to see you!" Dash greeted Summer. He looked sharp but overly heated in a striped Oxford shirt and red Bermuda shorts. "La Madre is in rare form," he added, with a nod over his shoulder at Georgiana. She stood at the bow of the boat, with her arms stretched out to the wimpy breeze like Rose in *Titanic*.

Professor Bell was right behind her. Summer actually felt sorry for Georgiana right now. No escape.

Wait. The professor wasn't going to push her, was he? Nope, worse. He was taking his manila envelopes out of his monogrammed boat bag.

It was too painful to watch. Summer turned away.

Beside her father, Juliette-Margot looked as if she'd jumped out of *Vogue Kids* in an adorable straw hat and sailor dress, with boat-shoe Mary Janes. "*Bonjour*, Summer, and Madame Dorothy. Have you seen the pretty fish?" She pointed to the glass bottom floor between their feet.

"My, aren't they beautiful?" Dorothy said.

"Papa, can Juliette-Margot have fish? Pretty ones, in beaucoup colors? We still have the aquarium *Grandmère* ordered for Skipperdee."

"Tropical fish are very hard to take care of, honey," Dash said, looking to Summer for help.

"You're on your own now, dude," she told him, over Juliette-Margot's head. "I'm done with animals."

"Doooorothy!" Gladys, dressed in full nautical gear, flapped over, playing the gracious hostess. If she were Dorothy, Summer thought, she'd be on her last nerve.

Actually, Dorothy seemed just fine with Gladys taking over on event duties. Her friend seemed a little book-clubbed out lately. Too bad Ernie wasn't here today for her to hang out with. But she and Dorothy did have to work on the case, Summer reminded herself.

"Whattaya say you go over with me, Dot, and help convince GH Hamel to read the professor's manuscript?" Gladys asked. "I've been spending a lot of time with him lately," she added, lowering her voice for once. "You know, for the investigation. He said he really needed reader reviews for test marketing, and he values my opinion very highly, of course. I've already read four hundred pages."

"Sorry, Mrs. Rumway," Summer said, taking her sleuthing partner by the elbow. "Dorothy and I need to talk to Parker over there."

As the two of them headed toward the cabin, where Parker was helping one of the boat crew bring out boxes with the food and plastic wineglasses, Summer stopped with her friend to eavesdrop on Georgiana and the professor.

It wasn't too difficult.

"I don't know how in blazes Lorella put up with you," Georgiana was saying, loudly as usual. She and Gladys sure had that in common. "But *I'm* not going to. You and your pathetic, self-described epic romance novel can take a dive into the ocean, for as much as I care. And if you keep trying to ingratiate yourself with me, I'll throw you overboard myself."

"Well," Dorothy muttered. "I think GH Hamel has made herself quite clear."

"Hello, everyone!" Parker called into the crowd. "And welcome to the S.S. *Hamel-Dunbar*. Before we get this party started, I'd like to make an announcement."

"Yes," Georgiana boomed in. "If anyone here has my writing notebook, I'm serving you notice that you will be dealt with to the fullest extent of the law. And my personal capabilities, which might be a lot worse."

Before she could get another word out, Dash ran up to her with a glass and a newly popped bottle of champagne. "Look, just for you, Mother. Someone put your name over the label. Wasn't that thoughtful?"

"Okay, so, here's the other announcement." Parker shot a nervous, sideways glance at Georgiana. "I have all the details on tomorrow night's festivities at Tangerine du Sol. It will be the last local event for GH Hamel, who will soon depart for New York, but good news: Because of growing enthusiasm for her new book, Carrie has agreed to extend her stay here in Milano for a few more weeks—so you won't have to say goodbye to her just yet!"

Summer stifled a groan. Beside her, she was pretty sure Dorothy did, too.

"Anyway," Parker went on, still looking urban trendy in her striped V-neck tee and short black skirt, "Maxwell & Perkins has agreed to sponsor tomorrow night's event, and it's going to be even bigger than we planned. In fact..." She paused. "GH Hamel's editor will be flying down from New York for this very exciting evening."

Casually, Summer turned, to check on Charles's reaction. Yep. The professor was practically foaming at the mouth.

"And if that isn't all, Maxwell & Perkins has also arranged a special sneak peek at the trailer for the major upcoming movie based on Georgiana's book *Good Night, Sweetheart*."

Ohhh. Summer suddenly remembered her dad's assistant had sent that same trailer to her in a box of stuff she hadn't really gone through yet. She was supposed to have watched it last week. Oops.

Well, she hadn't been home long enough to get the home theater installed. Besides, now she didn't even have a phone for the setup guys from Top This to reach her.

Dorothy nudged her in the ribs, and Summer snapped back to attention.

Georgiana was headed toward the tub of champagne bottles that had just been set out at the front of the boat. Now was her and Dorothy's chance to talk to her about their plan.

"It's still possible Georgiana just lost her own notebook, right?" Summer said as she and Dorothy made their way closer to the makeshift champagne bar at the S.S. *Hamel-Dunbar*'s bow. "I lose stuff all the time."

"Well, yes," Dorothy admitted. They couldn't rule out the idea that the author had killed Lorella herself, either. Maybe some kind of jealous rage—or some issue between the two of them that no one else knew about.

But so far, Georgiana didn't appear to have an obvious motive for disposing of Angelina St. James. One author wrote mystery, the other romance. And Lorella had hardly been a limelight stealer. She'd valued her privacy above all else, it seemed.

"Let me do the talking, dear," Dorothy said as they approached Georgiana.

She was a bit nervous about broaching their sting idea to GH Hamel. But the author heard Dorothy out as she sipped her bubbly.

"I couldn't help but notice that you have a new notebook in your tote, Georgiana. What would you think about tearing out any important material and replacing it with a few, nonsensical notes. Then you could let everyone know you've been jotting down some fresh, new ideas and set the tote—with the notebook inside—down in some semiobvious place?"

Georgiana cocked her head. "I see where you're going with this. It might work."

"Of course it will," Summer said.

Dorothy placed a light hand on her friend's arm. "Summer and I will watch the bag very carefully, and hopefully the thief"—perhaps Lorella's killer, she added silently—"will be revealed."

"Let's do it." Georgiana gave a sharp nod. "My money is on that insufferable Charles Bell."

"You could bring the notebook to the big party tomorrow night," Dorothy suggested.

"No," Georgiana said. "I don't want to wait. I need those notes. They were brilliant. I had a whole new plot outlined. I'll just make a few scribbles now as I enjoy this next glass of champagne."

At this point, Dorothy was almost ready for one herself. But it was much too early in the day, of course. And she needed to keep her wits about her.

Dorothy tried to relax a bit as she and Summer joined

Dash and Juliette-Margot on the cushioned benches set up near the middle of the boat. Their captain pointed out some lovely ocean landmarks of interest, as well as a charming pod of dolphins, and Georgiana put their plan into operation.

Everyone aboard seemed intrigued when the author let their fellow passengers know she had some maaahr-velous ideas for her next novel—even better than the ones revealed in that bloody TV interview.

Then Georgiana left her canvas tote with the propped-up notebook peeking out from under the skirted cooler beneath the drinks tub, as if she'd for-gotten it in a champagne haze. She played that part quite convincingly, Dorothy told herself.

She and Summer eagerly watched and waited as the captain told them about other various points of inter-est, including the new Milano Point Lighthouse. The updated but still classic-looking structure had replaced the crumbling, decommissioned metal one. The rem-nants of the former lighthouse became covered by the sea at high tide.

Fascinating.

But to Dorothy and Summer's extreme disappoint-ment as the flaming orange sun began to drop below the horizon, streaking the sky in shades of pink, blue, and lavender, no one took the notebook bait.

THIRTY

SUMMER FINALLY FELT like herself again, after a good twelve hours or so of sleep and a trip to the Horizon wireless store.

She had just finished setting up her brand-new, even better phone over at Dorothy's condo when it rang.

Dash. Again. What was it with that guy lately? Having his mom visiting sure stressed him out. On the other hand, if Harmony or Joy dropped into Milano, she'd probably be freaking, too.

"Hey," she answered. "What's up?"

"Major problem." His voice sounded different this time. Like, superworried and upset, not your regular panic. "Mother left in the Mercedes after the maid brought in the mail from our box this morning. There was an envelope with just her name printed on it that someone must have left there last night, because it was wet from all that rain we had."

"Was the envelope orange?" Summer asked, thinking of Trixie. Maybe she had mailed it earlier.

"No," Dash said. "White. No return address. No postage. It didn't go through the mail. Anyway, I didn't think much of it when Viola told me after I got home from a client meeting later this morning. Mother always gets fan mail here. She gave people our address."

"That's kind of funny," Summer said.

"No. It is not. Julian and I always return them straight

to sender. But anyway, Viola heard Mother mumbling something about going to get her notebook when she left. The first one, the one that got stolen."

Uh-oh. Summer put the call on speaker and hugged her knees. That wasn't good.

"When I heard that, my first thought was she remembered where she'd misplaced it," Dash went on. "But she hasn't returned home, and tonight is that big Maxwell & Perkins shindig down at Tangerine du Sol. She had a manicure and hair appointment scheduled at the house this afternoon, and she'd never miss them. Have you or Dorothy heard from her?"

Dorothy shook her head from the couch, where Mr. Bitey's giant orange head peeked out from between the cushions.

"Sorry," Summer said.

"Okay, thanks, I'd better go," Dash said. "I already tried to file a missing person's report, but they said it's too soon."

"Keep us posted," Summer said. "Dorothy and I will be on the lookout."

"Oh dear," Dorothy said, after she hung up. "I do hope nothing has happened to Georgiana. Maybe we should check with Carrie and Parker, over at the Verandas."

"But they're suspects," Summer pointed out. "That might be a bad idea."

"Try them anyway," Dorothy suggested. "Carrie gave me her card. It's there on the counter."

"Her number's in my cell already, trust me." Summer sighed as she hit Call Back. "No answer from either of them. I don't know if that's a good thing or a bad thing. Parker always checks her phone. Should we go over to their rental place?"

"Now that I remember, Parker mentioned something on the boat yesterday about a brunch she'd booked for Carrie with some influential bloggers," Dorothy said. "That could be where they are."

"Maybe," Summer said. "If Georgiana doesn't show up by tonight, should we still go to the party? We might need to help Dash look for her."

"No," Dorothy said. "If Georgiana doesn't make it there, we'll know for sure something's wrong. And if she's actually been kidnapped, which may be rather alarmist to consider just yet, our suspects will all be at Tangerine du Sol."

"Okay," Summer said. Time to plan something fabulous to wear. She might even wear Lorella's bloodstone ring.

THE PROMO PARTY at Tangerine du Sol seemed like an author's dream, Dorothy told herself—or it would be, if both guests of honor could attend. There was still no sign of GH Hamel.

Tastefully trendy and decorated in soothing shades of the ocean, the restaurant boasted a large deck featuring a steel band for those who wished to dance. A long boardwalk, lined by tiki torches, led down to the water and a boathouse draped with blue lanterns.

Parker had everything under control, it seemed, coordinating details with the Tangerine staff and introducing her client through the crowd. Carrie, Dorothy noticed, did not seem her usual, overly perky self.

Neither young woman had seen Georgiana. "I've just been telling everyone Georgiana has been detained, but she'll be here soon," Parker told Dorothy. "You know how GH Hamel likes to make an entrance. I think her editor is a little miffed, though." She nodded toward a very tall, elegant woman in pearls who was sipping white wine in the bar area.

As Dorothy watched, Georgiana's editor was approached by Charles Bell. She fled almost immediately to the ladies' lounge with her drink.

Dorothy scanned the crowd again. Many of the guests, including Summer, were camped in the bar area, entranced by the multiscreen video display. Currently, every screen displayed the live, dramatic capture of a giant python down at the beach. Camo. Finally.

Carrie wasn't watching the reptile show. The new author, who still seemed nervous or upset over something, had stepped onto the beach off the deck.

The young woman was alone, looking harmless and almost pitiful in her ill-fitting velvet dress with the little-girl sash. The band was on a break. There was no one else in sight, but this was still a public place. The perfect opportunity to confront Carrie about Lorella.

She might have to fudge a bit, Dorothy told herself, but she'd improvise, if needed.

"Hello, Carrie," Dorothy said, coming up beside her. "I need to talk to you."

Carrie knew she was cornered. "Um, sure, Dorothy."

"I know you stole plot ideas from Angelina St. James," Dorothy began. "Who was also Lorella Caldwell. And now you're trying to do the same with GH Hamel."

Carrie looked uncertain, her eyes darting between the beach and the restaurant. "What do you mean? I don't know what you're talking about."

"I have the evidence to prove it," Dorothy informed her. "Lorella kept backup files on the computer in the Hibiscus Pointe Business Center."

"What?" Carrie's left cheek twitched slightly.

It was a complete lie, of course, as far as Dorothy knew. But the ruse seemed to be working. "You gave the WMLO-TV staff Georgiana's spoiler copy for the teleprompter, didn't you? And you stole her notebook."

Carrie didn't answer. She looked as if she were about to burst into tears. This was working beautifully.

"But most appallingly of all, you killed Lorella Caldwell when she discovered what you had done. She planned to expose your treachery, even if it meant revealing her secret identity, didn't she?"

To Dorothy's surprise, Carrie burst into tears. "I've dreamed of being a famous author my whole life," she sobbed, sniveling into the sleeve of her dress. "Why are you saying this? It's not true."

"It certainly is," Dorothy said firmly. Hopefully, Carrie would write her next book—the story of her own crime—all by herself. From behind bars.

A minute or two of silence passed.

"Okay, maybe I did copy some of Lorella's work," Carrie said finally. "I disguised it a little, but not too much, and no one even noticed until you did. Oh, and Lorella." She hung her head. "The pressure was terrible. I'm just not talented enough, I guess. But I wanted to be famous."

Dorothy felt like slapping her. How heartless and selfish could one young woman be?

Carrie looked up again, her eyes still shining with tears in the tiki lights. "I stole Georgiana's notebook at the Algonquin, too. And I was sorry right away. That's why I didn't take the second one she left out on the boat."

Carrie might not be the world's best writer—who knew if any of her words were her own?—but she was no dumb bunny, Dorothy thought. She knew the second notebook was a trap.

"But I didn't kill Lorella, I swear," Carrie rushed on. "I could never hurt anyone like that. I didn't give those TV guys the teleprompter copy, either. I wanted to use that great scene in my next book."

Dorothy rubbed her temples. She couldn't believe she was hearing all this. And she wasn't about to let Carrie off the hook for Lorella's murder.

"I wanted to give Georgiana her first notebook back," Carrie said. "I left a note in her son's mailbox for her to meet me at a coffee shop so I could return it and apologize in person. You know, writer to writer."

"And what happened?" Dorothy crossed her arms.

"Georgiana was glad to have her notebook again, but she got superangry," Carrie said. "She called me some terrible names, but I guess I deserved them."

"Mmm," Dorothy said.

"And Georgiana threatened to tell everyone tonight at the party, in front of everyone. Even her senior editor at Maxwell & Perkins. Mine is only an assistant," Carrie added, with a hurt expression. "Anyway, now Georgiana has disappeared. And I know who's behind that."

Dorothy raised her eyebrows. "Really. Who?"

"Parker," Carrie said immediately. "She seems nice, and she's a great publicist, but she's, like, crazy power-hungry. I'd fire her, but I'm scared to death what she'd do to me."

Dorothy's mind spun. *Oh my.* Had Summer been right about Parker? Could Carrie possibly be telling the truth?

"It was Parker who encouraged me to steal Lorella's work," Carrie said. "And I'm afraid she killed Lorella Caldwell to keep her quiet. I know I should have gone to the police, but I was so scared of Parker—and, well,

I guess I was excited my writing career was really taking off."

This was outrageous, Dorothy told herself. Completely unbelievable…or was it? "Where is Georgiana now?" she asked, keeping her voice calm and steady.

"I don't know," Carrie said. "But probably somewhere close by. Parker didn't actually admit to me that she kidnapped Georgiana, but she told me GH Hamel probably wouldn't show up at the party until the very end. And I bet, if Parker does let her come here, she'll probably make her promise first not to say anything, or she'll kill her."

Of all the things Carrie had just told her, that made the least sense, Dorothy thought. Then again, she was obviously dealing with two extremely irrational young women.

"In the meantime, though, the spotlight will just be on me," Carrie said. "Like it should be."

As the deluded author spoke, a beam from the lighthouse on a nearby jetty flashed. In that moment, Dorothy was sure she knew where Georgiana was being held.

It was straight out of a scene from her favorite GH Hamel book. *Good Night, Sweetheart.* And wasn't Maxwell & Perkins showing that new trailer tonight from the upcoming movie version?

"I'd better get back to the party, Dorothy," Carrie said. "Parker will notice if I don't, and then she might get angry and hurt Georgiana. You won't tell her what I said, will you?"

Dorothy needed to return to the party as well—to get Summer and try to rescue Georgiana, if it wasn't already too late. They and the Milano PD would deal with Carrie—and possibly Parker—later.

"I won't breathe a word," Dorothy said.

THIRTY-ONE

SUMMER WASN'T WATCHING Camo the snake being extracted from the mangroves on the larger-than-life video screens. She was keeping her eye glued to the door, in case Georgiana showed up.

Whoa. Jennifer had just walked in with Garrett, the tennis pro from Majesty Golf & Tennis. Oh no. Was her former fake date the guy Jennifer had gone to dinner with, not Detective Donovan?

So her plan to set those two up had worked. That was a good thing. A superamazing thing, actually. She'd sort of blown it with the detective in the Milano PD parking lot, but maybe, if she sort of explained things... No. She couldn't do that. He'd think she was crazy.

He already thought that. And his grandma did, too. Peggy had been giving her the evil eyeball from her table all night.

"Summer, come with me," Dorothy said, at her elbow. She dropped her voice. "We need to rescue Georgiana."

Summer left her untouched apricot martini on the bar. "Where is she?"

"It's just a hunch," Dorothy said. "But I'll tell you on the way. We're headed to the beach."

It was raining now. Hard. Summer had grabbed an umbrella from the stand, but the wind kept blowing it inside out. Behind them, the steel band on the deck had packed up and all the guests had fled inside.

"Where did this awful storm come from?" Dorothy said, huddling against Summer under what was left of the umbrella as they hurried down the boardwalk. "It was so nice, just a few minutes ago." She sighed. "Tropical weather."

"So, where are we going?" Summer asked. Her dress was totally ruined by now, and it was sticking to her like mousetrap glue.

Dorothy pointed toward the jetty. "The lighthouse. Not the new one that's flashing. The old one next to it."

"What?" Summer said. "Didn't the boat captain tell us it gets covered up when the tide comes in? It's almost high tide right now."

"I know," Dorothy said. "And now it's stormy to boot. We'll have to borrow one of those little boats tied up at the dock over there."

Summer bit her lip. "Well, okay. But I don't know if those will handle big waves real well."

"We have to try," Dorothy said. "Georgiana's life may depend on it."

Summer ran over and untied the biggest boat she could find—which wasn't saying much—by the time Dorothy caught up with her in her Aerolite pumps. "You're sure you want to do this?"

"Yes," Dorothy said. "Push us off."

She wasn't able to tell Summer much over the noise of the engine. And the thunder. But that was okay, because Summer had to concentrate on navigating the rough waves. Every now and then one would come over the side and drench them.

Hopefully, they wouldn't sink before they found Georgiana. If she was even there.

When they reached the rocky jetty, Summer helped

Dorothy out of the boat. "This is too dangerous for you," she said. "I can catch you, but watch your step, okay?" The wet slime on the rocks could do them both in.

Dorothy nodded, and the two of them made their way to the metal ruins of the old lighthouse. Every couple of seconds, a flash from the other one lit their way. But the rest of the time, it was totally dark.

Summer's sleuthing partner was being really brave and strong, but she could really get hurt. "Stay right here, and let me go check," Summer said.

Before Dorothy could protest or follow, Summer ducked into what was left of the lighthouse. Hopefully, nothing would fall on her and kill her.

Between bouts of driving rain and occasional thunderclaps, she heard muffled noises. They were coming from not far away, in a corner near a big pile of jumbled rocks and metal.

Summer hurried over and found Georgiana propped against a broken steel beam, tied up and blindfolded. "It's okay, Georgiana," she said. "It's Summer and Dorothy. We're here to rescue you, but we've got to move fast. Are you hurt?"

The author shook her head, and Summer quickly untied her and removed the blindfold. "Where am I?" she said. "And who are you?"

That wasn't good. Dash's mom must have been hit over the head or something. "I'll explain later," Summer said. "But first let's get you out of here."

She helped an unsteady Georgiana to her feet and tried to move her as fast as she could out of the old lighthouse. "Watch your head," she warned. "This place is a mess."

They reached Dorothy in less time than Summer had

expected. Her friend was overjoyed to see Georgiana, and it seemed like the author recognized her. Well, that was a better sign. Maybe Georgiana had just been in shock, or disoriented.

"Oh no," Dorothy said suddenly. "Our boat is untied."

"What?" Summer followed her friend's gaze. Yep, the boat had become untied somehow from that old piling she'd attached it to. She was sure she'd quadruple-knotted it.

"The tide is rising," Dorothy said. "We have to get that boat."

"I'm on it." Summer ran to the highest point of the rapidly disappearing jetty she could find and dove off.

It took longer than she expected, and every last bit of her strength and ocean lifeguarding skills—good thing she'd taken that *Baywatch* training for fun a few years back—but Summer finally managed to get her hands on the half-wrecked boat.

She couldn't get in it from the water. The waves were too strong. Somehow she'd have to swim the boat back to the jetty, to rescue Dorothy and a very groggy Georgiana.

Her chances of making it weren't good. But she'd have to try.

As Summer battled the waves, Dorothy spotted another, larger boat on the other side of the jetty. Behind her, she heard a crunch of gravel, and a small rock rolled toward her feet.

Dorothy whirled around, keeping one hand on a still-disoriented Georgiana.

Carrie. The young woman, wearing a bright orange slicker, was dragging a small but heavy anchor behind her.

"Ahoy there, Dorothy," Carrie said. "And Georgiana, too. Perfect. Two birds with one anchor. I'll tie you up here together so you can watch the tide come in. And don't worry, Summer can join the party, too—as soon as I get that Maxwell & Perkins ring off her finger. If she hasn't drowned already, I mean. I hope not. I really want that ring, at least until they give me my own."

Dorothy was fairly sure Carrie couldn't lift that anchor. At least the girl wouldn't be able to hit her and Georgiana over the head with it, as she had Lorella Caldwell. She backed down the jetty slightly, bringing a dazed Georgiana along with her. "Where are we going?" the older author said. "I don't want to go anywhere."

"Yes, you do," Dorothy said grimly. "Trust me on that."

"There's no way you're getting away from me," Carrie said. "And all I have to do is jump in that nice big boat over there, and you'll drown. So you might as well let me tie you up. That way the Marine Patrol might find your bodies sooner."

"You won't get away with this," Dorothy said. Where on earth was Summer? She could still save herself. How could Dorothy warn her? Summer would never hear her shouts, over the wind and crashing waves.

"This is going to be so much easier than I expected," Carrie crowed. "Even easier than getting rid of Lorella. You had it all figured out, Dorothy, but I'm just a lot smarter than you. And that stress queen Parker doesn't have a clue. It was all me."

"You're not as clever as you think, Carrie." Dorothy tried to stall for time.

"Oh yes, I am," Carrie said. "This brilliant plan just shows you why I'll hit the mystery best seller lists in no time. I'll be sure to mention you and Georgiana in my Edgar Award acceptance speech next year, by the way. There won't be a dry eye in the house. And believe me…"

The crazed girl was still talking when Summer ran up behind her and threw a filthy, smelly fishing net over Carrie, bringing her straight down to the rocks.

Carrie struggled in vain against the rough-looking, tangled netting, covered in broken shells, seaweed, barnacles, and old fishhooks. "Ow!" she cried.

The water was rapidly rising. "What should we do with her?" Summer said. "Just leave her here?"

"We'll have to take her with us somehow," Dorothy said. "We can take her larger boat over there."

"Oh, I guess." Summer gave a heavy sigh. "If we have to."

Dorothy was sure her friend was joking. She hoped so, anyway. "We have to hurry, before the water rises any higher," she said. "We can't be sure how much time we have left until the entire jetty floods. Georgiana, can you walk to the boat? We can just drag Carrie, I suppose." She smiled down at the furious writer. "I'm not entirely serious, of course."

"Hey, look," Summer said, waving from the end of the jetty. "We have company. Super timing."

The Marine Patrol had arrived, with Detective Donovan close behind them in another tiny boat from Tangerine.

The detective pulled up to the jetty a few seconds before the Marine Patrol. "Is everyone okay?" he called. "We have medics."

A few minutes later, the Marine Patrol took Dorothy and a shivering Georgiana on board their vessel, and

Detective Donovan skippered Carrie's boat with Summer and a hastily cuffed Carrie as passengers.

"How did you know we were here?" Dorothy heard Summer ask.

"Parker," the detective answered. "She was pretty concerned when she saw Carrie leave the party in a boat. In the middle of a storm, no less. I'd just gotten to Tangerine with my grandma, and I didn't see you and Dorothy, so… I figured the worst. Do you see now why it's dangerous for amateurs to get involved in police investigations?"

"Well, everything turned out okay," Summer said. "We have Lorella Caldwell's killer right here."

The captain of Dorothy's boat started his engine, and Detective Donovan followed suit. But not before Dorothy saw the detective toss Summer a Marine Patrol sweatshirt for the trip back to Tangerine du Sol.

THIRTY-TWO

SUMMER BREATHED A sigh of relief as she looked around at all her friends and neighbors who had shown up to the viewing party at her condo. Everyone seemed to be having a great time.

At first those guys from Top This had refused to install the home theater system, after she'd blown off so many appointments by mistake. But then Detective Donovan had put in a word with his old coworkers, and presto! Tonight she was hosting the premiere of the *Good Night, Sweetheart* rough cut, courtesy of her dad.

All she had to do was write a review and get some focus group feedback from her guests. No problemo.

It was too bad Georgiana and Parker couldn't be here, but the two of them were already back in New York. Parker had a new client now and GH Hamel had a new independent publicist-slash—social media manager. A perfect partnership.

The author couldn't wait to get started on her new mystery novel, inspired by her recent adventures in Milano. According to Dash, she was still threatening to buy a place down here in town. Or, even better, move in with her son and his family so they could all spend some more quality time together.

Professor Bell was writing a new book, too, based on the notes from Lorella's files. GH Hamel had advised him to trash the first one. She'd even arranged a special

grant for him through Maxwell & Perkins. All he had
to do was take indefinite sabbatical to a secluded cabin
in central Maine. No phone, internet, or other forms of
communication.

Unfortunately, Trixie and Ray had skipped bail—
and no one knew where they were right now. Camo
the snake was safe at Safari Sue's, where Dr. Josie said
Summer and Juliette-Margot could visit her anytime,
along with Skipperdee. No, thanks.

Juliette-Margot was pretty thrilled about her new
pet, though. She was now the co-owner of Guinevere—
Grace's new therapy kitty. Ernie told her she could visit
whenever she wanted, too.

Jennifer and Garrett were looking cozy over in the
corner, sharing a bowl of popcorn as they waited for the
movie to start. And Detective Donovan wasn't here yet,
but he and Summer had a real date set up for Saturday
night. Not the Tick-Tock Diner, either—a cool Brazil-
ian place where they served all the food you could eat.

"What are you thinking about, dear?" Dorothy asked,
coming up with a glass of wine. Summer noticed her
sleuthing partner seemed a lot more relaxed lately, now
that things had gotten back to normal after they'd solved
the Caldwell case and Carrie was awaiting trial.

"Oh, nothing," she said, with a smile. "I'm just glad
everything worked out so well."

"Have you started your reading for book club yet?"
Dorothy said. "The next meeting is Friday, remember."

"I'm on it," Summer said. A lot of people had
dropped out of the Hibiscus Pointe Book Club after
GH Hamel left, but that was okay. Her sleuthing partner was happy that the smaller club meant they could
focus more on books. And Summer was happy because

there was more free food to go around. Plus, Gladys was thrilled to be the newly appointed events coordinator, which would hopefully distract her from pining over the loss of Professor Boring.

"You know, I couldn't help noticing your lovely new bookcase," Dorothy said. "And look at all those titles from the Lorella Caldwell Memorial Library. I guess you'll be spending a lot more time reading now."

Summer grinned. "Maybe. But I'd still rather solve a few real-life mysteries. What do you say, partner?"

* * * * *

To purchase and read more books by
Lisa Q. Mathews, please visit Lisa's website
http://www.lisaqmathews.com/#!books/cfvg

ACKNOWLEDGMENTS

I WOULD LIKE to thank my fellow mystery writers and blogmates at Chicks on the Case: Ellen Byron, Kellye Garrett and Marla Cooper; my incredible agent, Stephany Evans at FinePrint Literary; and of course the hardworking staff at Carina Press, especially my ever-awesome editor, Kerri Buckley. And as always, love and gratitude to my husband and kids, who always have my back: Rich, Kimberly, Stephanie and Rory—couldn't do this without you guys.

ABOUT THE AUTHOR

LISA Q. MATHEWS prepped for her career as an author by studying ads in the back of her mom's magazines ("We're looking for people to write children's books!") and investing her hard-earned allowance in pristine spiral notebooks. She also devoured every Nancy Drew book in her summer camp library, determined to outwit the perfect girl detective. She failed, of course, but years later she had another chance.

After graduating from college with a typing speed of twelve wpm, Lisa headed to New York to work as an assistant to four busy editors. Soon after, she became an editor herself—of new Nancy Drew books! She also wrote under a pen name for other kids' series, including *Mary-Kate and Ashley* and *The Lizzie McGuire Mysteries*. Eventually, she became Creative Director at Random House Children's Books.

But Lisa had always dreamed of writing mysteries full-time—for grown-ups. During an extended stay at her parents' floral-themed retirement community in Southwest Florida—and a chance elevator meeting with a memorable senior—The Ladies Smythe & Westin series was born.

A former figure skater and lifeguard, and mom to three grown kids, Lisa now scribbles in her notebooks from New Hampshire, where she lives with her husband, her own mom and a golden retriever puppy named

Farley. She is happy to report that her typing speed is much improved, and she and Nancy Drew are still fast chums.

To learn more about Lisa and her books, please visit her website and sign up for her newsletter at lisaqmathews.com. You can also follow her on Twitter, @lisaqmathews, friend her on Facebook, and share in her writing adventures at the group blog Chicks on the Case. Lisa hopes you'll enjoy The Ladies Smythe & Westin books as much as she enjoys writing them—and she looks forward to meeting you!

Get 4 FREE REWARDS!

We'll send you 2 FREE Books plus 2 FREE Mystery Gifts.

Harlequin® Intrigue books feature heroes and heroines that confront and survive danger while finding themselves irresistibly drawn to one another.

FREE
Value Over
$20

YES! Please send me 2 FREE Harlequin® Intrigue novels and my 2 FREE gifts (gifts are worth about $10 retail). After receiving them, if I don't wish to receive any more books, I can return the shipping statement marked "cancel." If I don't cancel, I will receive 6 brand-new novels every month and be billed just $4.99 each for the regular-print edition or $5.74 each for the larger-print edition in the U.S., or $5.74 each for the regular-print edition or $6.49 each for the larger-print edition in Canada. That's a savings of at least 12% off the cover price! It's quite a bargain! Shipping and handling is just 50¢ per book in the U.S. and 75¢ per book in Canada*. I understand that accepting the 2 free books and gifts places me under no obligation to buy anything. I can always return a shipment and cancel at any time. The free books and gifts are mine to keep no matter what I decide.

Choose one: ☐ **Harlequin® Intrigue**
　　　　　　　　　Regular-Print
　　　　　　　　　(182/382 HDN GMYW)

☐ **Harlequin® Intrigue**
　Larger-Print
　(199/399 HDN GMYW)

Name (please print)

Address　　　　　　　　　　　　　　　　　　　　　　　　　　　　Apt. #

City　　　　　　　　　　　State/Province　　　　　　　　　　Zip/Postal Code

Mail to the **Reader Service:**
IN U.S.A.: P.O. Box 1341, Buffalo, NY 14240-8531
IN CANADA: P.O. Box 603, Fort Erie, Ontario L2A 5X3

Want to try two free books from another series! Call 1-800-873-8635 or visit www.ReaderService.com.

HI18

Get 4 FREE REWARDS!

We'll send you 2 FREE Books plus 2 FREE Mystery Gifts.

Harlequin® Romantic Suspense books feature heart-racing sensuality and the promise of a sweeping romance set against the backdrop of suspense.

FREE
Value Over
$20

Get 4 FREE REWARDS!

We'll send you 2 FREE Books plus 2 FREE Mystery Gifts.

FREE Value Over **$20**

Both the **Romance** and **Suspense** collections feature compelling novels written by many of today's best-selling authors.

YES! Please send me 2 FREE novels from the Essential Romance or Essential Suspense Collection and my 2 FREE gifts (gifts are worth about $10 retail). After receiving them, if I don't wish to receive any more books, I can return the shipping statement marked "cancel." If I don't cancel, I will receive 4 brand-new novels every month and be billed just $6.74 each in the U.S. or $7.24 each in Canada. That's a savings of at least 16% off the cover price. It's quite a bargain! Shipping and handling is just 50¢ per book in the U.S. and 75¢ per book in Canada*. I understand that accepting the 2 free books and gifts places me under no obligation to buy anything. I can always return a shipment and cancel at any time. The free books and gifts are mine to keep no matter what I decide.

Choose one: ☐ **Essential Romance**
(194/394 MDN GMY7)
☐ **Essential Suspense**
(191/391 MDN GMY7)

Name (please print)

Address

Apt. #

City

State/Province

Zip/Postal Code

Mail to the Reader Service:
IN U.S.A.: P.O. Box 1341, Buffalo, NY 14240-8531
IN CANADA: P.O. Box 603, Fort Erie, Ontario L2A 5X3

Want to try two free books from another series? Call 1-800-873-8635 or visit www.ReaderService.com.

Get 4 FREE REWARDS!

We'll send you 2 FREE Books plus 2 FREE Mystery Gifts.

Love Inspired® Suspense books feature Christian characters facing challenges to their faith... and lives.

FREE
Value Over
$20

READERSERVICE.COM

Manage your account online!

- Review your order history
- Manage your payments
- Update your address

*We've designed the
Reader Service website
just for you.*

Enjoy all the features!

- Discover new series available to you, and read excerpts from any series.
- Respond to mailings and special monthly offers.
- Browse the Bonus Bucks catalog and online-only exculsives.
- Share your feedback.

Visit us at:

ReaderService.com